# BEYOND HIGHLAND SUNRISE

SPECIAL OPS SCOTS
BOOK 2

KAIT NOLAN

# CHAPTER 1

## CALLUM

"Oi! Callum. Are you waiting for an engraved invitation, mate?" From the back of the work van we'd pressed into service for the move, Finley Patterson wiggled his fingers in a give-it-here gesture.

I shoved the box I was carrying at him. "Just letting you finish rearranging. We all ken you treat this as a giant game of *Tetris*." It was easier to sling shite back rather than admit the truth—that I hadn't seen he was ready because he'd been on my bad side.

Not waiting for a reply, I headed back up the stairs to Alex and Ciara's apartment over The Stag's Head, the pub owned by her brother Ewan, our former squad leader and one of my best mates. Although that position was in question given he'd somehow weaseled his way out of helping them move. The sneaky bastard. The rest of us were on deck because Alex was our brother in all but blood. And there was a bottle of excellent single-malt Speyside whisky for each of us on the other side.

I moved through the mostly empty main room, hunting for the next box, and caught a glimpse of Alex and Ciara through the open bedroom door. As if they'd both forgotten we were in the middle of loading every bloody thing they owned into a van, Alex had his woman backed against a wall, one hand hitching her leg around his waist as he devoured her mouth.

For a moment I stared, feeling like a voyeur, not because they were half a dozen steps from shagging, but because they were so totally lost in each other. Their mutual joy fairly radiated off them. Alex had been through a lot, and I was happy he'd found someone who understood him, who wanted to spend her life with him. But I couldn't deny the whisper of envy twisting through me. I'd never have that. I didn't deserve that. Not now. I was far too surly and short-tempered. No woman should be saddled with my piss poor attitude and all the issues I'd brought with me into my retirement from the Royal Marines.

Taking a deliberately heavier step, I moved toward another stack of boxes. "Echo, the point is to christen the new place, no' the one you're leaving."

Alex shot up a middle finger and took his time finishing the kiss. By the time he lifted his head, Ciara's cheeks were as flushed from embarrassment as from the snogging.

"If you didn't insist on walking like the bloody ghost we named you for, perhaps you wouldn't end up with an eyeful."

*An eyeful.* I turned away at the sight of his wince. I was tired of everyone tiptoeing around the issue. I'd lost my sight in one eye. I'd been damned lucky not to lose my life. Objectively, I knew that. But it didn't do a damned thing to dampen my rage over feeling like a broken man. And my friends knew it. They wouldn't lighten up until I did, and I just... couldn't. Not yet. Maybe not ever. Hence the tiptoeing.

Damn it.

I hefted a box labeled *Kitchen* and headed for the stairs. Though this was at least the twentieth trip just today, I hesitated at the top, hating the need to check the location of the first step down. But I'd misjudged the distance on the first day and narrowly avoided taking a header all the way to street level. Thankfully, it had just been a box of clothes that had crashed instead of my skull. I had enough to deal with without adding brain damage to the list.

Angling my head to better see with my one good eye, I eased my foot down. Assured I had solid footing, I swung into motion, trotting down to the alley that ran behind all the shops on this side of the high street. Even knowing there shouldn't really be anyone else around, and that any of those who were hardly represented the kinds of threats I'd faced in the field, I kept my head on a swivel, constantly scanning, as if that could make up for losing half my field of vision. I barely registered the beauty of the Highlands stretching up behind the village proper, not beyond automatically noting vulnerabilities and tactical advantages. A low-grade headache was building in the back of my head, a sure sign I needed to give my eye a rest. But it would have to wait until we were finished. I'd take my whisky home and sit in the dark like the embittered hermit I was on my way to becoming.

Half an hour later, we'd finished with the flat and relocated ten minutes away to the house they'd leased on the other side of Glenlaig. I breathed a silent sigh of relief that it was only a single level. No more stairs to navigate. We congregated at the rear of the van. Finn opened the back, as Alex went to unlock the front door of the cottage.

"Oh! Ciara, hello! Finally moving in with your young man?"

I turned and spotted an older woman with a sweep of silver hair tucked into a bun. She had a wee black cocker spaniel on a leash.

"Mrs. Buchanan, hello. Yes, tonight will be our first in the new place."

I'd long ago learned that Ciara seemed to know everybody in the village. Partly because she'd lived here most of her life, partly because she'd worked as a server in Ewan's pub for her first few years after uni, and partly because she was a sociable creature who actually liked people. As the two of them fell into easy conversation—how the hell did Ciara do that?—I grabbed up the nearest box.

At the sudden motion, Mrs. Buchanan glanced toward me. She did a double-take, her eyes going wide before she took an unconscious step back. That step was a punch in the gut.

Fighting the scowl that wanted to set in, I moved around them and marched toward the house.

*Good job, Quinn. You look so terrifying, you're scaring little old ladies.*

I wished I could say it was the first time, but the locals had been giving me a wide berth since I moved to Glenlaig to go into business with my mates. It was no doubt a combination of the resting ogre face, as Finn called it, and the fearsome scar that ran down the left side of my face, right through my eye. No one ever knew how to react. The deliberate avoiding of it was just as bad as the stares, and there really was no in between. I had a permanent reminder of exactly how not normal I was. On top of the fact that I hadn't peopled well to begin with, it meant I wasn't fit for human company most of the time.

It was why I'd chosen to buy my own house well out from the village, away from everyone and everything. In my own home, I didn't have to worry about how I looked or what I said. I didn't have to interact with anyone at all. If I sometimes found that lonely, well, I offset it by all the time I spent with Alex and Finn at the outdoor adventure company we'd opened or being dragged to group dinners organized by Ciara or Ewan's fiancé,

Isobel. They could handle my bark and my bite without batting an eye.

Damn it, why were so many idioms sight based?

The adventure company had been my idea. A way we could all utilize the skills we'd gained in the military and keep active, which I knew would be key to us all staying sane. Finn and Alex had been all in, and through all the build-out we'd done to the building and setting up of things, everything had been fine. But the moment we'd opened the doors to actual customers, I'd felt out of my depth. I was struggling with a key part of our business, and I knew I was letting my business partners down. I couldn't abide that. I never wanted to let my team down. Ever. It might not be life and limb at stake now, but it was our livelihoods, and I couldn't be the one to tank that. My mates didn't have a fallback like I did if Out of Bounds Scotland failed. So I had to find some way to make this work. To be better. For them.

And I didn't have the first fucking clue how.

Alex passed me on the front walk. "You alright, mate?"

"Fine." I snapped the word, accidentally shoulder-checking him as I misjudged the distance when I moved by.

Rattled and a little ashamed, I wasn't properly focused on where I was going, and I rammed straight into the door frame. The box in my arms promptly collapsed, the bottom springing open and disgorging the contents all over the front stoop.

*Fuck!*

I wanted to scream it to the sky but managed to choke the words back down as I closed my eyes, breathing through the rage and embarrassment. When was I going to get used to having only one eye? The doctors had told me my brain would adapt to monocular vision, that depth perception wouldn't be as difficult as it had been right after the injury. But of course, they hadn't put any kind of time frame on it, and I was starting to think the whole thing was just a crock of shite they'd cooked up so patients didn't lose all hope. It hadn't done that for me.

At the sound of footsteps, I jerked my head around to see Finn and Alex approaching with far more caution than friends ought to. Fuck. Even my best mates were wary of me.

"I'll get another box," Finn offered. "Looks like that one's done for."

Alex started to reach for some of the scattered items.

"I've got it. It's fine." I was aware that my rage was creating a bubble around me, repelling everyone, but I couldn't seem to rein it in.

"Um, I think Ciara would prefer I gather it up."

At his careful tone, I glanced down to see what had been in the box. Toys. Of the kind kept in a bedside table that nobody outside the relationship talked about.

My lips twitched and a little of the rage bled off. "Aye, right. I dinna think I need to be touching that."

I turned toward the truck.

Ciara moved past, carrying a box. "What was in that one?" Her choked noise told me the moment she realized. "That's it. I can never look any of your friends in the eye ever again."

No one wanted to look me in the eye as it was. And that was something I was still learning how to live with.

# CHAPTER 2

## PARKER

I stood on the sidewalk outside the headquarters of Out of Bounds Scotland, bouncing with a sense of giddy anticipation and excitement.

After months of dreaming and planning, I was finally *here,* surrounded by scenic vistas at every turn. Everything about Scotland was so dramatic, from the sweeping mountains to the forests and lochs. I'd spent the entire series of trains and buses I'd taken to get here glued to the window, soaking in the views. I'd come so much further than the literal miles I'd traveled from Tennessee, and I'd had to do a few things I was less than proud of to make it this far. My guilt over that was going to be with me for a while, but at this point, the ends justified the means. I'd come to Scotland for an adventure, and I'd landed in the tiny Highland village of Glenlaig because the sister of a friend had raved about it.

Also, because no one would think to look for me here. I was supposed to be in London, after all.

But I was through doing only what I was supposed to. This wasn't the first step toward taking control of my life. I'd been making dozens of small ones in that direction for the past couple of years. But it felt like the biggest, if only because it was symbolic of how I wanted to live from here on out. No more thinking small. No more letting other people decide what was best for me.

*You've got this.*

Squaring my shoulders, I strode up the walk and stepped inside the building. A massive, broad-shouldered man stood behind the counter, the phone to his ear, his face set into a scowl that pulled at the wicked scar that bisected his left eye.

"I dinna ken who you think you are, but I've never heard of such entitled—"

My inner Southern debutante clutched her pearls in horror at the blatant rudeness, even as I marched across the room and took the phone straight out of the giant's hand. The handset was warm from his grip. I had absolutely no idea what I thought I was doing, but I was in it now, so I put on my best polite tone and focused on the call. "Hello? Hi. I apologize. Someone answered the phone who shouldn't have. How can I help you?"

"I was simply going over all the customizations I'd like to add to my package."

American guy. Definitely huffy. Probably thought the world revolved around him. I'd had plenty of experience with his ilk, and while they were annoying, it wasn't an excuse to be rude.

"Uh-huh." In all the time I'd spent combing the company's website, I didn't remember there being a single thing said about customizations, but it wouldn't hurt to write down his requests. "And what would those be?"

As the guy on the line, whose voice sounded solidly Silicon Valley, prattled on about high-end whisky tastings, gourmet catered meals, and a host of other things that he'd be far more likely to find at some kind of all-inclusive five-star resort rather than an outdoor adventure company, I grabbed a pen and notepad and began to scribble down his requests, murmuring encouraging replies to make sure he felt heard. The guy was an A-plus asshat, and I absolutely understood the frustration of the man whose stare I'd been concertedly ignoring through the conversation.

"Yes, sir. I understand. Well, I can't make any promises, but I'll see that all this gets to the appropriate people for discussion." It was the best offer I could make, considering I had less than zero power here.

"You've been most helpful. Thank you. Have a good one."

"Uh-huh. You, too. And I'm sorry for your experience earlier."

"Between you and me, whoever the first guy was deserves to be fired."

I wasn't about to voice an opinion on that. Time to wrap this up. "Uh-huh. Buh-bye now."

With careful deliberation, I hung up the phone and set down the pen, bracing myself to face the consequences of my impulsive action. The man I'd interrupted was even bigger up close, towering over me by the better part of a foot, with shoulders that would do any linebacker proud. His brows were drawn together, a furrow dug between them as he stared down at me. No doubt he wasn't accustomed to someone who stood only a few inches over five feet, daring to take charge.

Knowing I'd probably just killed any shot at getting what I'd come here for, I straightened and prepared to take my lumps. "I am so sorry. I know that was overstepping and incredibly inappropriate of me, but you cannot talk to people like that." If I'd already destroyed my opportunity, it wouldn't hurt to use this as a teaching moment.

He loomed over me, an intensity to his expression that I probably should've found alarming. "You're hired."

I went brows up, positive I'd heard him wrong. "I'm sorry?"

"As the new office manager," he explained. "When can you start?"

It was my turn to knit my brows. He couldn't be serious. "I... what?"

"Do you already have a job?" He took a half step forward before he seemed to catch himself. I probably should've been intimidated, but there was an unmistakable edge of desperation in his tone.

"Well, no—" I mean, I technically had a job, but it wasn't full time, and I could do it from anywhere.

"Do you need a job?"

I hesitated. I did need a job. Finding one had, in fact, been my number one priority after booking my Scottish adventure.

"Do you?" he pressed.

"Yes, but—"

"Then you're hired." He pronounced this with a tone of finality, as if we'd just solved world hunger.

Scooping a hand through my hair, I couldn't do anything but laugh at the absurdity of this situation. "You don't even know me."

"I know you just saved my business a potential client, and you're apparently no' afraid of me."

The rumble of his Scottish burr stroked over me like an almost physical touch, and I had to repress a shiver as I angled my head to peer up at him. No doubt there were people who were put off by that scar and the one milky eye. But I sensed no malice in him, only a deep well of frustration and pain. When was the last time anyone had acknowledged that for him? "Everybody has bad days."

"Every day is a bad day for some."

The words fell between us, vibrating with a ring of truth that I felt down to my very core. I understood that hopelessness. I'd been there myself. Still slid back from time to time. As I didn't think it was appropriate to wrap him in the hug I wanted to offer, I gave him the gift of holding space for his pain without flinching away. I suspected it was another thing he didn't experience very often.

The door opened behind us, and another man came inside. "We've got ten new kayaks. Finn's pulling around back. We need to open the loading bay door." He stopped when he caught sight of me. "Oh, who's this?"

The giant of a man didn't tear his gaze away from me. "Our new office manager. This is..." He paused, a fresh intensity coming into his expression. "What's your name, lass?"

*You can call me anything you like, if you'll just keep talking.*

Flummoxed by the thought and the job offer, I blinked at him. Surely, it shouldn't be this easy to execute my plan. I'd expected it to take weeks to find a job. I hadn't even checked postings yet, as I hadn't decided where I wanted to settle. Was this kismet? Maybe it was a sign from the Universe that I was in exactly the right place at the right time.

There was only one way to find out.

I extended my hand. "Parker. It's nice to meet you."

# CHAPTER 3

## CALLUM

"Parker. It's nice to meet you."

Instinct and long-dormant social training prompted me to take the hand she offered, but something far deeper struck me as our palms met. A sense of like recognizing like. Another moment of connection I hadn't anticipated. My fingers closed automatically around hers, so small in mine. Those big brown eyes widened fractionally, but she didn't pull away, and I couldn't seem to make myself let go.

"Right. Parker. Nice to meet you, as well." Alex's voice broke through whatever spell this woman had managed to cast. "Will you excuse us for just a moment?"

"Oh, of course." Cheeks turning a pretty pink, she withdrew her hand and stepped back. "I'll just be right here."

My palm still tingled from the soft rasp of her delicate fingers against my skin as Alex propelled me through the door to the back.

"Are you lot expecting me to unload all these kayaks by myself, then?" Finn demanded.

"It can wait," Alex insisted. "Did you post an ad for an office manager without telling us?"

Finn swung toward me. "What's this?"

"I didn't, no. But she's perfect." A gift from bloody God, the way she'd marched in and taken over without even batting those Disney-princess eyes. I was willing to go to great lengths to get her to stay. Up to and including paying her salary out of my own savings. It would hardly make a dent.

"Who's perfect? What's happening?"

"Callum thinks he's found us an office manager," Alex explained.

"Oh, well, we need one of those, for sure. Who is this woman?" Finn wanted to know.

Alex folded his arms. "Parker, of no last name, whom he's basically offered the job to without knowing a thing about her."

"I know what I need to know. She took over with a difficult customer on the phone before I could tell him to go fuck himself."

Finn blinked. "She... took over?"

"Grabbed the phone right out of my hand." Which I'd been too stunned to protest, then too fascinated by watching her in action to interrupt.

"Brave woman," Finn murmured. "However, leaving that aside, if you didn't post an advert for an office manager position, then she didn't walk in looking for a job. So why is she here? To book some of our services? Rent some equipment? Ask for directions?"

That was a fair point, but I couldn't shake the idea that she was exactly what we needed. What *I* needed to save my sanity and the business. "She said she could use a job. We need somebody."

"Aye, we do need somebody, but hiring someone who literally just walked in off the street doesn't seem like the best way to go about it. There are protocols for such things. Interviews to be conducted. References to check." Alex was big on protocols.

All of it sounded like a colossal waste of time to me. "I dinna need to check references. She can do the job." I knew I was edging into belligerent, but I just needed them to go along with this.

Alex studied me for a long moment. "Why her?"

"Apart from the fact that she waded in and simply handled the situation... she's no' afraid of me." The admission hurt, because it meant I had to acknowledge that plenty of people *were* afraid of me. And we all knew that would ultimately impact who'd be willing to work for us.

My mates exchanged a look.

Finn nodded. "Okay. Well, let's go talk to her to find out if she's even remotely qualified for this job. Then we'll go from there."

Some of the knots that had set up in my shoulders began to loosen a bit. We went back out front. Parker stood beside one of the picture windows, examining the array of photographs that lined the back wall, displaying the assorted services and adventures we offered. Sunlight broke through the clouds outside, limning her in gold and flashing off the nearly black strands of her hair. She glanced over as we came out, her lips curving into a faint smile. She looked so at ease. What must it be like to be that comfortable anywhere? When was the last time I'd felt at ease in my own skin?

Alex took point. "Let's backtrack a little. I'm Alex Conroy. This is Finley Patterson and Callum Quinn. We own Out of Bounds Scotland. And you are Parker...?"

"Lawrence." Her accent made the word sound like warm honey.

"Well, Parker Lawrence, I presume you didn't actually come in looking for a job today, so why are you here?"

Her faint smile dialed brighter, and it was as if someone turned up the sun in the room. "I was hoping to book an excursion with y'all."

"You're a tourist, then?" Finn asked.

My heart sank with the implication. I'd jumped the gun, made assumptions. I knew better.

Parker's gaze flicked to me. "Well, not exactly. I actually am looking to move over here, which will ultimately require a job. But I came in because I've been following y'all's YouTube channel and Instagram, and the trips look so lovely, I wanted to go on one myself."

"We can certainly help you with that," Alex confirmed. "But since it got brought up, would you be interested in a job?"

"Definitely interested, but I'd like some more details before I commit to anything."

She wasn't saying no. I took a firm grip on the hope that wanted to leap like a rabbit in my chest. Just because she felt like my salvation from having to people didn't mean she'd take the position.

Again, Alex took the lead. "What we're really looking for is an office manager. Someone to handle the phones, the filing, and organizational stuff. We have an online booking system, but as you've evidently already experienced, there are people who will call instead, and they need to be taken through the options. Hand-held, as it were. There are also equipment rentals to manage."

"Would that require physical wrangling of the equipment?"

"One of us should always be around to manage that. It's more the documentation side. Do you have any experience with that kind of thing?"

"Well, I've been a virtual assistant for a popular romance author for the past few years. There are a lot of moving parts to her business, and she'd rather someone else handle the details so she can stick to writing. That's what I do. Handle those boring details, so she can do what she wants to do. I like to organize things, and spreadsheets are my love language. I'm Southern, so I'm morally obligated to be good with people. The phone doesn't bother me, and I'm the picture of self-restraint when it comes to entitled stuffed-shirt blowhards who have more money than sense."

This last she directed at me, with a quirk of her mouth that made the corners of her eyes crinkle, as if she were inviting me to laugh with her.

I folded my arms. "He was a total wanker."

"He was," she agreed. "Bless his heart."

My lips twitched. "Is that the polite Southern way of saying 'fuck him'?"

"It's a multi-purpose phrase that's heavily dependent upon context and tone." She winked. "But if the shoe fits."

In my inexpert opinion, Parker Lawrence seemed like a fantastic fit for our needs. But that might simply be my abject desire to never have to answer a phone again. "Is this all something you'd be interested in?"

*Please say yes.*

"Well, it's kind of tough to say. Probably. But there are things like pay rates and work visas and I don't know what-all kinds of details. I literally just got to town today, and I wasn't prepared for any of this."

*Neither was I.*

"Are you looking for temporary work for a few months or something longer term?" Alex asked.

That was something I hadn't considered. That she could intend to work her way across the country. It was something I'd have expected of someone younger, closer to university age. But

I pegged Parker closer to late twenties. Was I off in my estimation? Or was she simply doing things in her own time?

Something clouded those big brown eyes. "I have six months to see if I can make this work, and I don't want to be going back to the States at the end of it. In the end, I'd like to settle somewhere."

What was in the US that she didn't want to go back to? A life she didn't like? A problematic partner? An unsupportive family? What made a woman like her up and decide to move across the world?

"What if we do a trial period of, say, two weeks?" Finn suggested. "That should be ample time to see if we all suit, if you like the area, and if you even like the job before we pursue the more complicated matter of getting you a work visa and such, if you decide to stay. And while you're here, we can take you on the excursion of your choice."

"That sounds very fair and reasonable. I appreciate the opportunity, gentlemen."

As my business partners began to hash out the details, I let out a long, slow breath. She was staying, at least for a little while. She'd be taking over almost all the shite about the business that I hated, and if she was as good as I suspected she'd be, maybe I'd never have to answer a phone again. That might be a bit of a pipe dream, but finding her felt like the first real win I'd had in a very, very long time.

I'd take it.

# CHAPTER 4

## PARKER

I had a job.

At least for the next two weeks.

Alex and Finley hadn't seemed nearly as desperate as Callum for me to take it. Not that they'd been unwelcoming, but I gathered finding an office manager hadn't yet been on their radar. Finley was a natural-born flirt, and Alex seemed perfectly at ease with people. It wasn't hard to guess that Callum didn't share those skills. He didn't strike me as a patient man. Definitely not one who had any tolerance for bullshit. I suspected that had been true even before whatever accident had taken his eye. The scar that bisected his brow and trailed down to the top of his left cheek was still pink. Not brand new, but not old, either. He was still adjusting to his new normal.

I understood what it was like to have the normal world altered forever in a second. Being forced to find a new way to live. I'd been doing that for a decade now, and there were still days I struggled. Maybe that was part of why I'd been so quick to say yes, even though I hadn't seen nearly enough of the country to decide where I wanted to ultimately land. Because I thought I could help him. Maybe not with the deeper issues. I wasn't a therapist, after all. But maybe I could take some of the burden off, so he had more bandwidth to focus on himself and whatever changes he needed to make. And, if nothing else, maybe he could just use a friend.

*A friend? Come on, Parker. The man isn't a stray puppy.*

But he pulled at my heartstrings just the same.

My head spun as I walked back through the village of Glenlaig from the Out of Bounds Scotland headquarters. Office? What did they even call the place? I'd have to ask.

On the way there, I'd casually strolled down the high street, glancing in shop windows and being generally charmed by the look of the place. But I looked at it through fresh eyes on the return trip, because visiting was one thing. Living here was another.

I knew a little about the village from my research prior to the trip. There were two estates in the area. Ardinmuir Castle, which had been a seat of the MacKean clan for some stupid long hundreds of years. It had been converted into an event venue, though I understood part of the family still lived there. The other, Lochmara, was newer—though that was relative. It, too, was several hundred years old. They were both the kinds of places I'd have expected to have huge tourist draw, but instead, I found the village proper to be off the beaten tourist path, geared far more toward the locals, though there were, of course, a handful of shops with the expected kitschy souvenirs highlighting Highland coos, wooly sheep, and tartans. Other than that, I spotted a small grocery store, a newsagent, a couple of takeaways, a charity shop, a bakery, and a tearoom. I'd only seen one pub, The Stag's Head, at the far end of the street. I hadn't yet ventured off the main drag, but what I could spot from here looked more residential.

The dramatic Highland hills rose behind the village, their

slopes thick with pines. The late afternoon sun painted them in shades of gold and deep green. Even from here, I could smell someone baking bread—probably from that little bakery I'd passed. Everything about Glenlaig felt cozy and intimate, like stepping into a snow globe version of a Scottish village. One on the verge of what they called spring. I'd already spotted half a dozen locals who'd given me warm, welcoming smiles as I'd walked past. One woman had even stopped sweeping her front stoop to ask if I needed directions, her accent so thick I'd had to ask her to repeat herself twice.

This place was *teeny*.

I was from Nashville, albeit one of the suburbs. At home, I had access to anything I could want within an hour's drive or less. Nothing here would be about convenience. I had no idea what the UK's version of Walmart was or where the nearest one was located. And I suspected the shipping of internet orders wouldn't be fast either up here in the Highlands. That would be an adjustment. But those were all first-world problems. I hadn't gone to such great lengths to get here because I was looking for more of the same as home.

I liked the idea of a close-knit community, where I knew the shopkeepers and my neighbors. As a people, the Scots seemed to be friendly and helpful. That was a great trait, considering I was here with no support system whatsoever. By my own choice. Too many of the supports in my life felt like chains. I'd elected to go solo or bust on this adventure. Reckless? Maybe. But I needed to prove to myself that I could stand on my own two feet.

Back at the B&B, I found my hostess had left a plate of freshly baked chocolate chip cookies out with the makings for tea. Snagging two, I carried them back to my room. I'd have a snack and a little lie down before going out to find something for supper.

As I toed off my Chelsea boots, my phone vibrated with a text.

PAISLEY

Get settled in okay?

PARKER

I did. And I have news.

PAISLEY

I've just emerged from the writing cave. Time for a video call?

I flopped onto the bed and toggled over to the proper app.

After only one ring, her face filled the screen. "What's the news? Is everything okay?"

I bit into a cookie, humming with pleasure as the salty, sweet flavor melted on my tongue. "Yeah, everything is fine. I already have a job offer."

Paisley blinked. "Well, that was fast. How did that happen?"

As she took me into her kitchen and began putting together food, I gave her the rundown. "Honestly, I can't really believe I just did it. It was kind of rude in its own right, but it paid off."

"Sounds like kismet. Tell me more about the broody hottie."

Paisley Parish was not only a friend, she was the romance author I worked for. She habitually saw the potential for love everywhere. Some might have thought it an occupational hazard, but she'd been a romantic all her life, despite two divorces before Fate landed her back with the first love who'd broken her heart at eighteen. Now she was living her best life with the former Army Ranger husband who adored her and the world's most adorable and friendly mutt. And when she wasn't matchmaking people on the page, she tested out her skills in real life, which I found generally amusing until it was aimed in my direction.

"Slow your roll. That broody hottie is now one of my bosses. A relationship is not on my itinerary."

With an exasperated huff, she leaned closer to the screen. "Come on! The grumpy-sunshine workplace romance practically writes itself."

Given how Paisley's brain worked, that was probably true. By the end of the phone call, she'd have the entire plot mapped out, down to the bonus epilogue with braw little Scottish bairns. Did they still call babies that here, or had I read one too many historical romances?

"This is my life, Pais—not one of your books."

"Exactly. All the more reason for you to leap in head first. That's the entire point of this adventure of yours and all the hoops you've jumped through to take it."

She wasn't wrong. I'd come here because I wanted to *live* my life, not just go through the motions. And that was going to upset a lot of people in my world.

"Speaking of those hoops... have you heard from Jade?"

It was part redirect, part legitimate concern.

Paisley settled at the kitchen table with her sandwich. "Oh yeah, and she's pissed you gave her the slip. I'd say 50% is that you would dare and the other 50% was that you pulled it off."

I winced. I wasn't especially proud of any of this. "I knew she would be. I'm sorry you're catching the flak for it."

Paisley waved that away. "Hey, I volunteered to be the go-between, so she didn't lose her shit and think you'd been kidnapped. I stand by that decision."

"Are you sure?"

"I mean, she's not going to hop on a plane to fly back to the States to interrogate me. That may only be because it would mean leaving you alone over there, but I'll take the reprieve. Either way, she's definitely on the hunt to track you down."

My heart squeezed. "Did you let anything slip?"

Paisley snorted. "What do you take me for, an amateur? We set up all new accounts she doesn't know about. You already got a new phone under my name, and the lodging and travel that's already been booked was paid for through pre-paid credit cards. I've made it clear that we're in contact, and that she can consider that proof of life, and that you're safe."

"Thanks for that."

"How long do you plan to wait before you tell her where you are?"

I considered as I started in on the second cookie. It was a good thing I was currently without a vehicle, because the walking was the only thing that would save me from the conse-quences of indulging in my temporary landlady's cooking. "I'm at least taking the two weeks to see if I want to stay here. Prob-ably longer. I need time—as much as you can buy me." God, I hated to do this to Paisley, but as she'd said, she'd volunteered for this.

"You know I'm on your side. How long do you think she'll wait before telling your parents?"

This was the riskiest part of my whole plan. If my very over-protective parents had any clue what I was actually doing, they'd promptly lose their shit and send out the National Guard—or whatever the international version of that looked like. And my father had the resources to do it.

"The blowback on Jade would be significant—" Something else I wasn't proud of. "—so I'm hoping she'll hold off. She's always been overprotective and just a little paranoid about theoretical threats that turn out to be nothing. Part of the job, I guess. So long as she's reassured that I'm in no legitimate danger, I should be fine." That was what I was telling myself, anyway.

"Well, I hope you know her as well as you think you do."

A furry head popped into the frame, offering some much-needed levity to the conversation.

I grinned. "Hey, Duke. Who's the best boy?"

He barked and wagged hard enough it shook his whole body.

Paisley draped an arm across his back and pressed a noisy kiss to his head. "This one says it's time for one of those things."

Duke glanced back at her with a look that said he knew perfectly well she was talking about a walk, whether she said the word or not.

"Go do the thing. I'm gonna get a nap."

"Keep me posted, and good luck, sugar."

"Thanks. I'm gonna need all of it I can get."

I ended the call and pulled out my planner and a legal pad to start making notes for everything I thought I'd need to learn for the job. I suspected I had a lot of work to do, and I couldn't wait.

# CHAPTER 5

## CALLUM

"You're no' just going to leave me here." I recognized the faint desperation in my voice but couldn't quite pull it back as I watched Alex and Finn gather gear.

Alex pulled one of the mountain bikes down from the rack. "We have clients booked. This whole thing was your idea, so you're in charge of onboarding Parker and getting her up to speed on where we are and what we need."

Finn grinned from where he was checking climbing rope. "Dinna tell me you're afraid of a wee lassie."

That put my back up, as he'd probably meant it to. "Of course not. I just thought there'd be more than me to welcome her on her first day."

"It's the nature of our business that we're out of the office a lot. She might as well get used to it." Alex's lips quirked into a smirk. "Besides, you seemed perfectly ready to welcome her all by yourself the day she walked in here."

He said it as if there'd been something going on besides the professional, and I didn't appreciate it. "That was pure desperation because she took over the phone." I wasn't ashamed to admit it. They knew how much I hated to people.

"And she'll take over the rest of it. But she's got to be oriented to what we have going on here before she can do it properly, so don't think you can hand off everything just yet."

That was logical. I guess I'd just thought one of them would be the one to do this bit, as they were both considerably better with people than I was. Parker hadn't shown any fear or discomfort with me the day we'd met, but that had been a relatively short interaction. Maybe it would change when she got stuck up close and personal with me and realized that my lack of sociability wasn't just in the face of entitled rich twats.

I didn't relish the idea of it.

But neither did I want to give my mates any more fodder for ribbing me. "I can handle it. But anything other than the basics of the booking system, I'm referring back to you."

Alex nodded. "Fair enough. I doubt she'll get that far today. I expect it'll take her all week just to make sense of our filing system."

"Lack of filing system," Finn corrected. "I really hope she works out. We're shite at the paper trail components of this business."

"You just want to play outside all day and get paid for it," I pointed out.

"That would be the high point of this job. Anyway, I've got to get going. I'm meeting my client for a rock climb in forty-five minutes, and I've got a drive."

Alex was right behind him after loading up three mountain bikes for his excursion. Then I was alone in the empty office. At least I'd have half an hour to get my head on straight before Parker arrived. She'd been told the workday started at nine. In truth, we kept variable hours, depending on bookings, but we had to put official hours on the website. After years in the military, none of us were late risers, so one or more of us were usually here by eight or earlier. Now that Alex had Ciara, it was more typically me and Finn.

I supposed if I'd had a beautiful woman in my bed, I'd prefer to start my day there, too. But there was definitely no one warming my sheets but me, and that was only when I managed to sleep. Sometime in the past many months, that balance had shifted to sleeping more often than not. Improvement, if not as much as I'd have hoped for. I wasn't a patient man under the best of circumstances. Not when it came to my expectations for myself. All the doctors and physiotherapists and the mandatory psychological professionals I'd had to meet with after the accident, while I transitioned to civilian life, had cautioned me to be patient, warning that these things took time. But I'd spent my entire military career demanding the most from my body and mind, and getting it. I refused to accept that I no longer had that degree of mastery. Because if I didn't, what did that make me?

I'd just sat down at my computer when I heard the bell over the door jingle. I closed my eyes. All I wanted was some peace and quiet. Couldn't the walk-ins wait until someone else was here to deal with them? I should've locked the door.

"Hello?"

My head snapped up. Not a random walk-in. Parker.

Shoving back from the desk, I strode out to meet her. "You're early." I realized after the words left my mouth that they'd sounded like an accusation.

"I know, but I brought coffee and pastries for everybody, and didn't want to slow anybody down from starting work, in case y'all had appointments first thing."

I stared at the little caddy of drinks and the box she carried under one arm. She'd brought *us* breakfast on *her* first day. I mean... it was nice. But who did that? Actually, we probably should've done something for *her* to welcome her to the office. I felt a little like a bawbag for not thinking of it.

Apparently undeterred by my lack of reply, she set the box on the counter and flipped back the top. "None of y'all struck me as the vegetarian type, so I figured sausage rolls would be a safe bet. I didn't know how anybody took their coffee, so I got two black and two flat whites. One of those is mine, though. The lady at the counter told me that's basically what we drink in America." As she spoke, she uncapped one of the to-go cups and began to add sugar.

The cheer fairly rolled off her. It was way too bloody early for that.

When I still didn't speak, she finally looked directly at me, studying my face. Then she passed me one of the coffees. "I can hush until you've had yours, if it helps."

The cup was warm in my palm, and the aroma wafting up urged me to take a sip. She'd handed me black. I probably seemed the type. Gruff. No frills. Certainly, I could and did drink it this way when it was the only thing on offer, but I preferred it with milk and a nigh ridiculous amount of sugar.

"Thank you."

The word came out rusty, but Parker beamed as if I'd done more than utter the barest of replies. "You're welcome! Where are Alex and Finley?"

"Out already."

"Oh."

A little bit of the smile dropped, so I grabbed a sausage roll. "Their loss. More for me."

That seemed to please her. I don't know why I gave a shite, other than she'd done this nice thing for us, and I didn't want her to feel unappreciated on her first day.

She took a sausage roll for herself and carefully bit in. The little moan she made struck me low in the gut. "I've been in the

UK for less than a week, and I'm already addicted to the pastries. Do you have any idea how lucky y'all are to have this?"

"They dinna have breakfast pastries in the US?"

"Not like this. And not as widely available. The options skew more toward the sweet breakfast pastries, like donuts, or bagels and croissants. I tried crumpets when I first got here because I wondered what the heck they were, and I'm obsessed. I think English muffins are supposed to sort of be that for us, but they just don't compare. Toasted with a swipe of good butter and some berry jam? Perfection." She made a chef's kiss gesture with her fingers, and I found my attention drawn to her mouth, pretty and pink and oh so appealing.

*No, nope. No way. She's an employee.*

I dragged my errant brain back to what she'd said. Had I ever given that much thought to breakfast food? Probably not. I certainly hadn't ever been that excited about it.

Her cheeks pinked, and she flashed a self-conscious smile. "Sorry, I promised to hush until you'd finished your coffee."

"It's... fine."

She moved around to the back of the counter. "I assume I'll be stationed out here to handle walk-in traffic and answer phones?"

When I grunted an affirmative, she put down her purse and began to explore the drawers. She found the post-it with login information that Alex had left for her and took care of that on her own, while I finished my first sausage roll and took another.

"Are there any rules or limitations around software I'm allowed to download?"

I must have looked confused, because she added, "More than likely I'll be downloading and customizing some project management software, unless y'all already have one you use."

"We don't."

"Okay, then. I'm familiar with several. After I have a

clearer notion of y'all's needs, I'll decide which one makes the most sense. It can be done for free, but there are, of course, more options on the paid plans. Those vary by number of users. Since it's a small company, the cost should be minimal, but if budget is a concern, I can stick to the free tier."

I didn't even know what project management software was. "That's an Alex question."

"I'll check with him when he gets back." She pulled a legal pad out of her bag. I noted the first few pages were already filled with what appeared to be neat, color-coded lists. "I took the time last night to do a more thorough review of y'all's social media presence. I've got notes on ways that could be improved or expanded to get you more organic reach. I need to do a bit more research on targeting, but I'm also familiar with Facebook ads, if you want to expand into that variety of marketing."

Already overwhelmed with everything she'd just said, I polished off the last of the coffee. "Let's start with the filing stuff first, aye?"

Again, she flashed that easy smile. "Of course. If you could give me an overview of the kinds of things you're keeping records for, how you're keeping them, where your friction points are, what you're getting behind on, that kind of thing, that'll be a great starting point."

Wanting to get this over with, I dove in to take her through it. In less than fifteen minutes, I was embarrassed by the state of things. She'd asked a half dozen questions I didn't know the answers to. Our version of organization had been more like vaguely themed piles we intended to get to later. Except later hadn't happened. Though she said nothing critical, the many, many more notations she'd added to that legal pad of hers seemed to call out our incompetence. I hated that, even as I felt like this underscored exactly how badly we needed her.

After we got through the paperwork, I pointed at the

computer. "I can show you the basics of the booking system, but any major questions you'll have to direct to Alex. He's the one who designed it."

Parker blinked. "Designed it? He wrote the software?"

"Aye. He's got a lot of skills in computers." That was underselling him. Alex was an extremely talented hacker. But that life was largely behind him now.

"Good to know. Well, I think this is certainly enough to get me started. Unless there's something else you'd like me to prioritize, I'm going to work on an improved organizational system."

"Godspeed." And without another word, I escaped into the back. Our whole interaction had used up at least a month's quota of words, and I needed some silence.

I settled in to check the sheaths of a pile of climbing ropes waiting to be rewound and added back into the rotation. I kept expecting to be interrupted with questions, especially when I heard the phone ring at least three times. But she left me alone. Eventually, I got curious enough to go check on her.

She'd emptied the file cabinets entirely. There were multiple piles spread out along the front desk counter, as well as on the seat of a couple of chairs she'd dragged over from the visitor's area.

"Oh, hey, how do y'all feel about purchasing some more filing supplies? I think I can come up with a better system than what you have going on here."

"Sure. I'll get you into the Amazon Business account."

"If you could go ahead and do that, I'll let you get back to whatever you were doing." She edged her chair to the side so I could access her keyboard.

"Aye, right." When I bent over to enter the credentials, I caught a whiff of coffee and something floral—her shampoo, maybe. My brain stuttered, and I found myself holding my breath, struggling to maintain some professional distance in the tight space because all I wanted to do was lean closer and bury my nose in her hair. "There we go."

"Great." As soon as I stood, she reached for the mouse and immediately began adding a lot of eye wateringly bright colored folders and post-its instead of the generic manilla we'd gone for. When it became clear she didn't need me, I left her alone again.

The next time I came out, she was dealing with a walk-in customer come to lease one of our mountain bikes.

"I know. It's so gorgeous here, isn't it? If I can just get you to fill out this contract here. It spells out the terms. I'll work on pulling everything else together."

As the man across the counter began reading through the paperwork I hadn't even shown her, she turned to me. "Oh good. This gentleman here is renting a mountain bike. If you could get him squared away with the equipment, I'd appreciate it."

"Of course."

I sized the guy up and went to the back to retrieve a bike and helmet, then circled it around front, where Parker already had the man checked out and laughing.

"Have a good ride!"

"I'm sure I will!"

I felt like a bumbling idiot after their easy interaction, but it was simple enough to make sure the bike was adjusted to his height and that the helmet fit properly. Then he was off, apparently electing to ride straight from here.

Back inside, Parker looked up from where she was making yet another notation. "Do any of y'all have allergies?"

"Allergies?" I repeated. "Why?"

"I just thought some plants would perk up the place."

"Plants?" She wasn't the first person to suggest it, but none of us had leapt at the idea because that meant we had to keep them alive.

"Yeah."

"I dinna think anybody has any allergies. I dinna really know. You'll have to ask Finn and Alex."

"Cool. If there's time tomorrow, when Alex and Finley get back, I'd really like to have a group staff meeting to go over my thoughts before I start just implementing things willy-nilly."

She'd been here less than eight hours, and she was already ready for all that? It had been a long time since I'd seen anyone approach a task with such quiet competence. The woman left me with a sense of awe, appreciation, and dread all at once. The need for control itched under my skin, but for once, I forced myself to step back and let someone else take the lead. I'd asked for this.

"Aye, right. I'm sure we can make that happen."

# CHAPTER 6

## PARKER

In my experience, the only thing more satisfying than making order out of total chaos was a good, hard, partner-assisted orgasm. Given I hadn't had one of those in longer than I cared to think about, I was potentially taking too much pleasure in the progress I'd made at Out of Bounds Scotland this week. With all the new color-coded filing supplies in hand, I'd completely overhauled the filing system into something that was both functional and attractive. As an added bonus, I hoped that the color coding would be a visual cue that helped Callum not overwork his good eye trying to find things. Not that he'd asked me for help. I suspected that man would rather choke than admit he needed help with anything. But I'd noticed the lines around his eyes by the end of most days and the subtle physical signs of a probable headache. If I could mitigate that, why wouldn't I?

I had a way to go getting them fully migrated to a solid digital project management system, but Alex was definitely enthused by the prospect of that. Over the course of the week, I'd gotten a feel for the rhythm of their business and their days.

As soon as I crossed one thing off my list, it seemed like I managed to think of three more things to add. I had so many ideas on how their systems could be improved, and even quite a few about how they could expand the reach of their business. But I was keeping those to myself for now. No reason to overwhelm them too quickly, and no reason to spend much time developing those ideas until they decided I could stay.

And I did want to stay. I liked the job. It was a good mix of the organizational pieces I loved and the social I was good at. I liked my three bosses. Finley was definitely the natural-born flirt, and I'd already learned he'd do anything to get out of the office. Alex was the grounded, responsible one. Clearly tech savvy. The booking system he'd built was a dream, and he'd already taken some of my suggestions into account and was working on the coding necessary to incorporate them. And Callum... I got the sense everyone else found him hard to read. Not that he was an open book for me, but I recognized what was underneath the gruff and the grump.

He was a man in great pain. I didn't know how much was physical and how much was emotional. I suspected a fair bit of each. But I'd made it my personal mission to try to coax a smile or a laugh out of him every day, because I kind of thought he'd maybe forgotten how. I hadn't gotten further than the barest quirk of his mouth, but I wasn't giving up.

I'd made notes of the areas that were pinch points for him because of his eye. The little things he struggled with that made him frustrated. I couldn't help with all of it, but I was researching accessibility options that might benefit him. Talking him into using those options would be a whole other project, but I needed to know what was out there first.

The bell above the door jangled, and I glanced up to see Alex's girlfriend, Ciara, step inside, her very enthusiastic puppy, Maeve, trailing after.

"Oh, are you looking for Alex? He's not supposed to be back for another hour or so from that trip to the Cairngorms."

She folded her arms and leaned on the counter, grinning down at me. "Nope. The gents are on their own tonight. I'm here for you."

I blinked. "Me?"

When Maeve whined and dragged at her leash to get to me, Ciara let her go. She scrambled for purchase, looking like a Looney Toons character until her little paws finally found traction. Then she rocketed around my desk, leaping into my lap. I wheezed out a breath but didn't even mind because her little tongue was lapping at my face. Laughing, I wrapped my arms around the dog.

"Who's a good girl? Who's a good pupper?"

"You're coming out with us tonight," Ciara announced.

That surprised me enough to hold the puppy away from my face. What was it with the people here declaring I was doing a thing? First Callum, now Ciara. "I'm sorry. What?"

"You're new in town. You need to meet people, and frankly, we want to interrogate you, so you're coming out with me and my friends."

Finley strode out from the back. "Pro tip: Dinna mention the interrogation before you have your quarry secured. Knowing it's coming tends to make them run."

She stuck her tongue out at him. "Nobody asked you." Her focus turned back to me. "Seriously, come out for girls' night at the pub."

I didn't know this woman. But she had a really cute dog. It was worth enduring some potentially nosy questions in order to get some more puppy snuggles. "On one condition."

"What's that?"

I cuddled Maeve a little closer. "Can Maeve come?"

Ciara grinned. "The chaos monster will definitely be coming."

And that was how I found myself on the outdoor stone patio of The Stag's Head in the middle of a bunch of complete strangers. The pub itself was everything I'd imagined a Highland pub would be—dark wood and worn stone, all set against the backdrop of wooded hills rising to the mountains. The sun hadn't yet set—I still hadn't gotten used to the fact that it stayed light until eight in April—but I could tell that when it did, twinkling fairy lights would add ambiance to the flagstone patio.

Ciara released Maeve's leash, and she immediately defected to a blonde in jeans and a sweater with a puffer vest over the top. "Everyone, this is Parker Lawrence, the new office manager at Out of Bounds Scotland."

The group waved. Ciara pointed to the blonde. "This is Saoirse MacGregor, one of our local vets."

"Sit, Maeve. Sit." Despite the Scottish name, the accent was pure London. The kind of smooth British accent attached to rich people and boarding schools on American TV.

When the puppy plopped her butt on the ground, Saoirse produced a treat from the pocket of her vest.

"That's a good girl."

A black woman with a cloud of enviable curls and large, dark-framed glasses was next.

"This is Pippa Wallace, our resident cheese genius."

"Cheese genius?" I asked.

"I make cheese," Pippa explained. "Ciara's something of a fan."

"She's underselling herself. Her cheese is amazing."

"So you're the person everyone wants for their charcuterie party." I nodded. "Got it."

The third woman, a brunette with blue eyes and a ready

smile, leaned closer. "And I'm the other resident ex-pat South-erner. Skye Stewart."

Hearing a familiar drawl, I instantly relaxed. "Where are you from?"

"Madison, Mississippi."

"Just down the road, so to speak. Nashville for me. How did you end up here?"

"I fell in love with my Scottish pen pal and moved here to be with him."

"You're leaving out the bit where you asked him to be your date for that wedding and ended up jumping his bones," Saoirse added.

Skye's cheeks flushed. "Well, I mean, that, too."

I laughed. "Must be nice."

"It does not suck," Skye agreed.

"Does that mean you, too, are single?" Saoirse asked.

"I am."

"Thank, God. I was getting lonely as the last holdout. Ciara's got Alex, and Pippa's boyfriend, Zeke, just moved here from Texas. All of them are disgustingly happy." But she made the declaration with a smile that made it absolutely obvious she was happy for her friends.

"If you'd stop working for five minutes, you could up your dating game," Pippa pointed out.

"What dating game? You lot have taken up all the single men worth having in the village." She pointed at Ciara. "And before you bring up Alex's mates, that's not an option. Tall, dark, and broody and I would kill each other, and Finley Patterson is the absolute last man I would go out with. I don't give a damn how hot he is."

"Ah, but you admit he's hot," Ciara grinned.

"I'm not blind. I just have standards."

Intrigued, I studied her. "What, precisely, is your problem with Finley?"

Saoirse rolled her eyes. "I'm sorry. I know he's one of your bosses. We just don't get on." She filled an empty glass from the pitcher of beer at the center of the table and pushed it in my direction. "Here, drink this. We're here to get to know *you*."

Dropping my hand to Maeve's head, I scratched between her ears, taking an immense amount of pleasure from the silky feel of her fur beneath my fingers. "What do you want to know?"

"How did *you* end up here?" Skye asked.

"I landed in Glenlaig in particular because the sister of a friend spent a fair amount of time here for a wedding and fell in love with the place."

"Who's that?" Ciara asked. When I only looked at her, she added, "I work for Ardinmuir Event Planning, so it's possible I met her."

"Oh, Swayze Parish."

Ciara straightened in her chair. "No way! You're friends with Swayze?"

"Not really. But I'm very good friends with her sister, Paisley."

"The romance writer? Oh my God, I love her books," Pippa gushed.

"So do I. I've been working as her VA for the past couple of years. Anyway, when I decided I wanted to give the UK a try, she asked her sister for recs, because Swayze's travelled all over, and she recommended here. As for the job... I think I was just in the right place at the right time."

"Were you ever. The boys need you. I dinna think they would've admitted it, but Alex has already been talking about the difference you've made just this week," Ciara said.

"That's nice to hear. They gave me the initial orientation

and kind of turned me loose, so I was hoping they'd be okay with the changes I've been making."

Saoirse picked up her own beer. "What made you decide to move to the UK?"

"Honestly, I needed to put some serious distance between me and my parents." At their varying looks of concern, I felt compelled to clarify. "They're not problematic or abusive or anything. It's more that they want to keep me in a bubble."

"Why?" Skye asked. "If that's not too personal."

I hesitated. But it wasn't as if these women were going to have any idea who my parents were to run and tell them where I was. "I've got a chronic illness I'm dealing with that sometimes limits me, and my parents try to stop me from pushing myself too far or too hard. They mean well, but it's just gotten really stifling." I couldn't remember the last time I'd been allowed to go somewhere alone.

"No one knows your limitations better than you," Saoirse murmured.

"Exactly. I knew I wouldn't really get the chance to sort out what those were on my own, unless I was too far for them to easily interfere. And I chose Scotland because I've always been kind of obsessed. It's beautiful and has such a fascinating history."

"Good for you," Pippa said. "Taking a leap into the unknown is always scary."

"It is that," I agreed.

"Has the transition been hard?"

"I'm still figuring it out. There's so much to love. My favorite thing so far is how dog friendly everything seems. And everyone's dog is so well behaved."

"Do you have dogs at home, then?" Saoirse asked.

"No, we never did. I always wanted one. Spent all my spare time hanging with my friends who had dogs growing up.

Maybe after I get settled. In the meantime, I'm taking advantage of loving on everyone else's." To underscore the point, I leaned down to scruff Maeve more thoroughly. Her back leg kicked in ecstasy.

"Scotland is amazing in a lot of ways," Skye agreed, "But the UK does kind of lag behind the US in terms of accessibility. I don't know what limitations you might sometimes have, but it's hard for them to retrofit stuff in and around all these old buildings, so if you need anything at all, do let us know."

"I appreciate that." I appreciated, too, that she didn't press for details on my condition. It wasn't visible on the surface, and most of the time, I preferred it that way. I didn't want people to look at me differently.

Ciara lifted her glass. "Let's toast to your adventurous spirit."

We all clinked our glasses and drank.

"Now, let's order some food. I'm fair starving."

As the other women began studying the menu, I quietly smiled to myself. I really hoped this job worked out, because I could really see myself making a life here.

# CHAPTER 7

## CALLUM

The nature of our business meant we frequently worked weekends. One day off was as good as any other to me, so I hardly cared when mine were. It wasn't like I had to worry about some kind of social calendar. Days off were for getting the hell away from people and mentally recharging or doing some work on the house I'd bought. Sometimes Alex, Finn, or Ewan would drag me out and force me to people. Other times, I caved up like some kind of mountain hermit. At least until one of them or their well-intentioned women threatened to oust me with a stick of dynamite.

After the week I'd just had, I was wishing for a chance to hermit. As much good as Parker had brought to the office with her superior organizational skills, having her there had also been... a lot. She was just so bloody... cheerful. All. The. Time. I didn't understand it. And while I appreciated that she now handled the phones and the lion's share of client interactions for booking, I could hear her all day when I was there. It just underscored how bad I was at that part of the business. I'd spent most of my adult life operating as one of the elite. I hated feeling incompetent at anything.

But there'd be no chance to cave up until tomorrow. Today I was booked for a guided kayaking excursion. If the client had experience, that might not be too bad. I could simply lead them around the loch, and it wouldn't require a lot of conversation. If they were a beginner, it could go either way. I didn't relish the idea of needing to fish a tourist out of the cold water if they managed to capsize. The days were growing warmer as the Highlands rolled into spring, but warm here was relative. The water itself remained frigid well into the summer. Not that I hadn't been trained for cold water rescue. It just wasn't on my list of things I wanted to do today.

I stepped through the front door of the office.

Parker looked up from her perch behind the front desk and flashed that warm honey smile. "Mornin'."

I grunted. Part of me hadn't expected to see her here today, but someone had to handle equipment rentals, and I didn't remember seeing anyone else on the schedule.

Her smile only deepened at my lack of real response, a pair of dimples popping out in her cheeks. Of course she had dimples like some kind of fucking cherub. It was almost as if she thought my shite attitude was amusing. Except that made absolutely no sense at all.

Scraping together some civility, I approached the desk. "Have you heard anything from my client? I'm booked for a guided kayak today."

"It's me."

"Huh?"

"Y'all said you'd take me on the trip of my choice. I figured it would be easier if I just put it on the schedule like a regular client."

Finn had said that. As she'd been largely in control of the schedule, it meant she'd been in control of choosing her guide.

"And you picked me?" Why the hell would she do that to herself?

Her brows quirked. "Yeah. Is that a problem?"

"No. No, I can take you." Shaking off the confusion, I flipped into professional mode. "It's still pretty cold out. We need to make sure you're dressed properly."

"Got that covered. I'm wearing synthetic long johns, hiking pants, and a fleece. I know we've got waterproof pants and jackets here."

"No cotton socks," I ordered.

"Nope, they're wool." She stood up and came out from behind the desk for my inspection.

I scanned her from head to toe. She actually had dressed appropriately.

"Have you ever kayaked before?"

"Not a day in my life. I'm a complete beginner."

I folded my arms and studied her. "Why do you want to do this?"

I expected her to have some kind of ready, flippant response, but instead she seemed to consider the question with an unusual amount of seriousness.

"Because it's something out of my comfort zone that looks like a challenge, but not so much of a challenge that I'd be in totally over my head. Not that I'm worried about getting in over my head. Obviously, you're very capable, so if anything goes wrong, you'll handle it."

I appreciated her vote of confidence in my abilities. I appreciated, too, this level of responsible caution. We'd had plenty of clients who'd oversold their expertise in various things. It never ended well.

"Okay. I'll start gathering up equipment. If you're coming out, who's on desk duty?"

Finn stepped out of the back. "That'll be me. Herself has given me homework to input my trip logs for the week into the new project management system."

"You'll thank me when you're fully switched over."

"That remains to be seen. But I concede you've already worked wonders, so I'm willing to trust you a bit further."

I left the two of them chatting and began pulling gear. Half an hour later, the kayaks were loaded on the top of my 4x4, and all the rest of the equipment was piled into the backseat.

"Do you have a dry change of clothes in case you tip?"

"I'm hoping not to tip, but yes."

I handed her a dry bag to stuff those into.

"I'll need one more. I brought snacks for us."

"Snacks," I repeated. I also had snacks, but somehow I thought her version was more than trail mix and energy bars.

"Yeah. I thought you might know a good spot for a picnic."

*A picnic. Christ.*

"We'll see."

She stayed miraculously quiet on the drive out to Lochmara. The estate was one of two large ones in the area, both owned by cousins of Ciara and Ewan. Scotland had a right to roam, but due to the potential liability issues, we'd made more formal arrangement to run excursions on their properties. I took a series of farm tracks past the assorted crofts leased from the estate and a number of cottages they'd turned into vacation rentals. We passed rolling hills and disappeared into the green dark of the forest. Parker drank up the view with rapt attention. A little while later, we emerged at the west end of the loch, which had a good shallow spot that would suit our orientation lesson.

I pulled down the kayaks and carted them over to the shoreline. Parker followed with the dry bags. I stowed them in their spot, and we both tugged on our waterproof layers. Then I had her get into her kayak on the ground and began to give her the overview of the equipment. She listened to me with the same rapt attention she'd given the view, asking questions and following every instruction I gave. She wasn't going to be one of those problematic clients who tried something reckless. Good. That would be less stressful for me.

"Right, then. Before we go anywhere, you need to get comfortable with the basic strokes." I positioned my kayak parallel to hers in the shallows, close enough to demonstrate, but not so near she'd panic if she wobbled. "First thing is your posture. Sit up straight, feet braced on the foot pegs."

Parker adjusted, her movements precise and careful. The sunshine yellow of her borrowed waterproof jacket was an assault on my good eye, but her form was textbook perfect. Which was... unexpected.

"Like this?" She looked over, all earnest concentration.

"Aye. Now, the basic forward stroke is like this." I kept my movements slow and exaggerated. Having to compensate for my blind side made me hyper-aware of my form these days. "Push with your top hand, pull with your bottom hand. You want to slice into the water about where your feet are, then pull straight back along the side of the boat."

She mimicked the motion, albeit tentatively. "I feel like I'm going to tip over."

"You won't." The calm certainty in my voice surprised me. "The boat's more stable than it feels. Try it again, but this time, engage your core. Think about the power coming from your trunk, no' your arms."

Her second attempt was stronger, more controlled. A quick learner, this one. And for once, the perfectionist in me wasn't screaming about someone doing it wrong.

"Better. Now let's work on stopping before you end up in Inverness."

I took her through the rest of it until I was confident she'd be able to manage in open water. She was such a good student that I felt some of the usual tension I carried when I was teaching bleed out.

"Ready to go?"

"I think so."

"I'll take the lead. Call out if you're feeling unsteady, aye?"

She grinned and gave a smart salute. "Aye, Captain!"

I caught myself almost smiling, and quickly schooled my expression as I dipped my paddle into the water.

The cloud cover dissipated as we went, until shafts of sunlight caught the ripples of our wake, scattering diamonds across the water. Parker kept pace beside me, staying just at the edge of my good eye's view. She'd picked up the rhythm quickly enough, and for the past hour, we'd moved in companionable silence. No inane chatter, no constant questions. Just the lap of water against our boats and the cry of a hunting osprey overhead.

I'd expected her usual sunshine disposition to spill out all over everything, but she seemed content to simply... be. To observe. Her head turned at each new sight—the flash of a king-fisher's wing, the looming crags of the hills, the ruins of the old crofter's cottage we passed. But she held her peace, absorbing it all with a quiet reverence that sat oddly with my mental image of her.

A flash of movement had me raising my hand in the signal to stop—one she'd memorized instantly during our safety brief-ing. Her paddle stilled. Twenty feet to our right, three sleek heads broke the surface. Otters. The whole family of them were out for their morning hunt.

"Oh!" The soft exclamation drew my attention from the

otters to Parker. Her face... Christ. Like someone had lit her up from the inside, pure joy radiated from every feature. She pressed her lips together, clearly trying to contain her excitement, but her eyes sparkled with it. One of the otters dove beneath her kayak, popping up on the other side with a fish in its mouth, and she bounced a little in her seat.

The movement sent her boat rocking, and my hand shot out automatically to steady her craft. But she'd already corrected, already found her balance again, all without taking her eyes off the wildlife show around us.

My chest felt tight. I told myself it was just the damp air.

We stayed where we were until the otters disappeared.

"That was absolutely incredible," she breathed, staring at where the last one had gone under.

"Aye, it was." But I was looking at her. Because all the tension I'd been carting around this week—hell, for months—had let go. I was more relaxed out here on the water with her than I'd been... maybe since my accident. And that was a bloody miracle.

I tore my gaze away from her. "C'mon. I think I know a place for our picnic."

We paddled for another half hour, until we reached the shore of a tiny, forested island far from any of the inhabited stretches of the loch. I directed her where to beach her kayak and watched her execute my instructions to perfection.

"Stay there. I'll help you out."

I beached my kayak beside hers and loosened my spray skirt so I could climb out of the boat. I splashed through the shallows, dragging my boat further ashore. Then I turned and held out a hand for Parker as she began to extricate herself.

"Should I pass you the dry bags first?"

"We'll get them once I pull the kayak. Hand." I flexed mine to emphasize the order.

She laid her hand in mine, and I held on as she wiggled free of the spray skirt and stepped out of her boat. She staggered a bit as her second foot got caught, and would have toppled straight into the water if my arms hadn't automatically tightened around her, banding her against me.

"Oop!" Her own arms wrapped tight around my waist, and she looked up at me with wide eyes, close enough now I could see the gold flecks in their depths.

Damn, but I wanted to drown in those eyes.

Parker took a tighter hold on me and for one mad second, I thought she'd rise to her toes and kiss me. I didn't think I had it in me to stop her because I desperately wanted to know what that smiling mouth tasted like.

Instead, she found her footing and straightened, releasing me. "Sorry about that."

Disappointment shot through me as she made her way fully onto the shore.

*For the best.*

It wouldn't do to start something up with the likes of her. We needed her for the business. I couldn't go fucking that up out of curiosity. And I would fuck it up. I wasn't relationship material. I wasn't any kind of human material these days, and I'd do well to remember that.

# CHAPTER 8

## PARKER

PARKER

You are on my shit list.

PAISLEY

Why?

PARKER

Because I sorta, kinda, maybe have a little crush on one of my bosses. 😬

PAISLEY

How is that my fault?

PARKER

First, because you were the one who went off on the grumpy-sunshine workplace romance, and got me thinking about it at all. Second, can we talk about the dozens of unicorn heroes you've written that give women expectations of the men in their life?

PAISLEY

:GIF of Lady Bridgerton exclaiming Tell me
everything!:

I checked my watch. Twenty minutes left of my lunch break.
I'd parked myself on a bench in a little patch of sunshine to eat
the sandwich I'd grabbed at the bakery. There was time to tell
her and make it back.

PARKER

I mean, there's nothing to tell. Nothing's
happened.

PAISLEY

So why are you crushing on tall, dark, and
broody?

PARKER

How do you know it's tall, dark, and broody?

PAISLEY

Opposites attract is a thing for a reason.

I huffed out a breath and began to text again.

PARKER

We went kayaking on Saturday. It wasn't a
date. Just the adventure I had booked.

The whole experience had been lovely. The loch was absolutely gorgeous, and watching Callum's broad shoulders flex as
he demonstrated proper paddling technique had been... educa-
tional. Getting out on the water, out in the middle of nature,
had felt so soothing. Less soothing had been that moment I'd
nearly fallen getting out of the kayak. But he'd been right there,
catching me before I could fall, as I'd always known he would.

I'd been extra grateful I had two days off after the trip,

because while kayaking had been amazing, that much activity had been hard on my body. I'd slept most of the last forty-eight hours, other than surfacing for food. I was a still bit achy and sore today, but functional, which I was counting as a win.

PAISLEY

And was that a bonding experience?

I considered the question. We hadn't talked. Not much. Yet I felt closer to Callum after the trip. Over the course of the day, I'd watched the tension sort of drain off him. I wasn't sure how much of that was just being out in nature in general, being away from people, and how much might have been due to the fact that—just maybe—he enjoyed my company.

PARKER

I don't know. Maybe? He's just... so much like a lion with a thorn in his paw. All big and snarly and strong.

PAISLEY

And you want to help heal the lion. I get that. I felt the same way about Ty.

Paisley's second-chance romance with her high school boyfriend, who'd broken her heart when he chose duty over her, was the stuff of one of her own books. They'd found their way back to each other again after nearly twenty years, and she'd been the one to help heal him. She didn't put it that way, but I'd heard Ty himself say she'd saved him.

Did I want to do that for Callum? I could see his pain, both physical and emotional, and I wanted to help him. But without making him feel broken or less, because, God knew, I understood what that was like. It was one of the reasons I didn't easily share my own condition with others. But this was more than feeling a bit of a kindred spirit. I was attracted to Callum, something I'd become overwhelmingly aware of when he'd saved me from toppling into the loch. I'd had such a rush of heat through my system, I wondered I hadn't started steaming right there on the shore. Even now, I could feel the warmth of his grip and the pressure of his arms around me, the press of that magnificent chest against mine, even though the life jacket.

PARKER

He's not Ty, and we don't have y'all's history.

PAISLEY

Doesn't mean there couldn't be something there.

PARKER

If ever there was a poster boy for Not Open To Relationships, it's him.

PAISLEY

I mean, nobody said it had to be an outright relationship. You could just have a hot, sexy Scottish fling.

PARKER

I am absolutely not flinging with one of my bosses. That would be messy in the extreme. I like this job.

PAISLEY

☹ Fine, no flinging with your boss. Which is just a crying shame. But I make no apologies for writing books that give women expectations of their partners. Men need to be held to a higher standard!

PARKER

I can't argue with that. And now I have to get back to work before you go off on one of your feminist rants. Plus, you have words to write.

PAISLEY

True story. At least you entertained me during my coffee. Duke sends wags.

She followed that up with a video clip of her pup wagging so hard it shook his whole butt.

I grinned.

PARKER

Give him snuggles from his Auntie Parker.

On the walk back to the office, my brain put those moments I'd fallen into Callum's arms on repeat. Again.

*Not helpful, brain. No flinging. Friends only.*

Alex looked up from a folder as I stepped into the lobby. "You're a genius."

"Am I?"

"I mean, it's a wee bit of a pain to fill all this out on clients on the front end, but having all this information on them will make it so much easier for repeat bookings."

Feeling a little smug, I stowed my purse in the drawer. "It'll also make it easier for you to target them when you run specials to encourage those repeat bookings. Your mailing list is my next frontier. But I want to finish the project management stuff first."

"That sounds brilliant. I look forward to hearing your ideas."

I checked the schedule. "Aren't you due out for another mountain biking excursion in half an hour?"

"Shite. Aye, I am. Thanks." He disappeared into the back, and I basked in the sense of a job well done.

I'd busted my ass at this job, and it was paying off. Everything was running smoother—anecdotally anyway—and bookings were up. I'd already been thinking about other ways to improve their process and means of reaching potential new customers, but I was sitting on those until I knew I really had the job. I still had four days to go before the end of my trial period. But it definitely seemed like the guys were happy with the work I'd done. They certainly weren't talking as if I wouldn't be back next week. But there were no guarantees in life but death and taxes, so I'd keep doing the job to the best of my ability and see what happened. To that end, I dove into inputting more of that client data to the database I'd set up.

The work moved steadily between client calls and forwarding booking queries to the guys. Alex headed out for his ride. Finn wouldn't be back until tomorrow. He was out on a backcountry guided hike, which I'd already learned was his favorite. I wasn't entirely sure where Callum was. He didn't have a booking on the schedule, so I wasn't sure if he was here.

A spate of swearing from the back answered my unasked question.

Rather than steer clear, I wandered back to find him in his office, rubbing his eyes. I could see the lines of strain and fatigue in his face. This didn't usually hit until the end of the day, but I knew he'd been trying to do the stuff I needed him to do for the project management side of things. I'd hated to put it on him, but I'd also known that he'd feel weird if I'd done his and didn't do Finn's or Alex's.

I leaned against the doorjamb. "Can I help you with something?"

"I need to respond to these emails." I could hear the frustration and simmering resentment that he still had to deal with people at all. That, at least, was something I could mitigate.

"Well, I can take dictation. You tell me what you'd like to say—unfiltered—and I can translate it into more professional, acceptable business speak." It might at least get him away from that monitor long enough to rest his eyes.

"I can write some damned emails," he growled.

I knew better than to rise to that bait. "Of course you can. But by your own admission, you don't enjoy peopling. This would minimize your having to think about ways to do it politely, and it would reduce the eye strain you're getting from staring at that screen for too long without a break."

It was the wrong thing to say. A muscle jumped in his scruffy jaw, and his hands fisted on the desk. "I can manage my own fucking eye. I dinna need you coming in here babying me!" He was all but roaring by the end. The lion indeed.

I absolutely understood that he was lashing out because he was in pain, but I had a line. Him using me as a ready target because he was frustrated was it. So I let the stiffness and upper-crust formality that had been trained into me practically since birth bleed into my tone. "I don't believe I'm babying you at all. Y'all hired me to streamline your business, and this is an area I can do that. It's your choice to be a horse's ass and hang onto something you hate on principle. I have other work. If you change your mind, you know where to find me."

Turning my back on him, I stalked back out front. For all my generally sunshiny nature, I absolutely had a temper. It just took a great deal to make me lose it.

Lowering myself carefully into my chair, I wondered if all my good intentions were worth it. I liked this job. I wanted to stay. But could I deal with Callum long term if he stayed like this? It was entirely possible that this angry, short-tempered state was his default and no amount of my attempting to help would change a damned thing. The depressing reality was he wouldn't change unless *he* wanted to change.

The phone rang, putting an end to my brooding. Shoving away my own irritation, I blew out a breath and put on my professional hat. It was time to get back to work.

# CHAPTER 9

## CALLUM

Shame hit me like a mortar round the moment Parker walked out. She'd just been trying to help. Doing the job I'd fucking hired her to do. And I'd gone and bitten her head off.

Playing the exchange over again, there was absolutely nothing in what she'd said that implied I wasn't capable. I did hate all of this shite. So why didn't I let her help?

My head ached, and I wanted to hit something. I needed some space. To get out of the office and release some of this rage before I said or did something truly unforgivable. Abandoning the emails, I slunk out the back like the coward I was and began to walk.

Our property backed up to a patch of woods that bumped up against the back side of the village. I wove through the trees, walking almost soundlessly through the vegetation that was finally starting to show real signs of spring. The ground sloped up, and I followed, relishing the faint burn in my thighs as I climbed. The past few days, I'd missed the punishing runs that bled off the worst of the rage and allowed me to function as something resembling human. Obviously, that had been a mistake. But I'd felt almost peaceful after my day on the loch with Parker.

It hadn't lasted. No reprieve ever did.

The trees gave way to pasture at the top of the hill. I scrambled up and over a cluster of big rocks. About thirty yards away, a stone circle speared up from the ground. It wasn't huge. Nothing on par with the likes of Stonehenge. A handful of sheep grazed in and around the stone dance, obviously unimpressed.

The sight of it stopped me in my tracks. In all my wanderings since moving here, I'd never stumbled across this place. It felt like stumbling into a secret. I strode over and circled the perimeter. There were no markings that I could discern. If there'd ever been any, they'd been worn away by time. The stones were well weathered, with moss growing up one side. It felt old. But if this was anything significant, why wasn't the village using it for tourism? I'd been here for months and had never heard a word about it.

Maybe this was a folly—one of those fake ancient-looking sites erected by the rich back in the 1700 and 1800s. Though I wasn't aware of any other estates in the area besides Lochmara and Ardinmuir, and we weren't near either. And even a folly would've been a tourist draw.

Parker would probably love this. I could just imagine her delight at finding it, how her eyes would light up at the sight of it. She'd probably whip out her phone to take a photo or try to research the history. Or maybe she'd just stand right there and absorb it, the way she had the family of otters on the loch, with wonder written all over her pretty face. Of course, she might well be just as delighted with the sheep. She seemed to find joy in almost everything.

Everything but me. Because I was an arsehole.

Fueled by a fresh wave of shame, I began moving again, headed toward the other side of the village.

I wound up at the pub. I didn't know exactly why I'd come here. There were people. There were always people at The Stag's Head. But it was well past lunch at this point, so it wasn't too busy. As I moved further inside, Laura Craig, Ewan's second in command, greeted me by name and waved an expansive hand toward the many open tables.

"Sit wherever you like. Or I can let Ewan know you're here."

Ewan. He was why I'd really come. My former squad leader had a good head on his shoulders. Maybe he'd have some wisdom to offer.

"I'll just go back. Thanks."

Laura waved me toward the hall off the largest dining room.

As I moved through the room, scents of fried onions and fish made my stomach growl. I realized I'd never had lunch. "Is the kitchen still open?"

"No' for much longer, but I expect we can scare you up something."

"Surprise me. Whatever's already ready or easiest."

"Got it."

I found Ewan hunched over the keyboard of an ancient computer, much as I had been earlier. "Hey."

"Hey. Come. Sit. Save me from accounting."

I dropped into one of the chairs opposite the battered wooden desk.

"How's the new girl working out?"

"She's working out great."

Ewan folded his arms and leaned back in his chair. "Then why are you scowling?"

Some variation of a scowl was my default expression these days, but this was more than that, and I knew it. I drummed my fingers on the arms of my chair, restless again. "Part of it is because she's come in and done all these things seemingly so effortlessly."

"What's the problem? Isn't that what you hired her for?"

This was exactly what I'd wanted when I offered her the job. My fingers stopped drumming and clenched the arms of the chair. I hadn't even admitted this to Finn and Alex, and saying it now was like speaking through broken glass. "Because it makes me feel incapable and way the fuck too dependent. I hate the idea of being dependent on anyone."

Ewan absorbed that, considering for a bit. "Did you depend on your squad?"

My brows drew together. "Of course. They had my back. I trusted them with my life."

"Did that somehow make you less?"

I'd walked right into that one. "Well, no. It's the nature of the job. If you dinna trust your team, you canna function properly as a unit."

"Right. So, how is this any different? You brought someone with a certain set of skills into the team to take over weak spots. She's done it and apparently done it damn well. So why is this really stuck in your craw?"

"I dinna know."

But I did know. I didn't want Parker to see me as less. Not that I was about to admit that to Ewan.

Laura knocked on the door. "Lunch is served." She brought me a to-go container of cottage pie.

"Thanks."

When she'd gone again, I poked at the food. It smelled incredible—anything that came out of Dom Bassey's kitchen was incredible—but my stomach was twisted in knots.

"I ought to go apologize, but I figure I'm just going to botch that, too."

"What exactly do you need to apologize for? Other than dodging the last three dinner invites Isobel or Ciara sent out."

More shame crawled up the back of my neck, heating my face. I was racking up a lengthy list of IOUs for apologies. "I bit Parker's head off when she was only trying to help."

"Well, we've all been getting a lot of that."

Fuck. That didn't make me feel any better. "Sorry."

"Right now, I'm no' the one who deserves the apology. I figure at this point, a botched apology is better than none at all."

He was probably right. I wasn't a man who apologized easily, because apologizing meant admitting I'd made a mistake, and I didn't like making those any more than I liked dealing with people. I'd made a big one with Parker, and I worried she'd want to leave.

A part of me wondered if maybe that was for the best, because this inconvenient attraction to her was a problem. I was her boss. As a former military man, I understood power dynamics. I'd never want to abuse that. Not that Parker was remotely a doormat. She seemed to have no trouble at all standing up to me in my shite moods. Damn if that didn't make me like her more.

I didn't want her to leave. Our business was better with her as part of it. Not just because she'd taken over so many things I disliked, but because she was truly good at what she did. We could grow and thrive with her help. But beyond all that, I didn't want her to leave because she didn't feel trusted or welcomed. Which meant I had four more days to find the right words to make her want to stay.

# CHAPTER 10

## PARKER

I settled in at my desk early on Saturday morning with a weird sense of dissonance. Today was the last day of the trial period. The guys had been so busy this week, there'd been no discussion of whether they wanted me to say on or if this was the end of things. And, honestly, I wasn't sure how I felt one way or the other. Despite the fact that I'd been all in on this job from the beginning, I was no longer sure it was the right fit for me. Or, more properly, I wasn't sure if I was willing to put myself into a position where I might be used as a verbal punching bag.

Not that Callum had done it again. In truth, he'd been scarce around the office ever since. Some of that was on me for making sure he was fully booked and occupied. Some of it had clearly been by his own choice. We were, I supposed, avoiding each other. Which had been fine for a day or two. But honestly, I'd expected better of him. Maybe it was my own romanticism making me think he'd come apologize.

He hadn't.

That shouldn't have stung as much as it did. What were we to each other, truly? I'd known the man for barely more than two weeks. He was one of my three bosses. Our outing on the loch didn't make us friends. I'd probably imagined that moment of connection the day we'd first met. For him, I'd been only a convenient solution to a problem.

Well, at least I could comfort myself with knowing I'd given my all these two weeks, and if they elected not to keep me, I was leaving them in better shape than I'd found them.

A noise from the back told me someone had arrived. More than one someone by the sounds of the footsteps making their way through the warehouse section of the building. Alex and Finn emerged from the back hall and converged on my desk. Finn held a familiar box under one arm.

"Good morning, Parker." He put the box on my desk and opened it. "We brought you breakfast."

I cautiously eyed the bakery box. "Is this a going-away pastry?"

Alex leaned on the counter. "We're hoping it's a you're-going-to-stay pastry, because we'd like to formally offer you the full-time position of office manager at Out of Bounds Scotland."

Finley closed in on the other side. "You've revolutionized everything in the time you've been here, and frankly we dinna ken what we'd do without you."

Their appreciation warmed something inside me. And yet, I didn't immediately say yes. Callum's absence from this offer was glaring. Did that mean he wasn't in favor of my staying? Surely his business partners wouldn't be making the offer if they weren't all in agreement.

"I appreciate all of that. Can I have some time to think about it? I need to consider all the aspects of really staying. From the visa application to the cost of living. There are a lot of moving parts involved in all of this, and I want to make sure this is the right move before I say yes. I wouldn't want to put you in some sort of position where you got left hanging."

The two men exchanged a look, obviously not having expected my reticence.

Alex broke the silence first. "Of course. Take all the time you need. And if we can answer any questions for you, or if you have any concerns, please don't hesitate to ask."

Did I imagine that little hesitation before he said "concerns?" Did I want to bring up my complicated feelings around Callum? No. He was their friend. Their brother-in-arms. Their allegiance would be to him—as it should be.

I mustered a smile. "Thanks. And thanks for the pastries."

When they might have pursued the issue, the front door opening put an end to the opportunity. The first of their clients were arriving. I offered a warm smile to the group of university students who'd booked a mountain biking excursion.

"Welcome to Out of Bounds Scotland. If I could just get y'all to sign in here and fill out this paperwork."

We all fell into our expected roles, getting the liability waivers signed, going over base-level safety instructions, and getting each participant kitted out with whatever equipment they needed to rent for the day. I appreciated the busy. It kept my mind off the decision I needed to make.

But eventually, the guys headed out, taking their clients with them, leaving me alone with my thoughts and the scones still perched on my desk. I nibbled on one as I input the new client paperwork from this morning's batch of adventurers.

"I'd like to speak with you."

At the deep male voice behind me, I startled so hard the scone went flying. Callum stepped into view, scooping up the ruined pastry from the floor. As he straightened to his full height—towering over me where I sat—I caught the familiar scent of coffee. He held a steaming to-go cup with the bakery's logo on the side.

I pressed a hand to my galloping heart and glared at him. "Are you *trying* to give me a heart attack? I thought I was here alone."

His mouth twisted in a wince. "Sorry. Stealth is kind of second nature at this point." He set the cup down on my meticulously organized desk, careful to use the coaster I'd added my first week. "I'll try to warn you I'm coming next time."

Next time? Did that mean he expected me to stay? And what was this coffee? Some kind of peace offering after days of silence?

The tension of our last real interaction still hummed between us, and I wasn't at all sure it was something I could live with long term. I hadn't been tiptoeing around him. That wasn't my way, and I wasn't afraid of him, no matter how loud his bark. But I had stuck to my job and avoided any additional effort to help him with anything, figuring that if he wanted to wallow, that was his business.

"What did you want to speak to me about?"

He shifted on his feet, glancing down at the floor before forcing himself to look back at me. "My behavior earlier this week was absolutely unacceptable. The work you've done here has been nothing short of miraculous, including all the small things you've done to make my life easier. I didn't know that color coding would help. And digitizing everything with the project management system so I could blow everything up to a larger size on any screen was... well, it was more useful than I would have imagined."

He continued to fidget, obviously uncomfortable. "I've been struggling with accepting help. Some days are worse than others, but that's no' an excuse. All that to say, I'm sorry I was an arsehole, and I want you to stay."

He did?

I was so stunned by the admission I said nothing at all.

Evidently compelled to fill the silence, Callum kept talking. "I'll understand if you dinna want to. If I've ruined the idea of that for you. But I hope I haven't. I promise I'll do better, and that I'll work on my reactions. Because you're good for the business and good for the team. And... you're good for me. Beyond the fact that you keep me off the bloody phones."

I couldn't help but snicker a little at that rueful admission.

"Please stay, Parker."

Leaning back in my chair, I absorbed all of this. By this point, I hadn't expected an apology at all, let alone a proper one that acknowledged what he'd done wrong. He hadn't struck me as the kind of guy who'd do that, because it required talking and admitting weakness, neither of which were things he tolerated well. But it was what I'd needed to hear.

The tension I'd been carrying around for days finally bled out, the wall between us collapsing. I had to acknowledge to myself that this job wasn't just about escaping my parents. If it had been, any job would have done. But I wanted *this* job in *this* place. And, for better or worse, part of why was the man standing in front of me.

I didn't know what that meant. Maybe nothing. But I felt, deep in my bones, that he and I were meant to be in each other's lives for a while.

"Thank you for the apology. And yes, I do intend to stay."

He visibly relaxed, his shoulders lowering, his posture shifting. "Good."

"I do have one really major issue I need to sort out in a hurry."

"What's that?"

"Lovely as the B and B is, staying there long term is cost prohibitive. I've got to find an actual place to live."

His shoulders straightened, as if with renewed purpose. "I can help with that."

# CHAPTER 11

## CALLUM

"I really appreciate you doing this." Parker shut the front door of the B&B, looking like a daisy in a bright yellow jacket. "It's not that I'm not capable of finding my own place, but I've been here long enough to understand that there are differences between here and the States, and I don't want to screw something up because I just don't know it's something I should ask about."

"No problem." It was the least I could do to make up for having been a total bawbag to her. I felt a wee bit guilty, too, that none of us had even considered the expense to her for lodging during the two-week trial period. That had to be a lot of money. While we were paying her fairly for the work she was doing, it wasn't enough to cover the exorbitant occupancy taxes and such that applied to places like inns and bed and breakfasts. So, I was here today to ferry her about and make sure she found something affordable that met her needs. "Are you ready?"

"I am."

Drawing on the manners I'd gotten far too rusty at using, I

made an after-you gesture. Parker flashed a smile and moved automatically to the left side of the pavement, nearest the road. My instincts screamed because on that side, I couldn't see her or any potential threats that might come from that direction. I made it about a half-dozen steps before I gently, but firmly, gripped her arm and moved her to my right.

She glanced up at me, eyebrows raised in question.

I wrestled with myself for a few moments before finally admitting, "I canna have you on my blind side." I couldn't deal with anyone on that side but my former squadmates, because I knew they could handle themselves.

"Oh. I didn't think of that. Of course. No problem." She continued on a few paces before I got my arse moving again.

"The estate agent is Mr. Harrison?"

She wasn't going to say anything more about it. At the realization, I gradually relaxed. "Aye. He's the same one we used to find the business property."

Harrison's office was on the high street, halfway between the pub and the newsagent.

Parker peered at the listings posted in the window. "They definitely do things differently here."

"They dinna post the properties where people can see them in the US?" I tugged the door open and held it for her.

"Not in a window. It's all online, with lots of pictures and sometimes video tours. And the architectural styles are wildly different from what I've seen here."

Harrison rose from his desk as we stepped inside. "Mr. Quinn. Good to see you again."

I shook the man's hand and made introductions to Parker.

She flashed him that sunny smile. "Nice to meet you, Mr. Harrison. I appreciate your time today."

"Of course, of course. Do you have a wishlist for what you're looking for in a property?"

She glanced at me. "I'm not sure what Callum may have told you, but of course, I'm looking for a place to rent. An apartment—flat—or a small house. I'd prefer somewhere that's furnished and within walking distance of the Out of Bounds Scotland office. Preferably on the first floor—wait, no, that's the second floor here. The ground floor."

Harrison blew out a breath. "Well, you ken it's a small village, so we dinna have a multitude of options, but I'll show you what we've got, and we'll see how many of your criteria we can meet. Come on out to my car. I'll drive us over."

The first place was half a mile down the road from our office, the bottom floor of a two-story house that had been converted into flats. It wasn't furnished. As we walked through the space and Harrison went on about the features, Parker stopped in the kitchen.

"Okay, what is it with the UK and having to turn on all the plugs? And why is there a random red Don't Touch Me switch on the kitchen wall?"

"That's the main breaker for the boiler. Since it's radiant heat, that controls the master heat and the hot water for the shower," Harrison explained.

She stared at him. "Then why's it out here instead of hidden away in a breaker box in a closet, where it can't get accidentally turned off?"

"Uh... because no one here would touch it?"

"So weird," she muttered.

My lips twitched a little. "The rest of it is because our electricity is a lot more expensive than what you have in the States, so we shut it off at the source unless we need it."

"Well, with that in mind, I can see I'm going to need to adjust my budget to account for more expensive utilities, so tons of furniture is definitely not in the cards." Her smile took any sting out of the words. "What's next?"

The next place was a bit more promising. It was furnished. Single level. Not a big place, but it would be plenty for her. As Harrison was going over the features and pointed out the washer, Parker spun a circle. "But where's the dryer?"

"Most people line dry their clothes," he explained. "There's a rack out back."

She stared at us. "In a country that rains this much, y'all line dry your clothes?"

"Well, plenty of people have dryers in their own homes, but it comes back to the cost of electricity. Many people will wash their clothes at home and then take them to the laundrette in the village to dry."

"They're... just toting bins of wet clothes around?"

She shouldn't have looked so damned cute with that perplexed expression on her face.

When Harrison and I just shrugged, she shook her head. "I'm feeling very American right now. Okay, Callum, thoughts on this place?"

I had to remind myself she wasn't asking for a tactical assessment. "The flat itself is fine, but I'm a little concerned with the distance. Two miles is nothing in good weather, but I dinna like the idea of you walking that far in the winter, so unless you're planning to buy a car by then..."

"Fair point. I don't know where my budget will be by then, and beyond that, I'm not sure I'm up for learning how to drive on the left side of the road. Next?"

Harrison circled back toward the village, to a side street not too far from work. "This one is closer and furnished. Single level."

The block held eight flats and didn't look great from the outside. The white painted exterior was stained, and rust showed through where paint peeled from the railings and stairways leading to the first floor. The moment we stepped inside, I smelled mold. It took me less than a minute to find the source—a leak over the kitchen window. The bathroom faucet dripped, and stains in the bowl of the toilet told me it ran more often than not. The floors were rough and scarred, and I absolutely couldn't imagine a woman like Parker living with furniture that looked as if it had been scavenged from a charity shop dumpster.

"No."

Harrison trailed off whatever selling point he'd been making. "I'm sorry. These are the only listings I've got."

Parker caught her lip between her teeth. "Well, I've got to have something. I suppose the—"

"I may have another idea. Hang on." I stepped outside to make a phone call.

Hamish Colquhoun answered on the first ring. He'd been the attorney to handle the closing on our business property. He'd also been Alex's landlord. Though the place had sat empty more often than not after Alex had moved in with Ciara, Alex had continued to pay the lease.

"Hamish, this is Callum Quinn."

"Callum. Good to hear from you. What can I do for you?"

"Have you leased the flat above your office?"

"No, actually."

"Would you be willing to show it to our office manager?"

"Aye, of course. I can meet you there in, say, half an hour?"

"Perfect."

Ending the call, I headed back inside. "I've got one other option I think will suit you better."

"I'll just take you back, then."

The short ride back to Harrison's office was a little awkward, but Parker smoothed things over by warmly thanking the man for his time. As we hit the pavement again, she moved to my right this time, without being asked. She'd remembered and didn't make a big thing of accommodating me. Because I noticed her flagging a little, I shortened my stride.

"Okay?"

"Just a little tired." She shot me a what was no doubt meant to be a reassuring smile, but this one didn't quite reach her eyes.

Had I said or done something wrong? Had Harrison said something to offend her while I'd been outside making my call? The man had seemed fine when I'd met him before, but he'd hardly try to mess with me. Parker was a sweet, trusting woman. I shouldn't have left her alone.

"Hey, where did your brain go just now?"

I looked down to where Parker's hand lay on my arm. "What?"

"You suddenly started scowling like you wanted to punch someone."

"Was Harrison inappropriate with you?"

She blinked, her eyes widening in surprise. "No. Why?"

I couldn't very well say that her smile wasn't right. "You just seemed a little... off somehow."

"Like I said. I'm a little tired."

I could have left it alone. Probably should have. But instead I paused. "Is that all it is? Are you having second thoughts about staying?"

The hand on my arm squeezed gently. "No. I'm fine. I promise."

"Would you tell me if you weren't?" I was pushing boundaries. I was her boss. But I felt responsible for her, somehow.

Her answer was too long in coming. "If I need any help, I promise I'll ask for it."

Which wasn't at all the same thing as being fine. But clearly I wasn't getting anywhere else with this right now.

A little while later, we met Hamish in front of his office. I made introductions again, and Parker charmed him in that way of hers.

"Let's go up." Hamish turned to unlock a door.

"Up?" Parker asked.

"Aye, the flat's above my office." Opening the door, he gestured up the stairwell.

There was a strange almost-anxiety about her as she took them in. Was she that tired, or were stairs a problem for some other reason? I didn't ask, not wanting to put her on the spot, and pretty sure she wouldn't tell me either way. We followed Hamish up.

"The flat's not huge. Just one bedroom, with a lounge area and small kitchen. We'd been debating whether we wanted to try the Airbnb thing or stick with long-term leases. It is furnished."

We stepped inside. It looked much as it had when Alex had lived here, minus the desk with the bank of multiple monitors that had taken up one wall.

Parker brightened as soon as she came through the door. "Oh, this is adorable."

Hamish reeled off the relevant details about price and specs, but I didn't think she was fully listening. I could see her mentally settling in. She moved over to the little two-person table beside the window that overlooked the high street. I could just make out the edge of her smile as she looked out at the view.

"What do you think?" I couldn't quite stop myself from asking.

Again, there was that hesitation before she finally answered. Her gaze skittered back toward the stairs. "It's perfect. I'd have preferred ground level, but this is by far better than the other options." She turned to Hamish. "What is your policy on pets?"

"Alex had a cat. Honestly, we're fine with pets. There's just an additional deposit."

"Good to know." This time, the smile she turned on me made it all the way to her eyes. "I'll take it."

A sense of satisfaction settled over me. I'd found her a place that was safe, affordable, well-maintained, and within walking distance of the office. It felt like I'd done something to help make up for the fact that I'd been an arsehole.

"Wonderful. Let's just go down to my office and we can sign the lease."

# CHAPTER 12

## PARKER

"Don't keep me in suspense! Show me your new place," Paisley ordered.

I flipped the camera around on my phone and began walking through the apartment. "It won't take long. It's just one bedroom, one bath."

I took her into the tiny room, panning over the full-size bed and dresser. "I just moved in yesterday, so until I have time to make a trip to one of the bigger towns, I borrowed a sleeping bag from work. I did pop by the local charity shop and grabbed a few knickknacks. I got this great stoneware bowl." Wandering back out into the main living space, I showed her the kitchen that took up one wall, along with the bowl on the counter I'd filled with fresh fruit. I completed the tour by showing the dinette set tucked beside the front window, and the lounge area, which had a decently comfy sofa, coffee table, and armchair.

"I'm super grateful it came furnished. And furnished with some decent pieces instead of some el cheapo weird stuff. My landlord and his wife have good taste."

"They do. It looks cozy and comfortable."

I flipped the camera back around. "It still needs some of me in it, but it's mine." I'd paid for the deposit and first month's rent entirely on my own, with money I'd earned myself. The amount of pride I felt at that might have been just a shade ridiculous, but it was something I hadn't been sure I could do when I came here.

"Congrats, Parker. Seriously. In a matter of just a few weeks, you've achieved your primary goal. That's months faster than you expected."

I flopped onto the sofa. "It definitely feels like the Universe is smiling on me."

"And will you be taking that as an auspicious sign to tell everybody back home? Or, perhaps more importantly, when are you going to come clean to your guard dog?"

Some of my pleasure in my accomplishment dimmed. I'd known there'd be consequences for the decisions I'd made. At the time, I'd judged them worth it. I knew the longer things went on, the worse it would be, but I just... wasn't ready yet.

"I'm not sure," I hedged. "I just need a little more time. Please." I needed to be sure that no one could drag me out of my new life. Because I knew they'd absolutely try.

Paisley did not look pleased with this request.

I held in a wince. "In other news, I got all your newsletters scheduled for next month, laid in the socials leading up to your next release, and sent you an analysis of the ad spend and audiences from your last big Facebook marketing campaign."

She opened her mouth, and I knew I wasn't getting away with the subject change. But before she could speak, someone knocked on my door.

"Apparently somebody's here. I've gotta go. I promise I'll be in touch soon."

She sighed. "Talk soon."

"I owe you!"

"Yeah, you do. Love you. Be safe."

I ended the call and went to answer the door, curious who it might be. No one but the guys knew I'd moved in yet.

Saoirse stood at the top of the steps, a bottle of wine in one hand, a leash in the other. At the other end of the leash was a gigantic white floof of a dog.

"Oh! Aren't you gorgeous?" I instantly crouched down. The dog wriggled with joy, kissing whatever bits of me he could reach, while I scruffed his ears and chest.

Saoirse stepped inside after the dog. "I see where I rank in all this." Her tone was dry, but a smile took any sting out.

"Sorry. You distracted me with cuteness. Who is this adorable pile of fluff?"

"This is Falkor. My current problem child."

"Problem child?" I continued to rub Falkor's ears as he leaned against me. "He seems like a total doll."

"Let's open this wine I brought as a housewarming gift, and I'll tell you about him."

"You're in luck. Dishes and basic cookware were part of the furnishings."

I wandered over to the kitchen and retrieved a pair of glasses. "How did you even know I was here?"

"Alex told Ciara. Ciara told the group chat. We want to add you to that, by the way, but I thought we'd better ask before we just did it. Because we're a talky lot, and once you're added, it's hard to leave."

Warm fuzzies bloomed in my chest that they wanted to include me. "I'd love that." Hunting through the drawers, I nodded toward the dog. "He's a Great Pyrenees, right?"

"He is. About two-and-a-half years old."

My search turned up a corkscrew. Falkor followed me step for step, looking up in adoration. God, he was adorable.

Saoirse did the honors with the wine, and we settled in with our glasses. Falkor sat at attention, sweeping that big poof of a tail as he stared first at me and then the empty stretch of sofa beside me.

I bit my lip. "Is he allowed on the furniture?"

"That's your call."

"Well, since you're bringing me the gift of puppy cuddles along with the wine..." I patted the sofa beside me. "Falkor, up."

He leapt gracefully onto the sofa, turned one circle, then collapsed in a rag-doll heap so his head landed in my lap.

"Oh, he's in heaven now."

"So am I." I grinned and stroked his head and silky ears as he continued to try to lick any part of me he could reach. "So what's his story?"

Saoirse sipped at her wine. "Falkor is a failed mobility service dog."

"Failed? He couldn't do the job?"

"Oh no, he does the job beautifully. He's just too friendly." She sipped her wine and sighed. "It was inevitable with his name, I suppose. He misunderstood the assignment. Instead of luck dragon, he thought he was supposed to be a *lick* dragon. The group that was training him failed him. He's not suitable for dealing with livestock, and he's not been 100% trained and certified for work as a service animal, but he's also not happy *not* working. So I've been trying to figure out what to do with him."

"Poor baby." I moved my scritches down to his chest, wondering how anyone could see that face and those big liquid eyes and not fall instantly in love.

"I was thinking you might like him."

I stopped petting and stared at her. "What?"

"Well, since you're staying now. You didn't say too much about what sort of chronic situation you're facing, but you did say you were sometimes limited because of it, and I thought I'd see if you two might suit. You clearly love dogs, and I thought he could be both help and companion."

My throat tightened with emotion at the offer. I was carving out a place here, but I still got lonely.

Falkor licked my wrist, reminding me I wasn't finished with my adoration duties. Absently, I resumed petting him, feeling grounded by the contact. I hadn't told anyone here the specifics about my condition, but in the face of this incredibly kind gesture, it seemed I ought to.

"I have fibromyalgia. Most of the time I can function reasonably normally. I'm well versed in how to manage my symptoms. But when I flare, I do have some mobility challenges. There are days my legs simply won't work." I hadn't yet had one of those here, but I knew it was only a matter of time.

Saoirse showed no pity, simply nodded, as if that solidified her logic for bringing the dog. "He can help with that. He can answer the door to let someone in, retrieve things for you, assist you in getting up and down stairs. Those are all things he's trained for."

I'd never considered a service dog before. The bad days were simply bad, and I adapted as needed. But at home I'd had help and a safety net I didn't have here in Scotland. And yet...

"I hate to take a service dog that someone else needs more."

Saoirse shook her head. "He's never going to be a service dog like that. He failed the program. Think of him as a pet with bonus features. Here. Let me show you. Falkor, come."

The dog scrambled down and sat at Saoirse's feet, waiting for orders.

"Brace," she commanded. The dog immediately planted himself, stiff-legged and steady. "This is how he helps someone stand up from a seated position or maintain balance." She demonstrated, using his sturdy frame as support. "Go ahead, try it."

Tentatively, I called him over and placed my hand on his back. He didn't move a muscle, completely stable, as I pushed myself up from my couch.

Next, she tossed her keys across the room. "Fetch."

Falkor bounded over, snatched them up, and brought them back, dropping them gently in her outstretched palm. "He can retrieve anything you drop—your mobile, the TV remote. He can even help you with laundry."

When she commanded "Step," he sidled close to her leg, providing a living banister. "This is for stairs or anywhere you need extra support while walking."

I watched her put Falkor through his paces, fascinated. What impressed me most was how focused he remained throughout the demonstration, his brown eyes alert and eager to help. He wasn't just following commands; he genuinely seemed to enjoy the work.

"The difference between him and a full service dog is mainly his temperament," Saoirse explained. "He's a bit too friendly for public access work. But for in-home assistance? He's perfect. And he's very protective, which is never a bad thing for a single woman living on her own. What do you say?"

Big brown eyes looked lovingly up at mine as his tail swish swish swished across the hardwood floor, and I was an absolute goner.

"Well, I always wanted a dog."

Saoirse grinned in triumph. "Excellent. I've got a bed and the rest of his supplies in my 4x4."

# CHAPTER 13

## CALLUM

I hated quarterly tax paperwork. So did Finn and Alex, so it was a task we'd agreed to take turns on. I'd come in early to get a start on it without distractions. If I could get it to a certain point, I'd probably be able to train Parker to at least gather the requisite numbers. I worried a little that we'd overload her. We'd already foisted so many things off. But so far she'd seemed to thrive, and I had to believe that she'd speak up if she felt overwhelmed.

The jangling of the bell out front alerted me to her arrival. It had to be Parker. Alex and Finn always came in the back, as I did. I'd gotten used to the sound of her arrival each morning, the quiet rustling as she settled in for the day.

But something was different this morning. Her voice drifted back, pitched low and gentle. "Okay, you have to be a good boy. Understand?"

Who the hell was she talking to?

The murmuring continued, punctuated by what sounded like some kind of clicking against the hardwood floor.

Oh Christ. Had she brought in a stray? I thought we were

done with that, since Alex had adopted the wee kitten we'd found during renovations. This was a business, not an animal rescue. Never mind the fact that the building had started its life as a pet spa before we'd gotten hold of it.

Abandoning the spreadsheets on my monitor, I shoved back from the desk and went to investigate. The brighter fluorescent lights stabbed at my good eye as I emerged from the cave of my office.

And there she was, all five-foot nothing of her, practically dwarfed by an enormous white... something. The creature looked more like a polar bear than a dog, with thick, fluffy fur and a tail that could double as a feather duster.

I could only shake my head. "What—?"

Her usual brilliant smile held a nervous edge as she laid a hand on the animal's head. "Good morning! There's someone I'd like you to meet."

The beast's tail started wagging with enough force to generate electricity.

"This is Falkor. My new dog." Her tone held a mix of pride, affection, and a little bit of defiance, as if she expected me to challenge her right to pet ownership.

I remembered her asking Hamish just days ago if he allowed pets in the flat, but I hadn't expected her to get one so quickly. Or one quite so... massive.

The dog gazed up at me with liquid brown eyes, and I took an instinctive step back. Not because I was afraid—I'd faced down insurgents, for Christ's sake—but because that look promised an imminent tongue bath I wasn't in the least prepared to receive.

"Right. Why is he here?" It seemed the most diplomatic of all the questions crowding my mind.

Parker pressed her lips together and widened those long-lashed, Disney-princess eyes in a hopeful expression that I suspected she'd perfected since she was a toddler. Damn if it wasn't effective.

"Well..." She twisted her fingers in Falkor's fur. "I didn't want to leave him alone at the flat all day, and I figured it would be less disruptive to bring him here instead of me needing to go home to let him out a couple of times a day." The words tumbled out in a rush. "This seems like such a dog-friendly village, and I swear he's a good boy. He won't cause any problems."

As if to prove her point, she unclipped his lead. The beast immediately padded over to me, tail swooshing like a metronome. Before I could dodge, he'd swiped his tongue across my hand, leaving behind a trail of warm slobber.

I jerked my hand back with a grimace and wiped it against my jeans.

"Oh, no." Parker's face fell. "Do you not like dogs?"

Christ, she looked so distressed you'd have thought I'd kicked the dog. Or maybe her. Those big doe eyes had gone all soft and worried, and something in my chest clenched.

"I like dogs fine," I grumbled. "I just dinna care for being slobbered on."

Her shoulders relaxed slightly. "We're working on that." She shot the dog a fond look as he returned to her side, plopping his butt to the floor. "He just has a lot of love to give."

That made two of them. Parker radiated warmth like a miniature sun, and this polar bear of hers seemed to be cut from the same cloth. God help me.

The sound of the rear door opening echoed from the back. A minute later, Alex and Finn strode in, deep in conversation about some equipment order. They both stopped short at the sight of the massive white beastie.

"Well, what have we here?" Finn's face split into a grin. The traitor immediately dropped into a crouch, and Falkor bounded over, treating him to the same enthusiastic greeting I'd received. The difference being Finn seemed to welcome it.

"This is Falkor. He's my new dog. Consider him the new office mascot."

Alex hunkered down, too, his eyes lit with amusement. "Were we in need of a mascot?"

Parker caught her lip between her teeth, drawing my gaze unerringly to her mouth.

"—unconventional. But I didn't want to leave him at home all day. Since I don't have a car, it would take too much time to go back and forth multiple times to let him out. I thought he could stay here with me. I mean, I know this is my workspace." She gestured to the front area she'd turned into command central. "But I swear, he won't be any trouble with the clients."

I watched my partners exchange grins. This was precisely the sort of thing we should have discussed beforehand, made a proper policy about. But between Parker's hopeful expression and Alex already down on the floor getting his face washed by the beast, I knew I was outnumbered.

"Course he can stay," Alex said, as I'd known he would. The man loved anything with four legs and fur. "Could do with a mascot around here."

"He seems friendly enough," Finn observed, still fussing over the dog.

"Too friendly," I muttered, though apparently not quietly enough because Parker shot me a look.

The beast had already charmed my partners. I could see how this was going to go—he'd have the run of the place by the end of the week. And somehow, watching Parker's face radiating joy as she watched the dog make himself at home, I couldn't bring myself to argue about it.

Over the next hour, I couldn't help noticing things about Parker's new companion. The dog might have been overenthusiastic with his greetings, but there was no missing his training. He stuck to Parker's side like he'd been glued there, particularly when she moved around the office. More than once, I caught her with her hand resting on his back as she walked, almost as if she was using him for balance.

When she dropped her pen, he retrieved it before she could even bend down. Every movement was precise, practiced. As if the dog was anticipating her every need.

"Where exactly did you get him?" I finally asked, after watching him fetch her water bottle from where she'd left it on the counter.

"Oh." Parker looked up from her computer, that same hand automatically finding its way to Falkor's head. "Saoirse brought him to my flat last night. She thought we'd be a good match."

"Did she know you were looking for a dog?"

A slight flush crept into her cheeks. "Not exactly. We'd talked about how I wanted to get one once I was settled here, and then she came across him at her practice." Her whole face softened as she looked down at the dog. "He's such a sweet, wonderful boy. Aren't you, Falkor?"

The dog's tail thumped against the floor, and he gazed up at her with pure adoration. That made two of us, then.

Shite. Where had that thought come from?

The dog chose that moment to leave Parker's side and pad over to me. Before I could object, he'd settled his head against my knee, those brown eyes looking up at me expectantly. My hand moved of its own accord, fingers sinking into his thick fur. He was surprisingly soft.

The tension I'd been carrying in my shoulders—courtesy of too much time squinting at spreadsheets—began to ease. Even the persistent headache that had been brewing behind my good eye faded a bit as I stroked his head.

Maybe having an office dog wouldn't be the worst thing in the world.

But there was something else going on here. Something in the way Parker watched the dog work, in the careful way she'd explained his presence. I just couldn't put my finger on what it was.

Then again, Parker Lawrence had been a mystery from the moment she'd walked through our door. Why should her dog be any different?

The dog kept making these... rounds, I suppose you'd call them. Every so often, he'd get up from his spot near Parker and do a circuit of the office. Check on each of us in turn. Professional behavior wrapped in a blanket of barely contained enthusiasm.

Around eleven, my head was pounding again—the screen's glare doing me no favors. I'd been fighting with the same set of numbers for twenty minutes when I felt that now-familiar weight on my knee.

"What?" I growled, not looking down.

Falkor didn't move, didn't react to my tone. Just stayed there, a steady presence, until my hand dropped to his head of its own accord.

The repetitive motion of stroking his fur drew my focus away from the frustration that had been building. My breathing slowed to match his, and gradually the vice grip around my temples began to ease.

When I finally looked down, he was watching me with those intelligent eyes. No judgment, no wariness—just quiet companionship.

"Alright," I muttered. "You've made your point."

His tail thumped once against the floor, and he stayed until my shoulders had completely relaxed. Then he rose, gave my hand one last gentle lick, and padded back to Parker's desk, where I knew he'd settle at her feet.

An office mascot. Right. This dog was something else entirely. But having seen Parker's quiet smile as she worked, noting how much smoother our morning had gone with him here—which was saying something given Parker ran a tight ship —I supposed I could live with a bit of dog hair on my trousers. And maybe—though I'd deny it if anyone asked—even the occasional tongue bath.

# CHAPTER 14

## PARKER

PAISLEY

PAISLEY

It's official. Jade is at the end of her patience.
Frankly, so is Ty. He says if you don't tell her
where you are, he will.

My fingers trembled as I typed out my reply.

PARKER

He wouldn't.

PAISLEY

Yeah, at this point he would. He's tired of
seeing me caught in the middle. And
honestly? So am I. Jade is out of her mind
with worry, and I'm running out of ways to
reassure her you're okay without telling her
where you are so she can see for herself.

I squeezed my eyes shut, as if that would do a damned
thing to stop the tension headache from taking a grip on my
skull. A warm weight settled on my lap. I automatically dug my
fingers into Falkor's fur, breathing through the anxiety because

I knew my time was well and truly up. I had to do... something. Asking Paisley to continue wouldn't be reasonable.

PARKER

I'm sorry. I shouldn't have involved you.

The typing bubble appeared and disappeared four times before her response finally came through.

PAISLEY

Look, I agreed to be your buffer gladly, because I get why you needed to do this. But you've done it. You've done exactly what you set out to do and in far less time than you expected it to take. Which is amazing. It's time to show everyone else.

She wasn't wrong, but I was so deathly terrified that the moment Jade had my location, she'd show up ready and willing to drag me home, away from this new life I was gradually building. I needed to find a way to prove to Jade that I was okay—thriving even—without giving away my whereabouts.

PARKER

Give me 24 hours. I need to think about what to say.

I only hoped it was sufficient time for me to come up with a plan.

I started to simply do a web search on how to make an untraceable phone call, but stopped myself. Did I really want a record of that at my workplace? I had no reason to think any of the guys would dig into my search history, but they were all former military, and Alex, in particular, was an uber computer guy, given what I'd seen of his programming skills. What if he had some kind of system in place to flag suspicious search behavior?

*Okay, now you're just getting paranoid.*

I paused.

He probably knew about this kind of stuff. I hadn't asked because it was none of my business. But he could probably help me. I just needed to figure out a way to ask him about it that didn't come off as sketchy.

Book research. Paisley's default answer for any kind of strange query was that it was book research. People told her all kinds of things out of a desire to be helpful to a real live author. I didn't think Alex would be particularly motivated by that, but he still might answer the question without thinking it too odd.

Shoving up from my chair, I headed down the hall to Alex's office. He sat at his desk, fingers flying over the keyboard with the kind of focused intensity that suggested he was in the middle of something important. I started to pull back without disturbing him, but he called out, "Need something?"

"Not directly. I'd just like to pick your brain for a minute. I can come back later if I'm interrupting."

He lifted his hands from the keyboard and shifted his gaze to me in the doorway. "Nothing I can't take a wee break from. What's up?"

I stepped into his office, Falkor trailing behind. My faithful shadow padded across to nose Alex for pets, and I fought the urge to fidget with the hem of my cardigan. I wasn't doing anything wrong by asking about this. Still, my palms began to sweat.

"Remember, I told you I work for a romance author on the side?"

"Aye." He leaned back in his chair.

"She has a research question I thought you might be able to help with." Knowing I looked as uncomfortable as I felt, I lowered myself onto the edge of the chair across from his desk, fighting the urge to wipe my damp palms on my skirt. "In the book she's working on, she has a heroine who needs to contact someone who's looking for her, but without revealing her location. Like a 'proof of life, I'm fine, but don't come after me' sort of thing. The heroine doesn't want these people stopping her from completing her mission."

Did that sound plausible? From the multitude of novels I'd read, it did to me, but I still had to consciously make myself keep breathing normally instead of holding my breath for his answer.

His dark eyes sharpened with interest. "That depends on what resources are available to the people trying to find her."

"Well, I don't know exactly what the plot is, but let's assume more than the average bear." I tried for a breezy tone, but my heart hammered against my ribs.

"Easiest way would be a burner phone. Brief conversation, not long enough to be triangulated."

"Burner phone?" I'd already effectively done that with the cell phone I'd picked up when I made my escape.

"Sure. Either a full-out phone or a replacement SIM card for an unlocked phone. They'd be readily available at a lot of places."

"Okay, that makes sense. Is there anything else?"

He reeled off several other options involving VPNs and IP addresses that went straight over my head, but I nodded along like I was taking mental notes. "And how long could the conversation be? Before being tracked, I mean?"

"Texts would be safer. Though that does leave its own sort of record if the information needing to be communicated is of a sensitive nature."

I shook my head. "I think it needs to be a talking conversation. Because otherwise, how would the receiving person know it's really the heroine and not somebody pretending to be her?"

"In that case... three minutes, tops." He flexed his fingers over his keyboard, clearly ready to get back to work. "That help?"

"Yeah, thanks. I'll pass that along." I stood, smoothing my skirt. "And if she has any follow-up questions..."

"You know where to find me."

Back at my desk, I struggled to get back to actual work. My mind was too busy spinning on logistics. My phone was unlocked already. That was how I'd switched phone numbers to begin with back in London. The corner convenience store in the village had those prepaid SIM cards on a rack behind the counter. I'd seen them on a previous trip to pick up snacks. I could get another and swap it out, make the call, say what needed to be said.

Falkor settled his head on my knee, peering up at me with big, liquid brown eyes. I scratched behind his ears.

Three minutes.

Three minutes to convince Jade I was okay, that I was safe, that none of those nebulous security concerns had come to pass, and that I was succeeding at being truly independent for the first time in my life. Three minutes to make her understand why I'd done what I'd done without making her more determined than ever to track me down. Three minutes to try to salvage our friendship.

It was a lot to cram into three minutes.

But it would have to be enough.

# CHAPTER 15

## CALLUM

I shouldered open the back door to the warehouse not too far ahead of closing time. The intermediate climbing expedition I'd been on had been just what I needed to level myself out. Challenging enough to feel like I'd done something without wearing me out.

"Oh, good, you're back." Alex emerged from the hall, his expression dialed to a level of serious I didn't like. Something was up. "Want a hand bringing in equipment?"

I placed the coiled climbing ropes and harnesses into the bin to be rechecked before being stored for next time. "Later. What's going on?"

He kept his voice low. "I had a weird conversation with Parker earlier today."

My hands stilled on the carabiners. "What kind of weird conversation?"

Alex leaned against the doorframe, arms crossed. "She asked me about hypothetically helping someone communicate with someone without revealing their location. Said it was research for the romance author she works for."

"And?"

"And I don't think it was research."

Every sense went on alert. "Why?"

He scratched his jaw. "Something in her manner when she asked... it didn't sit right. She seemed nervous, but trying to hide it. Probably would've worked on someone without our training. She's been fine the rest of the day, but..." He shrugged. "Has she mentioned anything to you? Any problems?"

I shook my head. Anything outright? No. There wasn't a single specific incident or remark I could put my finger on. But there had been moments. Little things that hadn't quite added up. I'd filed them away, let them go. But maybe it was time I did a little more recon. If she was in some kind of trouble, I wanted to help.

"Well, it may be nothing, but I thought you'd want to know."

I secured the last of the gear and glanced at the clock on the wall. She'd be heading home in about ten minutes. "Right. Thanks."

Alex's lips quirked as I started for the back door. "You planning on tailing her?"

"Aye. If someone's hassling her, they willnae be doing it for long."

I didn't wait around to see if he had opinions on the matter. The man had known me for years. He wouldn't have told me if he hadn't expected exactly this.

I waited just out of sight at the side of our building, downwind, so the dog wouldn't pick up on my presence. Melting into the shadows was second nature, something I'd always excelled at. My callsign had been Ghost for a reason.

When she emerged from the office a few minutes later, Falkor predictably at her side, she turned toward the village proper. I waited thirty seconds, letting her get just far enough ahead that I could fall into step without her noticing. Even from this distance, I could tell her shoulders were knotted with tension. Her stride was determined, her chin up, but there was an element of a gallows walk to the whole thing. Once she reached the high street, she ducked into the corner shop. I positioned myself across the street where I could see through the windows. She went straight to the counter. I couldn't hear the exchange but there were obviously pleasantries being traded, conversation about the dog that made her smile despite whatever was weighing on her. Then the shopkeeper turned and grabbed one of the prepaid SIM cards off the back wall.

She already had a UK number. Why did she need a burner? Alex had said she'd asked about contacting someone without revealing her location. Who did she need to talk to without being traced?

Parker exited the shop and crossed over to my side of the street. I stepped into the doorway of the charity shop, but her head was ducked, not paying a bit of attention to her surroundings. I'd be having a word with her about that, too. But later.

She strode down to the church, following the cobblestone path around to the walled garden in back. I followed, easing around to the opposite side of the garden, where the other gate was open. Without a sound, I slipped inside, ducking into the space between the wall and an overgrown hedge. I could just see her through the branches. She sat on one of the stone benches and swapped out the SIM card with fumbling fingers. Once done, she sat for a long couple of minutes, petting the dog as if the great beastie could offer strength. Then she scrubbed both hands over her face, blew out a breath, and dialed.

"It's me."

Even from my place in the shadows, I could see her wince at whatever reply she received.

"I'm not telling you where I am." Her voice carried on the wind. "I'm safe. I'm happy."

She listened, her free hand clenching into a fist in the dog's fur. "I have not been kidnapped or joined a cult. No one is holding me against my will." Pause. "Because if I tell you, then it'll get back to them, and they'll try to force me back." She sucked in another breath, her voice getting stronger with conviction. "I can't go back. I won't."

The hell anyone would force her back to anything while I was around to stop it. My hands curled into fists as I fought back the instinctive rage.

She paused again, listening. "I know. And I'm sorry. But this is as good as it's going to get for now. I'm not ready for anything else. I'll touch base again soon."

Without saying goodbye, she ended the call and immediately popped out the SIM card, replacing it with the original. The next breath she blew out was less than steady.

Only then did I move, separating from the shadow of the wall to close the distance between us. "Who's after you?"

Parker jolted to her feet, whirling toward me with a chalk-white face. "Callum! I—" She swallowed hard, those big brown eyes wide with fear and shock and an unmistakable thread of guilt.

I had to fight the instinct to reach out and touch her. I wasn't the sort of man anyone came to for comfort. But I could give her this.

"Listen to me verra carefully." I kept my voice pitched low, trying not to spook her any further. "No one—and I mean *no one*—is going to force you to do anything you dinna want to do. No' while I'm around." I edged a half-step closer, ducking my head a little to look her in the eyes so she'd understand exactly how serious I was. "No one."

She stared at me with something like wonder. As if no one

had ever offered to stand between her and trouble before. The thought made my chest ache. She looked at me like some kind of hero. It had been a long time since I'd been that for anyone, and the role didn't sit exactly comfortably anymore.

At last, she swallowed and nodded once, wrapping her arms around herself. "Will you come back to my place? I'd rather talk in private, if you don't mind."

Christ. What kind of mess was she in? But I nodded. "Lead the way."

As we walked, I positioned myself between her and the street, hyperaware of my blind side and the need to keep her safe. Whatever was going on, whatever she was running from, she wasn't alone anymore.

We made it back to her flat without incident, and I didn't miss how she seemed to lean on Falkor for support going up the stairs. Inside, she let the dog off his lead and shrugged out of her coat, hanging it on a row of hooks on the wall. The place already looked different than it had when we'd walked through just days ago. Colorful pillows had been added to the sofa, and a crocheted blanket that looked like something someone's nan had made was draped over the back. I spotted a few cheerful prints propped against the walls, waiting to be hung. A blue glass vase of wildflowers added a pop of color to the table by the window. She was making herself a home.

"Can I get you something to drink?" She picked up the kettle.

"No." I wanted answers more than tea.

She glanced up at me, then away as she put the kettle under the tap to fill it for herself. "Will you please sit down? You're looming."

Every instinct screamed to pace, to move, to *do something*, but I forced myself to drop into the armchair. Falkor padded over and licked at my hand in his version of silent support as we both waited for her to make tea. I stayed quiet, figuring she needed the ritual of it to settle herself.

A few minutes later, she sank down on the sofa, hands clasped around a speckled blue ceramic mug. "I haven't been entirely honest with y'all."

"I gathered that."

Despite my effort to keep my tone gentle, she winced. "I didn't lie. I just didn't tell you the full story. I did come here to have some adventures and build a new life."

"Away from who?"

Her eyes flicked up to mine. "My parents." She sucked in a deep breath. "They're... extremely overprotective. They mean well, but they've tried to put me in bubble wrap since I was diagnosed as a teenager. Nothing I do is ever without supervision or approval or commentary. They never want me to overdo, but by their standards, I can never really *do* anything. I just hit my wall with all of it. Saved up the money from my VA job with Paisley, made this plan, and came over here to start that new life. And I had to give my bodyguard the slip to do it."

There were so many things I wanted to ask, but I prioritized the one question that likely had the most to do with her safety. "Why do you have a bodyguard?"

She flashed a humorless smile and sipped at the tea. "My family... is pretty prominent in the business world. Not just in Nashville or the US. Globally. Let's just say my father has a lot of very prominent people in his Rolodex, and his reach is... long. The bodyguard thing started when I left for college, after some threats that had been made against my father. Threats that have never been acted upon, for the record. But Jade's been with me ever since. She's part bodyguard. Part assistant. Entirely my friend." Parker paused and grimaced. "Or was before I completely betrayed her trust to come here."

"If she'd sell you out to your parents, that's hardly a friend."

Parker shook her head, quick to defend. "It's not like that. I know I put her in a really tough position, because they're the ones who pay her salary. Officially, she has to answer to them. I don't know what she's told them."

"Where do they think you are?"

"We were supposed to be taking a six-month trip around Europe together. Because she's been with me for so long, she knows how to handle my... particular issues when they arise. So my parents finally agreed to let me go live a little. Have an adventure. They gave an inch, and I took an ocean."

Issues. Diagnosis.

I looked at Falkor, resting patiently by her side. "He's no' just a pet. He's a service dog."

Parker reached down to scruff his ears. "Sort of. He failed out of the program for being too friendly. But he does have the training. Saoirse knew exactly what she was doing when she brought him to me."

Did that mean Saoirse knew what health problems she was dealing with?

I bent forward, bracing my elbows on my knees. "You're no' obligated to tell me what you're dealing with, but I could help better if I knew."

She hesitated. "I'll tell you if it becomes relevant. Please?"

"Aye, fair enough." I understood about keeping some things close. God knew I had my own demons I wasn't ready to share. "I meant what I said before. Nobody's going to force you to do anything. I understand about needing to get out from under the thumb of family."

Her eyes sharpened with interest. "I feel like there's a story there."

Not one I wanted to get into now. "Perhaps another time. We're talking about you. Now, I'm assuming Jade isnae likely to just give up because you said so."

"No. Paisley's been running interference for me since I got here, but that option has run its course. I know I'll have to let her in on things, eventually. I'm just not ready yet."

"We can talk to Alex. He can set up a means for you to communicate regularly with her without revealing your location." When she hesitated, I pressed on. "He'll do it without having to know all the details, if you dinna want to share them."

"Okay."

Because I couldn't sit still any longer, I pushed to my feet. Parker rose when I did, setting her mug aside. Before I realized what she was doing, she'd wrapped her arms around my middle and pressed her head to my chest. I froze, caught between wanting to return the embrace and knowing I shouldn't.

"Thank you," she whispered. "You have no idea how good it feels to have someone finally know the truth."

The words hit me like a punch to the gut. How long had she been carrying this alone?

I gently closed my arms around her, figuring it made me a total bawbag if I didn't hug her back. She relaxed against me, and we stood that way for far too long. One part of my brain debated when I ought to let her go, even as the other was cataloging the vanilla and lavender scent of her hair and the feel of her pressed against me, as if she belonged there. The thought should have terrified me, but instead it felt... right. The military had trained the need to protect into my bones, but with Parker, it went deeper than duty. It was personal in a way I wasn't ready to examine too closely.

Eventually, she loosened her hold and stepped back. This time, the smile she gave reached her eyes. "You're a good man, Callum Quinn."

I didn't know about that, but I was a man who believed in loyalty. For better or worse, Parker Lawrence had mine, and I'd stop at nothing to keep her safe.

# CHAPTER 16

## PARKER

True to Callum's word, Alex came through without asking for a single detail. He'd set up some kind of VPN on steroids so that I could effectively video chat from my laptop or phone without revealing my location. The confidence with which he explained I was effectively untraceable by anyone with fewer toys than the NSA made me want to ask all kinds of questions about exactly what his job in the military had been. But I left it alone, simply expressing my gratitude that he'd done what I needed.

Neither he nor Finn was treating me any differently, though I had noted all three men were just a little more watchful, and they'd been deliberate in marking off the schedule so that I was never left in the office alone. Overkill? Maybe. But it made me feel protected and cared for. Well, that was how Finn and Alex made me feel. Callum made me feel so much more.

I'd spent the last three days replaying his declaration that no one would force me to do anything I didn't want to do, in that devastating, over-my-dead-body tone. He'd looked ready to go to war, fierce and furious and possibly the sexiest thing I'd ever seen. It hadn't done a damned thing to help with my crush. Neither had that probably ill-advised hug before he'd left my flat. But God, it did something to me, knowing he'd defend me. Because I understood him well enough by now to know that meant he'd let me past some of those mile-high walls of his. Not into his inner circle. I wasn't sure he let anyone that far in—not even his former squad members. But we were... something other than strangers and mere coworkers. I'd be lying if I said I hadn't fantasized about being more. A lot more. And I didn't really know what to do about that.

I mean, objectively, I should do nothing at all. He was my boss. But he was also... a friend. Perhaps not like any friend I'd ever had, but a friend nonetheless. Given this new life I was building, I couldn't afford to screw that up. But that hadn't stopped my dreams from rivaling the steam of the radiators I'd finally figured out how to use in my flat.

"Get it together, girl. You have more important things to worry about. Like setting some ground rules with Jade."

At the sound of my voice, Falkor's tail began to swish, and he tipped his head back against my leg, begging for pets. Of course I complied. Who was I to resist that face?

"Let's do this thing, buddy."

Scanning behind my spot on the sofa, I made sure there was nothing that would betray my location. Then I wrapped my favorite comfy cardigan around myself and settled with the laptop, following the steps Alex had given me to make a video call to my bodyguard.

She picked up almost immediately. Her fine-boned brown face filled the screen, so close I could easily spot the lines around the dark eyes that were filled with relief. "Parker." With a gusty exhale, she dropped her head, running one hand over her cap of tight, natural curls. "Girl, do you have any idea how worried I've been?"

"I can guess." I had the good grace to look chagrined.

"It's good to see your face."

I offered a half smile. "Yours, too." It had been a little over three weeks since I'd executed my plan, faking a flare and sending her out to sight-see while I slipped out of our Airbnb and made for King's Cross, leaving just a note behind for explanation. God, at this point, it felt like a lifetime, and the guilt weighed a ton.

"Are you planning on running away again after two minutes?"

"No. We can talk as long as you want. But I'm still not telling you where I am."

Jade pinched the bridge of her nose and fixed me with what I always thought of as her serious Dora Milaje expression. Deeply unamused and dangerous. "Parker Lawrence, what the hell do you think you're doing?"

"Look, I'm sorry. That's the first thing I want to say. I know I put you in a really tough spot by disappearing the way I did."

Just the faintest incline of her head acknowledged the apology. In Jade-speak, that meant, *I hear you, and I haven't decided if I'm forgiving you yet.*

"Why did you feel like you needed to concoct some elaborate plan and give me the slip?"

I fought the urge to squirm under her gaze, digging my fingernail into my thumb hard enough I knew it would leave a crescent-shaped indention in the skin. No matter how uncomfortable this conversation was, I still believed I'd done the necessary thing. "Because I wanted the chance to be completely normal. I wanted to prove that I could find a job, get a place to live, manage all my own affairs without a trust fund, without an assistant, and without a bodyguard."

"You don't think I'd have helped you with all that?"

"That's exactly the point. I wanted to be able to prove to

myself that I could do it on my own. I needed to prove that I can live like a normal person."

Her face softened. "Honey, I understand that desire. But you are not a normal person. Apart from the fact that you have some limitations because of your fibro, you're not just any person because of who your family is."

"No one knows me here. No one has any idea who my family is. And it's nice. People just see me for me."

It felt oddly thrilling to have this sort of secret life, and even more so to have someone like Callum in on it. Someone who understood why I needed this independence and would fight to help me keep it.

"How have you been managing the fibro?"

"Doing pretty well. It's that thing where, as long as I maintain momentum, I'm usually good. I've been making sure to get adequate rest and whatnot. And, well, I have a little help." I patted the space beside me on the sofa, and Falkor immediately leapt up, dropping down to snuggle with his usual rag-doll collapse.

Her eyes went wide. "Did you adopt a yeti?"

"This is Falkor." I explained his backstory and how he'd come to me. "He's well-trained for mobility assistance."

Jade looked reluctantly impressed. "Actually, that's a really great idea."

"He's been wonderful. He's great company. Sweet as can be. And you know I always wanted a dog."

Apparently, the acquisition of a pet drove home the seriousness of my intentions to stay in a way nothing else had. She settled back in her chair. I couldn't tell where she was. Indoors. There was an exposed brick wall behind her.

"Okay, you're not going to tell me where you are. What are you willing to tell me? How are you?"

"I meant what I said the other day. I'm good. I'm happy. I

found a job. I found a place to live. I'm settling in, doing exactly what I wanted to do." For the first time in my life, I felt truly in control of my destiny, and that knowledge straightened my spine.

"What are you doing, exactly? What kind of job?"

I'd considered this and kept things vague. "I'm working as an office manager. It's similar to the kind of stuff I do for Paisley, keeping things organized, answering phones, maintaining a schedule."

Jade snickered. "That kind of thing always did make you unreasonably happy."

Given she was just starting to unbend a little, I hated to ruin it all, but I needed to know. "What have you been telling my parents?"

As predicted, all signs of ease disappeared. She pursed her full lips, looking frustrated and more than a little uncomfortable. "I've been maintaining your social media presence and sending email updates to them from your account to keep them from panicking and sending out a search party."

I blinked in shock. "Really?"

Her brows drew down into a scowl. "What do you take me for? They may pay my paycheck, but my allegiance is to you. And you know that none of this is about my job."

Twist, twist went the guilt knife. Because, yeah, I knew all of that. But I'd already apologized and beating that dead horse wasn't going to improve the situation.

"Look, I'm not ready to disclose where I am, but I will agree to regular contact, so you know I really am doing okay."

Jade absorbed that and considered. "What am I supposed to be doing in the meantime?"

"Exactly what we said we were going to do. Explore the country. Take some time for yourself for once. You've been joined to my hip since college. Do something you'd like to do."

"Uh-huh. And when exactly are you planning to tell your parents about all this?"

"I haven't decided. I'd rather be a little more firmly established before I do that, because you and I both know they're not going to take it well."

"That's an understatement. And what about your security? You've just admitted that your new dog is more likely to kiss a threat than to take him down."

I snorted because, for all his wonderful traits, Falkor would one hundred percent present his belly for rubs if a burglar showed up. "I am perfectly safe. My bosses are all ex-military, and they're very protective."

Jade's gaze sharpened with obvious curiosity at that. "Okay. I will agree to this for now. But if I determine that there's any kind of threat, we reevaluate."

"I can live with that." We lapsed into a silence made all the more awkward for its rarity. I leaned closer to the screen. "I miss you."

"I miss you, too, Parks. Be safe."

"I will. Talk soon."

# CHAPTER 17

## CALLUM

After years in the military, I couldn't shake my habit of rising at o'dark thirty. With the lengthening days, it meant I had ample time for a run on the trails that snaked through the woods surrounding my house before I left for work. Usually my demons kept pace with the pounding beat of my feet, but the past few days it had been Parker occupying my thoughts. No matter how many miles I ran, I couldn't escape the scent of her hair, the shape of her smile, or the warm feel of her pressed against me for that unexpected hug.

The woman had gotten under my skin, into my dreams, and I didn't know what to do about it.

I didn't exactly *want* to do anything about it. She was a damned sight better than the nightmares that so often plagued me. But given the direction of those dreams, I could hardly take a single look at her mouth without going hard. Given how often she smiled, that was a fucking problem. I was her *boss*. And I was apparently the only one she'd told most of the truth.

I wasn't sure what to do with that, either. But it felt like that made us something more than boss-employee. So did my protective instincts. I'd have intervened for any employee I deemed needed help. That was simply the right thing to do. But the lengths to which I was prepared to go for Parker were something else entirely.

She'd become important to me. And not only because she'd made my life easier. I supposed that made us... friends of a sort. It had been longer than I cared to admit since I'd had any of those beyond the men I'd served with.

I was still brooding about it as I finished my coffee in the garden behind my house. The place didn't look like much. I'd done the bare minimum, hacking back the overgrowth once winter hit, and otherwise I'd just put a single chair outside, so I could enjoy the view to the woods beyond. Most of my focus had been on getting Out of Bounds Scotland up and running. But signs of fresh growth were popping up here and there around the space. I should probably do something for all that, too, but gardening wasn't exactly in my wheelhouse.

My mobile rang. I fished it out of my pocket, expecting to see Finn or Alex or Ewan on the display, but it was Parker's name flashing on the screen. She'd never called me before, and when she'd texted, it was almost exclusively about work.

"Parker?"

"Hey, Callum. I'm sorry to bother you, but have you left for work yet?"

"No' just yet."

"Would you mind swinging by to pick me up and driving me to work?"

Parker always walked. Even in the rain, and that wasn't a factor today. Though it was cold—we were having a bit of a wintery snap again—the sky above stretched an endless, uninterrupted blue. Our office was only a little over a mile from her flat. What was going on?

But I didn't ask. She needed me, so I'd go.

"Give me twenty minutes."

"Thanks."

I made it in slightly less, parking at the kerb beside the law office. I thought about texting to say I was here, but there'd been something... not right in the tone of her voice when she'd called. Her usual brightness sounded too forced. So I got out and pushed the buzzer at the outside door. From inside, I heard the door upstairs open, then the syncopated rhythm of footsteps. A moment later, the bottom door inched open.

Falkor stood on the other side. Had the dog opened the door? As there was no sign of Parker, I could only assume he had. I grabbed the panel, and he woofed, bolting back up the stairs. With a sense of unease, I took them two at a time, stepping into her flat in time to see her struggling to get off the sofa. Her cheeks were paler than usual, and lines bracketed her mouth and eyes in a way I clearly recognized meant pain.

That sense of unease dialed up to straight up alarm. "What happened? What's wrong?"

I closed the distance between us, stopping only when she shot me a fulminating glare.

"Nothing's wrong. At least nothing that you can do anything about."

Falkor pressed close, braced to take her weight as she used him to lever herself to her feet. She made it, but not without obvious effort.

"Parker?" Though I wanted to snap it, I kept my tone soft. "What's going on?"

She sighed, and I remembered her reluctance to talk about whatever condition she'd been diagnosed with as a teenager.

"I have fibromyalgia. I'm having a bit of a flare, and my legs aren't really cooperating terribly well at the moment. That's why I need a ride. I can't walk all the way to work today."

"Should you be coming to work at all? Do you need a sick day?"

Her brows drew together into a remarkably effective scowl. "I'm still a functional human. I just need a ride."

The whip of her usually sweet voice was so redolent of one of my own tantrums, I instantly understood. It was something else, being on the receiving end, seeing someone I cared about struggling with something, and knowing I couldn't fix it. I didn't know much about fibromyalgia, other than it had something to do with chronic pain. A million questions flitted through my mind, but I voiced none of them. And I wouldn't, because she'd given me the same respect. At the end of the day, the whys and hows and whens didn't really matter.

She wanted to protect her autonomy. I had to respect that, even though it took everything I had not to pick her up and tuck her into bed or wrap her in cotton wool. That was, no doubt, exactly what her parents had done for years. What she'd come here to escape.

"Okay. Just tell me what you need."

"Just the ride. And if you could get the door."

"Sure." I moved over to hold it open and waited as she made her agonizing way slowly across the room, leaning heavily on the dog.

The stairs were even worse, and I finally understood why a single-level home had been on her list. But she made it to the bottom. And as I held open the door to my 4x4, I could tell that it had taken a toll. But I bit back anything I wanted to say. I recognized her kind of stubborn, and the need behind it.

Once she was secure and Falkor had leapt into the backseat, I climbed into the driver's side. "Do you need anything? Breakfast? We could stop by the bakery or whatever on the way."

"No, I'm fine. I had some breakfast before I left."

"Okay."

I drove the short distance to the office, parking around back. She was visibly relieved that Alex and Finn hadn't arrived yet. And no wonder. She was moving like she was eighty as she made her way inside and to her desk. I didn't think she'd have made it without Falkor, and I sent up a prayer of thanks to Saoirse MacGregor for her forethought.

As soon as she'd settled, stowing her purse and turning on her computer, I went to the beverage station and put on the kettle. I knew she habitually made a cup of tea when she came in. I could handle that for her. While I waited for the water to boil, I strode back to her desk.

"What do you need? What will help you get through today better?"

I could tell she didn't want to say a thing. Fuck, it was impossible not to understand how frustrated everyone had gotten with me for the same reason.

At length, she sighed. "Is there a space heater in the office somewhere? Fast temperature shifts to cold make it worse."

And she'd elected to move to Scotland? Shite.

"Aye. I'll get it."

By the time I came back with the unit, the kettle had popped. I poured boiling water over a tea bag and set a mental timer.

"What else?"

"I'm probably going to need y'all to come to me instead of me coming to you for things."

"Done. Just ping us on the group chat."

I left her to her morning routine, taking care of unlocking the door myself, and watering the plants that had crept into the lobby. By the time I finished, her tea was steeped. I added cream and sugar, as she liked it, and brought the mug over. The oversized green one I'd noted she favored.

Her eyes went suspiciously shiny as she accepted the drink. "Thank you."

Because I was in no way prepared to handle tears, I made a quick getaway to the back. Alex and Finn had just arrived. I caught them just inside the door.

"Can either of you trade off with me for the cycling tour I'm booked for this morning?" A schedule change meant I could stay here all day, just in case she needed me.

"Aye, I can do that." Finn was always ready to leave the office.

"Good. Also, you're going to need to go to Parker today instead of waiting for her to come back to you. So pay attention to the group chat."

Alex's brow knit in concern. "Okay. But why?"

I thought of her reticence to even admit her condition to me. "That's not my story to tell. Just do the thing."

"Understood."

I strode back out front. "Finn's taking my cycling trip this morning."

Parker shot me a long, indecipherable look over the rim of her tea before reaching for her mouse and updating the schedule without a word.

We all got on with our day. Every time she winced, my muscles tensed with the need to help, to protect. But I forced myself not to hover, because I knew she'd hate that. And because I understood that how I handled this today would likely set the tone for how much help she'd willingly take in the future. Probably the only reason I managed it was because Falkor absolutely had her back. He did a lot of ferrying of paperwork back and forth in the color-coded folders she'd bought when she first started. Thankfully, they were plastic, so they protected the paperwork inside from his slobber. If I hadn't already known he was a service dog, this would've clued me in. If Alex noted the training, he didn't comment on it. But he did go out and grab lunch for all of us from the bakery.

By the end of the day, Parker and I were alone, but for the dog. Finn had gone straight from his last appointment to home, and Alex was still out with his client. I threw the lock on the front door with some measure of relief. I'd been stressed all day worrying about Parker. But the lines of strain on her face had eased, and she seemed to be moving with less difficulty as she gathered up her things. Maybe the flare was passing?

There was no question I was taking her home. I didn't ask what else she needed. I knew she'd hit her limit on how many times she could hear it before grinding her teeth. If she needed help, she'd ask for it. I was relieved to see her make it into the passenger seat on her own. Falkor leapt into the backseat again, as if he did this all the time. I slid behind the wheel, still wrestling with my urge to take care of her.

"Want me to pick up dinner on the way home?" I frowned at my own words because that made it sound like I expected to eat with her.

She rested her head back against the seat and flashed the first smile I'd seen on her all day. She had different smiles—the bright one she used with clients, the satisfied one when she solved a problem, and this softer, more vulnerable one that seemed reserved for moments like this. "That's sweet, but no. I'm literally going in and going straight to bed. I'll be better tomorrow."

"Okay."

We drove the short distance in silence. As soon as I was parked, I released my safety belt.

"You don't have to walk me up. I can make it."

It was my turn to level her with a look.

Parker huffed a laugh. "Okay."

I saw her up, relieved that, though she seemed exhausted,

her gait seemed less pained. Falkor stuck to her like Velcro. The pup had absolutely earned his kibble today.

"Is he good? Does he need a walk to do his business?"

"I've got him." She tossed her purse onto the coffee table. "Thank you for today."

"Anytime." I paused. "Pick you up in the morning?"

She hesitated only a moment. "I'd appreciate that."

"Okay. Then sleep well, and I'll see you in the morning."

Then, before I could give in to the urge to do something outrageous, like cuddle her until she fell asleep, I headed for the stairs.

# CHAPTER 18

## PARKER

PARKER

Thank y'all for the food!

CIARA

Of course. There's nothing like having a home-cooked meal you didn't have to make yourself when you're under the weather.

PARKER

Of course now Pippa's gone and gotten me addicted to her cheese.

PIPPA

And so you've been introduced to my nefarious plan.

PARKER

Devious. Skye, your chicken and dumplings were incredible.

SKYE

Thank my mama for that one. It's her recipe. It was nice to have an excuse to make some.

SAOIRSE

I feel bad for not contributing.

PARKER

Don't be ridiculous. You're the reason I have
Falkor, who is a godsend.

SAOIRSE

I'm good for the alcohol when you're feeling
up to a night at the pub.

PARKER

Soon!

I'd more or less recovered from my flare, so I might could've done it tonight, but I decided I'd best not push it. I'd been especially fortunate that I hadn't had many since coming to Scotland. I knew it was just a matter of time, because they were never too far from the norm. Rest and routine were paramount, and I'd mostly managed both thanks to the girls. I knew I'd have more challenges later in the year, once winter was on the way, but I had time to figure it out.

Until this morning, Callum had played chauffeur every day, driving me to and from work, and even helping me with groceries. He was unquestionably looking out for me, taking care of me. But it was different from how I'd been taken care of most of my life. My parents always wanted to coddle me. Callum didn't do that. He was brusque and direct, asking what I needed. If I said no, that I'd do the thing, he let me do it, even if that meant I struggled. So when I'd said I wanted to walk today, he hadn't argued.

I knew that was hard for him. I certainly felt the same way around him. I'd kind of missed that brief stretch of alone time with him, though. Not that we usually did much talking in the car, but it was just nice to kind of exist in the same small space. The office wasn't the same.

We were nearing the end of the day. Alex and Finn were off with clients. Callum had rearranged most of his schedule this week to be here for me. Something that would change starting next week, but I appreciated the effort. I knew since he'd stayed in the office it meant he'd begun tackling a lot of things on the computer that he'd usually avoid or hand off. Knowing the toll that usually took, I snagged a bottle of water from the fridge and a bottle of headache meds, and walked back to his office.

A couple of weeks ago, I'd had Alex install a dimmer switch and change out the lighting. Callum had taken advantage of that today. He sat behind his desk, lit mostly by the glow of the monitor. I could see the lines of strain around his eyes and the furrow between his brows. Circling around to his side of the desk, I put the bottles directly in his line of sight.

He frowned at them, then up at me. "How did you know?"

I shrugged and leaned back against his desk. I wasn't leaving until he took the meds. "I understand pain. I recognize it when I see it."

He studied me for a long moment before palming two pills and tossing them back with water. Satisfied, I could have left him to it, but something kept me glued to the spot. Maybe that intent gaze he fixed on me.

"I've heard of fibromyalgia, but I don't really know what it is."

I'd opened this door. The least I could do was explain. "It's a chronic condition that causes pain and tenderness throughout the body, along with a fun array of other symptoms. There are conflicting theories about where it comes from. The one that makes the most sense to me is that it's a symptom in and of itself. Like a fever. Lots of things can cause it, which accounts for a lot of the variability in people's experiences."

"You said you were diagnosed in high school?"

I blew out a breath. "Yeah. I was in a really bad car accident my sophomore year, and the recovery went poorly. Physically, I recovered in the sense that I got muscle control back and regained strength and that sort of thing. But the pain receptors effectively got turned on and never turned off again."

He frowned at that. "So you're in pain all the time?"

I shrugged again. "To some extent, yeah. Most of the time it's like white noise. I can tune it out. But sometimes the volume gets pumped up, as it were."

There was no mistaking the flash of sympathy, but he didn't offer false platitudes. "I would never have known."

I smiled a little. "Well, that's part of the point. I don't want people to know, because no one ever knows how to react. There's always either the pity that I don't want or a lack of understanding because I don't have some visible mark that shows that I have a limitation. There have been periods of my life when I was more open about it, but because I don't *look* 'sick', some assume I'm faking or exaggerating. Or they just assume I'm exactly like them and fine, which I vastly prefer to the alternatives."

He considered that, frowning. "I think I'd prefer that. Having something no one could see."

Oh, this man tugged at my heartstrings. Did he even realize how much shame he carried around his condition? "I get that. I get you. That's why I don't get irritated when you get snappish or frustrated. I understand what that headspace is like."

He shifted in his chair, obviously uncomfortable.

"Callum, I don't need you to talk about it. I don't need you to tell me what happened. I just want you to know that I get that it's hard, and that when I do stuff like this," I pointed to the meds, "I'm just trying to make it easier for you."

His gaze met mine, unflinching. "You have." His voice was

a rasp that stroked over my skin like a cat's tongue, making me shiver.

He reached out, tentatively covering my hand with his. "Is this okay?"

Tingles raced up my arm from where he touched me, along with a cacophony of physical reactions that struck me so hard, the last thing I was feeling was pain. He was making a connection, and I wasn't about to stop him. I turned my hand up to clasp his. "More than."

Gaze still on mine, he rose from the chair, moving to stand in front of me where I still leaned against the desk. He was so much taller, it should have felt threatening to have him looming there, but in the dim room it only felt close. Intimate. Vital.

"This is a terrible idea."

He rumbled the words, releasing my hand, only to grip the desk on either side of my hips instead, caging me in. But I didn't feel trapped. No, my heart was pounding for entirely different reasons.

"Why is it a terrible idea?" I whispered.

He searched my face, his own twisting as he wrestled with something. His honor maybe. "I don't want to hurt you."

By now, I understood him well enough to know that he meant that on multiple levels. Because that was a big part of why he didn't people. He acted as if he didn't like them, when really, he worried about how he affected them.

He wasn't wrong. This was an absolutely terrible idea. And still I reached between us, giving into the urge to frame his face. The scruff on his cheeks was a delicious rasp against my palms. I stroked my thumb along the ridge of his cheek, feeling the bump of scar tissue as I passed over.

"I'm no stranger to a little pain. That doesn't make it not worth it."

Straightening, I closed some of the distance between us,

until I could feel the warmth of his breath. I was terrified of putting myself out here like this, but I also couldn't... not. There was something between us, and if he was willing, I wanted to see what it was.

For a small eternity, he only stood there, breathing, and I was certain he was trying to devise some kind of way to let me down. Then his hands ghosted over my cheeks, combing into my hair, and he found my lips with his.

*Oh God.*

I shuddered at the contact, because this kiss was nothing like I'd imagined. It was soft and sweet in a way I never would have dreamed from a man as ostensibly hard as him. He was so careful, so patient. Not in a way that made me feel breakable. It felt like reverence. And that was an incredibly potent drug. I sank into the taste of him, heady and dark, such a contrast to those feather-light hands. I wanted to drown in it. In him. Because he'd effectively wiped away everything else.

As gently as it had begun, Callum eased back. Not far. Just far enough that we could breathe. And that's all we did for what felt like long minutes, neither of us making a move to release the other.

I was the one who finally had to break the silence. "Well, that's a thing that happened."

"Aye." He pulled back far enough he could look into my face. "Do you regret it?"

The thunder of his heart beneath my palms gave me courage. "Only if we never do it again." Ill advised? Maybe. But it was the God's honest truth.

His face underwent a miraculous transformation, softening in a way I'd never seen before. With one hand, he stroked my hair back from my face. "I wasn't looking for this. I wasn't looking for you. But here you are, anyway."

"I wasn't looking for you or this, either. But here we are."

"I dinna know that I can go back to resisting you."

"Then it's a good thing I'm not asking you to."

His lips curved in the first true smile I thought I'd ever seen from him. The dim light caught the planes of his face, softening the usual harsh lines, and my breath caught. God, that smile should be registered as a lethal weapon. His hand slid to cup my cheek, and I turned into the touch, the warm strength of his hold soaking into me in a way that made me want to feel those work-roughened fingers everywhere.

"You know what you are, Parker Lawrence?"

"What's that?"

"Trouble."

I grinned. "Somehow, I think you're just the man to handle it."

# CHAPTER 19

## CALLUM

My focus was absolutely shot. My office had become utterly useless because every time I set foot inside, I started reliving that kiss with Parker. Remembering what it was like to cage her in against the desk. How she hadn't been afraid at all. How she'd looked up at me with want in her eyes. How she'd been the one to take the step toward me. And that mouth. God. I'd been fantasizing about it practically from the moment we'd met, but reality was so much better. She was sweet—of course she was. But I'd tasted heat underneath, and I suspected that she'd be willing to move a lot faster than I was. Which meant I had to be the one to keep my head, because if I'd learned anything about Parker Lawrence since she'd come into my life, it was that she was willing to leap because she trusted I'd catch her if she fell.

That trust was a heady thing. Something I wasn't entirely sure I deserved, but I'd do my fucking best to earn it. To keep her safe. Even if I did feel like I was in some kind of free fall myself. I had no idea what any of this meant long term, but I'd let Parker in, and, for once, I was in no hurry to kick her back out.

She'd had me round for dinner last night, which ended with us cuddling on the sofa and talking.

Me. Callum Quinn. Cuddling. Having willing, enjoyable conversation.

Fuck me, but I liked it. I liked her.

Movement in the doorway caught my attention.

Instead of the object of my distraction, I found my business partners standing shoulder to shoulder, staring at me with suspicion.

"What?"

"You were smiling." Finn's words came out as an accusation.

"What the hell are you on about?"

"We saw it. It's gone now, but you were smiling. You never smile."

Damn it, he was right. And I could feel the strain in my cheeks from muscles that hadn't been used in I had no idea how long. "I dinna ken what you're talking about."

"We're just keenly aware of your usual temperament, and this is a change," Alex said carefully.

I scowled, and somehow the expression felt less comfortable than it used to. "I'm just sitting in here, existing, while you two wankers are standing there, harassing me for no reason." I put extra snap into the words, both because they clearly suspected something was going on, and because this reaction was expected.

Parker stuck her head between them, peering in and raising one delicate eyebrow in a way that asked, *Is that really necessary?*

My inner hackles settled immediately. "Sorry," I muttered.

Her sunshiny smile seemed to have a little extra warmth as

she nodded. My fingers twitched with the urge to reach for her, to draw her smaller frame against mine, and find those lips again. But I kept my hands firmly on the desk. Just because I couldn't stop thinking about how perfectly she'd fit against me last night didn't mean I could act on it at work.

Alex and Finn looked from her to me.

Finn widened his eyes in exaggeration and whispered, "She has superpowers."

Alex was speculative. "Seems she does."

Parker lightly popped both of them on the arm. "Don't be mean."

"Were you coming back here to wrangle the children or did you need something?" *Please say me.*

"I've decided what I want to do for my next adventure."

My brain started down an extremely graphic list of suggestions before she began speaking again.

"I've been reading up on mountains in Scotland and how they're all broken down into height levels, from Munros to Corbetts to Grahams. The bigger ones are probably out of my skill set right now, but I'd like to climb a Graham." Her cheeks pinked. "That sounds really suggestive in a way that I did not intend."

Damn, if I didn't wish my middle name was Graham right now... I'd be happy to let her climb me any way she pleased.

"Well, none of us are Grahams, so I think you're safe on that front," Finn snarked.

Parker looked at me. "Are you game for that on my next day off?"

I thought immediately about the flare she'd had last week. I didn't want to stress her out or bring attention to it, so I simply asked, "You think you're up for that?"

I could tell she recognized what I was really asking.

"Yeah, I think so. I want to try, anyway."

Then I'd do anything in my power to help her succeed. "Okay, I'll sort the details. Block off the calendar."

The faint jangle of the front doorbell sounded.

"Duty calls." As Parker left to deal with the walk-in, both my mates continued to stand in the door.

"What?"

They simply waited. I knew this tactic. They expected me to fill the silence. I'd been trained better than that. But despite my silence, I could feel heat crawling up the back of my neck. Because I knew what they weren't outright asking. Parker and I hadn't discussed what we were or if we wanted to tell people. The only thing we were clear on was that we didn't want to stop at just one kiss. Or, well, there'd been a few more at her place last night. But I was hardly going to blurt that out, was I?

The pair of them still stood there, staring at me, when Parker came back a few minutes later. "I've got a guy who needs to rent a bike out front. Can one of you help with that?"

Finn straightened. "Aye. Sure."

"Of course," Alex added.

"Before you go, you should know—I kissed Callum. Is that a problem for you?" There was no mistaking the look of challenge on her face.

Alex's gaze flicked to me, then back to her. "Did you feel coerced?"

I was too busy goggling that she'd just put that out there, bold as brass, to be offended at the implication.

"Not in the least."

"Uh huh." Alex looked at Finn, who shrugged.

"Right. Well, it's no' a problem for us, if it's no' a problem for you."

Parker nodded. "Good. Now, can you come help me with a bike for this gentleman out here?"

Alex followed her back out front.

Finn slouched indolently against the doorjamb, a shite-eating grin on his face. "I knew it. I knew you had a thing for her. No wonder your mood has improved."

I didn't appreciate the implication. "Watch it, Nomad. I can still kick your ass if you're disrespectful."

He lifted his hands in surrender. "Nothing but respect, mate. For either of you. I'm happy for you. Truly."

As he walked away, I had to admit to myself that I was happy for me, too, for the first time in longer than I cared to admit.

# CHAPTER 20

## PARKER

"Alex told me, but I needed to see for myself." Ciara leaned against my desk and pinned me with a stare. "You've been holding out, girl."

I jolted back in my chair, my hand automatically going to Falkor's head. "What?"

"You and Callum! This is a thing that is happening, and you haven't told the group."

Heat licked its way up my cheeks, and I couldn't stop myself from glancing toward the back, where the man in question was currently doing inventory. "We're taking things slow. We haven't had any discussion about defining anything. Bringing it up in the group chat felt like making it some kind of official."

Her grin spread wider. "Pretty sure announcing to his business partners that you snogged him made you some kind of official."

"Gah!" I buried my face in my hands. This was not how I'd planned for this to reach my friends. Though, of course, I should've known Alex would've told her. Honestly, it had been slightly more than a week. I was surprised it had taken her this long to call me on it.

"Whatever stage you two are at, you officially have plans for the night."

I eyed her with caution. "We do?"

"Aye. It's time for the monthly dinner."

"What monthly dinner?"

"The squad dinner. It rotates between mine and Alex's place and my brother, Ewan, and his fiancée Isobel's house, once or twice a month. Callum has skipped the last three, so I'm here to be sneaky-sneaky and issue the invitation, because if you say yes, he has to go."

"That doesn't seem entirely fair."

Ciara only laughed. "I never said anything about playing fair. So you'll come?"

Okay, yes, we'd spent basically every evening together since that toe-curling kiss in his office, but that didn't mean I had the right to make decisions for him. "I—"

"He's missed, and we want to see you, too. Plus, Isobel is dying to meet you. You'll love her. Besides, if you don't come, it'll throw our numbers off. Please say yes!"

My mouth opened to say I needed to ask Callum, but what came out instead was, "I suppose we will. What can we bring?"

*Wait, no! You can't speak for him like you're a real couple!*

"Oh, grab a bottle of wine or some beer. Whatever is fine. We'll see you at six at my house." Before I could gather my wits, she waggled her fingers and flounced out the door.

I looked at my dog. "Oh, boy."

Falkor wagged his tail, his brown eyes alight as if to say, "I get to go, too, right?"

Callum came down the hall. "Was that Ciara?"

"It was."

He frowned as he took in my expression. "Why do you have that look on your face?"

"Um." Unaccountably nervous, I wrapped my arm around Falkor to dig my fingers into the thicker fur at his chest. "Don't get mad."

"Why would I get mad?"

"I think we just got shanghaied into dinner. Apparently, there's some kind of squad dinner thing you've been avoiding. And Ciara just did an end run and kind of browbeat me into it, assuming I could answer for you, in a couply kind of way." I winced. "I'm sorry. I wasn't trying to make assumptions, I just didn't know how to say no. She manipulated my Southern sense of the polite."

Rather than irritation, his grey eye warmed, and the corner of his mouth kicked up in a half smile. "Boxed you in right neatly, didn't she?"

"Yeah."

"She's a devious little minx. Her brother's the same." He shrugged. "Well, I couldn't avoid it forever. It'll be better having you with me. What time are we meant to be there?"

He wasn't upset. The knot in my gut relaxed, and so did my fingers on the dog. "Six. We're supposed to bring wine or beer or something."

"Okay, then we'll go. But we canna stay late. We've got an early start in the morning."

I beamed at him. "I know. I'm really excited about our hike."

"Weather should be fine for it, by Scottish standards."

"Meaning pack for three seasons?"

He tapped the end of my nose. "You've been paying attention. Go on and wrap whatever you need to here. I'll give you a lift home, then pick you up five 'til six for dinner."

That didn't give me long to get ready, but it would be more time than if I walked home. "Sounds good."

But when I stood in front of my closet forty-five minutes later, I was struck by an unreasonable nervousness. This dinner felt like our first official appearance as a couple. Which was stupid. We hadn't defined ourselves as such. We were just... seeing each other. Still, I wanted to look nice, and I had no idea what to wear. Not that my options were extensive. I had only what I'd packed, which skewed heavily toward layers and outdoorwear, with a handful of nicer things filed under the heading of *just in case.*

Before I could overthink it, I called Jade.

"What's wrong? Are you okay?"

As her voice came over the line, I tucked the phone between my ear and my shoulder. "Hello to you, too."

"Sorry. Hi. You're calling outside your pre-scheduled time."

"I am. And I'm fine, but I do need your help. I've got this dinner tonight."

"A dinner?"

"Yeah, it's a thing." *Way to be descriptive, Parker.*

"A thing?" she repeated. "Like a date thing?"

"Kind of like a group date thing? Sort of."

The suspicion in her tone turned to interest. "Girl, are you dating somebody?"

"Sorta. Maybe? Kinda." I couldn't think of any other way to describe whatever I was doing with Callum. Trying not to climb him like a tree was not, in fact, a relationship status, even if it was accurate.

"Tell. Me. Everything." But the demand came out as bestie, not bodyguard, and it made me ache with missing her.

"It's new. Like, really new. We haven't defined anything, but we've got this group dinner with his friends. I want to make a good impression, but I have no idea what to wear."

I heard her clap and rub her hands together in glee. "I've got you, boo. Is this an eating out sort of dinner or an eating in?"

"Eating in at someone's house. We're tasked with bringing booze."

"So this isn't like a fancy, sent an engraved invitation sort of shindig."

I laughed. "Definitely not. I gather this is a recurring, round-robin style sort of dinner."

"Their version of a cookout, then. You want casual and cute. You packed the lavender V-neck long-sleeved T-shirt, right?"

"Yeah."

"Your boobs look amazing in that shirt. Pair it with the gray flyaway cardigan and jeans. Or those black stretchy pants, if you're feeling fancy."

"Pretty sure those are in the laundry, so jeans it is. Thanks, J."

"No problem. I haven't heard you sound this nervous-excited since that New Year's Eve gala you went to with Harry Bronson."

I winced and put her on speakerphone so I could change. "God, I hope this turns out better than that."

"Bronson ended up being a douchecanoe, but you did look incredible that night."

"I don't think he appreciated the sparkly Chuck Taylors I wore with my evening gown."

"Shut up. You were adorable." She paused. "It sounds like you really like this guy."

I dragged my shirt over my head. "I do. He's... not like the other guys I've dated." Not that there had been many. Between my fibro and my family ties, I'd led a remarkably sheltered life for being twenty-seven.

"Where'd y'all meet?"

I was hardly going to admit he was one of my bosses. "Nice try, J. I've gotta go. Talk soon, okay?"

"Fine. And Parker?"

"Yeah?"

"Have a good time."

I had just enough time to finish changing clothes and freshening my makeup and hair before Callum arrived. The slow survey he made of me from my head to my toes and back again had every inch tingling. And that was before he stepped up to curl a careful hand along my ribs, neatly avoiding the tender spots on my hips. "You look beautiful."

Whatever super articulate response I might have made melted out of my ears when he lowered his mouth to mine in a lingering kiss that was no doubt designed to leave me muzzy headed and revising our plans for the night. It almost worked. Almost.

"You're unfairly good at that," I murmured, body pressed to his, fingers curled into the front of his navy button-down shirt. "But we're still going to dinner."

He hummed a note of acquiescence. "Was worth a try."

"Please feel free to try at every available opportunity."

Callum chuckled, sliding his hand around to the small of my back in a touch that shouldn't have branded me but did, anyway. "After you."

My brain didn't kick fully back online until we loaded Falkor into the backseat. "Oh! We forgot the wine."

"I didn't."

A few minutes later, Callum parked behind Finn's truck in front of the cottage that I gathered must be where Alex and Ciara lived. Multiple other vehicles were in the drive and at the curb. At five after six, I had to fight the instinctive feeling that we were late. We hadn't spent *that* long kissing. It was fine. This was fine.

Callum came around to open my door and sprang Falkor from the back. He went brows up as I slid out of my seat. "Okay?"

"Fine." But even I didn't believe myself.

He had a bottle of something tucked in one arm, but took my free hand with his and led me up the front walk. Butterflies struck up a synchronized aeronautic routine in my stomach. The front door flew open before either of us could knock, and Ciara beamed. "You're here! Welcome. Come in. Mind your step. We're still unpacking a bit."

The moment we stepped through the door, the scent of wood and fresh lavender enveloped us. The main room—the lounge, I'd learned they called it over here—had richly colored walls and exposed beams along the ceiling. A stone fireplace dominated the space, surrounded by comfortable, well-worn furniture, with a multitude of the obligatory tartan pillows. There were still boxes stacked in the corners, but it was already a warm and inviting room. The kind of place that made you want to curl up on the sofa with a book and a mug of cocoa. As we followed Ciara through the space, I noted that one wall was dominated by photographs. I caught glimpses of sun-drenched landscapes and smiling faces, several of which I recognized. There were at least a dozen of Ciara and Alex. Candid moments that captured the essence of their relationship.

The lounge opened into the kitchen, where every horizontal surface seemed to be covered with food. A massive white dog that made Falkor look small nosed the edge of a charcuterie board.

"Havoc, no! Out!" A blonde woman who looked vaguely familiar waved her hands toward the open back door. "Out. You know better than to counter graze."

With a slow blinking look of affront, the big dog sighed and lumbered out the door. I saw Maeve streak by, nipping at him in an effort to start a game of chase.

"Falkor is welcome to go play in the back garden," Ciara added. "Havoc would no doubt appreciate assistance in distracting the chaos monster."

My faithful pooch had sat obediently beside me, his dark gaze taking in everything and everyone, his tail the only sign of his vibrating excitement. "You wanna go play, baby?"

He looked up at me with hopeful eyes.

"Go on out. You can go play. I'm good."

He took two dancing steps toward the door before he came back and whined.

"Go play. Make friends." I waved him away.

Falkor looked up at Callum.

"I've got her."

Damn if that rumble of a promise didn't make me shiver. Evidently satisfied that I was covered, my pup gave both our hands a lick and pranced out the door.

That was when I realized two things: Callum and I were still holding hands, and we were being stared at.

"Right, I should make introductions." Ciara gestured to a hulking guy I recognized from the pub. "This is my big brother, Ewan, and his fiancée, Isobel. This is Parker."

The blonde tucked at his side beamed. "I've so been looking forward to meeting you."

I shook her offered hand. "Nice to meet you." There was something about that face. "Has anybody ever told you that you look an awful lot like Elizabeth Duncan, the violinist?"

Everyone burst out laughing.

"There's a reason for that," Isobel said. "I am Elizabeth Duncan."

My mouth dropped open. "Holy shit. That's... wow." This woman was literally world famous. "I love your music."

"Thank you."

Because Callum still had a grip on my hand, I gravitated back to his orbit. At this point, I wasn't sure if the contact was for him or me, but I wasn't about to complain.

Ewan toasted the pair of us with the bottle in his hand. "Nice of you to finally join us, Quinn. I see it took a woman to get you out of hiding."

Feeling protective of Callum, I tucked closer, ready to come to his defense. But Callum only chuckled, the vibration of it seeping into me where his chest pressed against my back. "Nah. I heard it would be open season on Finn as the lone single guy. Didn't want to miss my shot."

As more laughter broke out around the room, I could only focus on what he'd said. The lone single guy. As if Callum didn't consider himself single anymore. Did that make us...?

I looked over my shoulder and caught his eye. There went the corner of his mouth again.

"Did I hear my name?" Finn came ambling into the room. "See! There it is! He's doing it again. Someone get a camera."

Callum didn't tear his gaze from mine. "Shut up, Patterson."

And that was when I knew tonight was going to go just fine.

# CHAPTER 21

## CALLUM

"I could have carried more." Parker's complaint was interrupted by the huff of her labored breath.

"This hike is a five-mile loop, and you're no' used to hiking that far at all, let alone with a loaded pack. You said yourself that if you overdo, you'll pay for it, so we're being smart about this."

I'd been researching fibro a bit in my spare time, and I was worried that most hiking gear would rest right on the multitude of tender spots that would set off a flare. For today's outing, I'd kitted her out with nothing but a camelback water bladder and some trekking poles. If she handled that well and enjoyed it, I'd look into getting her some well-padded, ultralight gear. For now, I carried most of the extra supplies, save for the water and wee first aid kit attached to the tactical harness she'd bought for Falkor. It was a far cry from the heavy packs I'd carried during my military service.

"I'm doing fine."

"You're doing beautifully."

The trail I'd chosen wasn't especially arduous by hillwalker standards, but I'd still made sure we took frequent breaks. Now that I knew about her condition, I had a better idea what to keep watch for. So far, I hadn't seen any signs that she was pushing too hard. There'd been a few difficult, boggy spots we'd had to traverse early on, but she'd taken her time, utilizing the poles, me, and the dog, as needed, to get through. The volume of mud Falkor was wearing now was a little alarming, but I already had a plan for taking care of that, so she didn't have to wrangle a hundred pounds of smelly dog into her postage stamp of a shower after today.

"How much further?" Parker asked.

"About ten minutes, give or take." I glanced back at her. Despite her breathlessness, her eyes were bright with determination. "We can take another break if you need."

"No, I want to push through. Unless you need a break?" The teasing lilt in her voice made my lips twitch.

"Cheeky wee thing."

"I'm not wee. I'm perfectly average-sized. You're just a giant."

"Average-sized for where? The Shire?"

She let out a surprised laugh. "Did you just make a Lord of the Rings reference?"

"I've read books." I tried to sound offended, but her delighted expression made it difficult to maintain the grump.

"You totally don't strike me as someone who'd be in to fantasy."

"Shows what you know. I've got layers."

Her grin widened. "Like an onion?"

"Christ, now you're quoting *Shrek* at me?"

"I can't help it. You keep setting yourself up." She paused at a switchback to catch her breath. "Besides, making you smile is worth the effort."

Resisting the urge to rub at the warmth unspooling in my

chest, I reached back and offered my hand, telling myself it was just to help her over the uneven ground. "Come on then, Hobbit. Let's get you to the top."

We had the top to ourselves. One of the benefits of our day off being a Monday. The summit offered a sweeping view of the glen that stretched out below in a patchwork of deep greens where spring was just beginning to touch the mountainside. The morning mist had burned off, leaving the sky a bold, crystalline blue that seemed to stretch to the horizon and beyond. A light breeze carried the rich scent of peat and evergreens, and somewhere far below, a stream caught the sunlight like scattered diamonds.

But I couldn't take my eyes off Parker.

She stood at the edge of the trail, Falkor pressed against her leg, her face tilted up to catch the sun. The wind had pulled strands of dark hair free from her practical braid, and her cheeks were flushed from the exertion of the climb. Her eyes were wide with wonder as she took in the view, her lips parted in a soft 'oh' of appreciation.

I'd been up here a few times since we'd opened Out of Bounds Scotland, led a handful of tourists up here to experience it. But watching her drink it all in, seeing the pure joy practically radiating from every pore, made me feel like I was seeing it for the first time. The way she reached out, almost unconsciously, as if she could gather the whole magnificent landscape into her arms, struck something deep in my chest.

This. This was why I'd chosen this path after leaving the Marines. Not the tourists with their selfie sticks, but the chance to share something real, something profound, with someone who truly appreciated it.

"Worth it?" I asked, my voice rougher than I'd intended.

She turned that beaming smile on me. "Absolutely."

When she held out her hand, I took it, letting her pull me

close. We flowed into each other, our mouths meeting on mutual sighs, and I tasted that incandescent happiness on her lips. This moment right here was worth every mile, every minute of planning.

With a little hum of pleasure, she dropped back to her feet. "Thanks for bringing me up here."

I tucked a loose lock of her hair behind one ear. "Anytime, Hobbit. Let's have a snack and a wee bit of a rest before we start down."

"That sounds good."

While she unclipped the collapsible bowl from Falkor's harness and filled it with water, I pulled out the lightweight waterproof picnic blanket from my pack and spread it on a relatively flat spot, sheltered from the worst of the wind by a cluster of boulders. From the depths of my pack came a couple of stainless-steel containers. The first held sliced chicken and apple with local cheddar. The second had oatcakes and the wee chocolate biscuits I knew she'd developed a fondness for. I'd also packed dried fruit and nuts, plus two insulated bottles— one with more water, one with hot tea that I'd brewed just before we left.

Nothing too heavy, but I'd put some thought into it. I wanted her first proper hike to be memorable.

Parker settled onto the mat with a grateful sigh, her eyes lighting up as I began to open each container. Falkor flopped down beside her, still panting from the climb but alert, his eyes scanning the horizon.

"This is perfect." She selected an oatcake and layered it with chicken and cheese. "I was expecting protein bars and trail mix."

I tried not to look too pleased with myself. "Aye, well, had to make it special, didn't I?"

"Mmm, this is Pippa's cheese."

I lowered myself to the blanket beside her. "Already a connoisseur, are you?"

"I feel like once anybody's had Pippa's cheese, they can't go back."

"True enough."

The wind caught her hair again. She looked so fucking right up here, surrounded by nothing but sky and mountains.

"You know, you're really fucking impressive."

Parker gave an exaggerated flip of her hair. "I know. I have highlighters and spreadsheets, and I know how to use them."

"Not that." I paused. "Although, aye, that. But you have this condition that most would argue is a disability. Yet you dinna let it define you or stop you."

She sobered, her eyes shuttering a little as she built another wee sandwich.

I knew I was treading on a different kind of boggy ground as I continued. "I realize I've been doing both those things with my own situation."

Her expression softened, and she laid a hand on my leg. "Believe me, it took a while. I've had years more time to get used to my situation than you have. Be gentle with yourself."

"I'm no' exactly a gentle man."

"Liar." But her smile took any sting out of the accusation. "You're selectively gentle."

"Aye, well, you're the exception."

"Still counts," she declared. Since I wasn't moving toward the food, she built a little sandwich for me and handed it over. "Here."

I accepted the food with a nod of thanks. "How is it you can stay so positive all the time?"

She poured some of the tea into one of the collapsible cups. "It's a choice. I can't change that I have this condition, but I can choose not to let it rule my life. That doesn't mean I don't accommodate myself, and I have to make long-term forecasts for contingency plans for anything I do in a way that most people don't." She looked back at the sweeping valley below. "But doing this? This was a huge accomplishment for me." Fierce satisfaction dripped from every word.

Driven by an urge I didn't want to analyze too closely, I snagged her hand in mine. "You make me want to be better. To make different choices."

The smile she turned on me warmed something in my chest that had long gone cold. "Good." And when she kissed me again, I vowed I'd keep making those better choices, so long as she stayed in my life.

# CHAPTER 22

## PARKER

The long drive back from our hike lulled me almost to sleep, such that I didn't realize we weren't headed to my flat until Callum put the Range Rover into park. I started to sit up from where I'd slumped against the window and winced. My muscles had locked up, and the thought of moving again made me want to whimper. Biting back a hiss of pain, I peered through the growing dusk at the stone house set back among the trees.

"Where are we?"

"My place." Callum killed the engine. "Thought we should get himself cleaned up before he destroyed your flat."

My cheerful pup had managed to find what seemed like every speck of mud and every puddle on the trail. Falkor's wet dog smell had thoroughly permeated the SUV's interior, and even the hour-long drive back hadn't been enough time for us to go nose blind. We both glanced back to see he'd left muddy paw prints all over the back seat. So much for the towels we'd tried to protect it with.

"Oh, Callum, your car."

"It'll clean up."

As if in challenge to his assertion, Falkor chose that moment to shake, spraying more muddy water across the interior. "Gah!" I threw my arm up in an ineffectual shield that made my shoulders scream. A moment later, I peeled my eyes back open to find Callum watching me.

"It'll clean up," he repeated and got out.

Taking advantage of the fact that he couldn't hear me for the moment, I hissed my way through straightening in my seat. I'd be better once I got moving again. He came around to my door, and I caught the slight hesitation before he opened it.

"It's no' much. And I haven't..." Color rising in his stubbled cheeks, he gestured vaguely at the general state of things, encompassing the overgrown vegetation and the weeds sprouting between the stones of the path leading up to the front door.

I closed my hand around his. "You don't bring people here." In the weeks I'd been in Glenlaig, I'd gathered that Callum never had visitors. Ever. Not even his best friends. Yet he'd brought me to his sanctuary.

I squeezed his hand and slid out of my seat. "No judgment."

The moment I was out, Falkor tried to come through the seats to follow, but Callum was quicker. He yanked open the back door, catching him around the middle. "Oh, no you don't, you great muddy beast." Despite the dog's size, Callum hoisted him up like he weighed nothing. "Come on."

I followed the pair of them, grinning as I spotted Falkor's happily lolling tongue over Callum's shoulder. At the front door, Callum paused, shifting his hold on the dog to dig keys out of his pocket. Then we were in the inner sanctum.

The last of the evening sun shone through the bare windows, dimly lighting the interior. There were no curtains, no photos on the walls. But the hardwood floors gleamed. Everything I could see was neat, organized with military precision. I trailed him down a hall and into what had to be his bedroom. The king-size bed was made with hospital corners that would've made a drill sergeant weep with joy.

Callum stepped through another doorway into the main bathroom. "Watch your step." For what, I didn't know. There wasn't so much as a stray sock on the floor to trip over. "The tub's deep enough we should be able to contain most of the mess."

His bathroom was easily three times the size of mine—not a high bar—with both a glass-walled shower and a deep soaking tub that instantly gave me visions of relaxing baths. Then my brain took a sharply sexier turn into less relaxing fantasies. Blinking those away, I noted the bathroom was just like everything else I'd seen—pristine, if spartan. No decorative towels or fancy soaps. Just the essentials.

Falkor began to squirm, smearing more mud across Callum's shirt.

"Into the tub wi' you." He bent to deposit his smelly bundle into the basin.

When Falkor might've leapt straight out, we both closed in. His eyes shone with manic glee. He wasn't a service dog in this moment. He was a filthy pup, trying to escape the consequences of his actions.

"Don't even think about it fluffball. Behave," I ordered.

Falkor looked at Callum, who only pointed. "No."

My dog gave a beleaguered huff and sat.

"Good boy."

It took both of us to get him clean, though mostly I just held his collar while Callum did all the work scrubbing off the muck. Once the last of the dirty water spiraled down the drain, Callum lifted Falkor out and reached for a towel. Before he could grab it, the dog gave a mighty shake, instantly soaking us both.

Callum blinked, droplets of water clinging to his unfairly long lashes. Falkor wagged at him, unrepentant.

"You're a menace." Plucking at the wet T-shirt that now clung to his chest like a second skin, he shrugged and tugged it off over his head. "Right. So we're next on the clean up list before dinner."

My brain was too busy short circuiting over the sight of all that muscle, interrupted only by a dusting of dark hair across his pecs and down the center of his abs.

"Dinner?" Was that my voice, dim and distant?

"I figured you'd be hungry."

My mouth was watering, but it had nothing to do with food. "Um." A rumbling growl filled the room. Alarmed, I laid a hand over my belly, which apparently didn't appreciate being forgotten. "Starving."

"We'll dry off the dog, get cleaned up, and I'll fix us something to eat."

There were so many possibilities in that statement, I didn't even know where to start. But I didn't want my runaway libido to be making assumptions, so I waited to follow his lead.

Callum did not drag me into the shower. More was the pity. Though, if he had, I wasn't sure I'd have been able to fully enjoy it. Fatigue weighed down my limbs, as if I'd shrugged on a suit of chain mail since we came down off the mountain. Instead, he set me up with a clean towel and some dry clothes.

"They'll probably swallow you, but at least they dinna smell like wet dog."

"Thanks."

I shut myself into his second bathroom and stripped out of my filthy gear. I had relatively clean outer layers and some spare socks in a bag in the Range Rover, but no extra pants or underwear. Looked like I'd be going commando in Callum's sweatpants. That felt remarkably intimate in ways I wasn't sure he'd thought through. But I was thinking through them as I pulled on his clothes after my shower, feeling the soft cotton stroke over my skin, catching the faint whiff of cedar and spice that I associated with him. Lord, it was hard not to imagine it was his hands whispering over me instead of his clothes.

*Get a grip, Lawrence.*

By the time I emerged from the bathroom, Callum was already in the kitchen, dressed in a similar pair of sweatpants and T-shirt. But where I'd had to do a lot of creative rolling and tying to keep them on, they hugged him like a second skin. His brown hair was still wet and spiky from his shower.

He turned, a skillet in his hand. "Better?"

I made an incoherent noise that was half between a whimper and a choke.

His focus narrowed. "Tired?"

"Uh-huh." Far better for him to believe I was incoherent because I was exhausted rather than that my brain was short circuiting with lust. And it wasn't a lie. I was tired.

"Give me ten, and I'll have dinner thrown together."

"'K."

I found my dog sprawled out on a pile of towels beside the radiator. He still smelled of wet dog, but without the bog stench added to it.

"I gave him some of the food from his pack. He seems to be down for the count."

As I sank down onto the big leather man sofa that dominated the lounge, I didn't manage to hold back the little moan. "I don't think I'm that far behind him."

"Ten minutes," he said again, and turned back to the stove.

In less than two, my eyes were already drooping shut.

"C'mon, Hobbit. Time to eat."

"Mmm?" I cracked my eyes to find Callum crouched before me, a plate in his hands.

With some difficulty, I struggled to sit up. "Oh, this looks great."

He'd gone with a classic breakfast for dinner. Scrambled eggs, sautéed potatoes, and sausages.

"Nothing fancy, but you'll need the protein and carbs to refuel." He retrieved his own plate and joined me on the sofa. "Feeling it?"

"Mmm."

"Think you'll flare?"

"Maybe. If I do, it was worth it." It took way more effort than it should have to scoop the food into my mouth. The fork felt more like a shovel than a utensil.

We ate in companionable silence until I set the empty plate aside. "Not gonna lie... I'm not sure I can move again tonight."

"I don't have a guest room."

Snuggling down into the sofa, I murmured, "That's not a problem for me. I don't have the energy to take advantage of you, anyway."

"You want to take advantage of me?" The dark rumble of that voice did something to me. Or would, if I wasn't so damned tired.

On a yawn, I mumbled, "I mean, have you seen you?"

Good God. My filter was positively gone.

But Callum only chuckled. "I think we can do better than the sofa."

Gently, he scooped me up as if I weighed nothing. With a sigh, I curled against the magnificent warmth of his chest. "Mmm, this is definitely better."

He carried me down the hall, into his room, and tucked me into his bed. His lips ghosted over my temple. "Sleep well, Hobbit."

I used the last of my strength to grab his hand as he started to pull away. "Will you stay with me?"

"Aye. Just a minute."

He disappeared from the room, probably going through the house to turn off lights and lock up. I was already drifting again when I felt the give of the mattress behind me. His big hand curved around my ribcage.

"Is this okay?" he whispered.

In answer, I wriggled back into the shelter of his body, tucking his arm more firmly around me. Then I slid straight into blissful, exhausted sleep.

# CHAPTER 23

## CALLUM

Sleep and I had long been uneasy allies. Too many years on ops and too much training kept me from sleeping deep or long, and that had only gotten worse with my retirement. I couldn't remember the last time I hadn't been awake before sunrise, so when I opened my eyes to sunlight, I thought I was still dreaming. The warm weight wrapped around me like a koala only added to the sensation. With a sigh, I turned my head, burying my face in hair that smelled of my shampoo. As it was a far cry better than what usually occupied my dreams, I lay there, content to drift as long as it lasted.

Only when my companion shifted, pressing a cold nose against my shoulder, did I realize I wasn't dreaming.

Parker.

Parker had spent the night in my bed. And I'd... slept. Not the whole night. I'd gotten up once to swap the laundry I'd started before bed over to the dryer, so she'd have something to wear home that wasn't covered in trail muck. But otherwise, I'd slept and hadn't stirred.

It had been a long time since I'd had anyone in my bed. Not

since before the accident. I'd never brought a woman here—for sex or anything else. But that indefinably intimate scent of sleep-warmed skin was doing things to me beyond inspiring a whole host of erotic ways I could wake her. It was making me imagine what it would be like to have this every day.

How the hell had we gotten here?

How had this walking ball of sunshine ended up all warm and cozy beside me in a completely platonic way? I thought of what she'd said last night about being too tired to take advantage of me. I didn't think she was joking about wanting to take advantage. So maybe not so completely platonic. Still. What had I done to deserve any of this? To deserve her?

I didn't know exactly where this was going. We hadn't formally defined things, though she hadn't balked at my allusion at dinner the other night that I didn't consider myself single anymore. Given she had no problem calling me out on anything else, I wanted that to mean she wanted this. Wanted me. For... whatever it was we were doing. But I didn't want to push for too much, too fast.

I thought about getting up, getting started on my day. Removing myself from the temptation she presented. But I didn't move a muscle. She'd told me her body needed extra rest after major exertion, and yesterday had been a lot. I'd let her sleep as long as she wanted. There was the small matter of it being a workday, and I'd need to get her back to her flat to change, at the very least, but I was the boss, damn it. If I couldn't grant lenience, what was the point? I'd get shit from Finn and Alex, but I didn't give a damn about that. So long as they directed it at me instead of Parker.

The dappled sun had crept further across the room by the time an alarm sounded from the other room. Her mobile phone, probably. Parker's head jerked against my shoulder and she groaned, curling tighter against me. "Five more mins," she slurred.

Unfortunately, given the phone's position, the alarm only continued to sound. Falkor popped up from the blanket I'd left folded on the floor last night and crossed over to nose at Parker's back. She whimpered.

My little sunshine wasn't a morning person. At least not straight out of bed. I stroked my fingers along her upper arm and brushed a kiss over her temple. "Time to get up, Hobbit. We've got work."

She moaned again in protest, and Falkor whined.

"Himself needs to go out. I'll take him."

"M'kay."

I carefully extricated myself, and Parker rolled into the warm spot and snuggled in. She'd be asleep again in less than thirty seconds. I'd give her as long as I could.

"Come on, lad. Let's go do your business."

With a quick detour to turn off the alarm on Parker's phone, I headed out back with Falkor. He didn't dally, finding a spot at the far edge of the garden, then trotting back, his tail waving like a banner. To give Parker a few more minutes of shuteye, I started the coffee and retrieved her clothes from the dryer. As predicted, she'd slid right back to sleep, sprawled on her stomach across my side of the bed.

Crouching down, I brushed the hair back from her face. "Rise and shine, Hobbit."

Her eyes were slow to open, and when they focused on me, I didn't just see fatigue. I saw a haze of pain. A furrow dug between her eyes, and the corners of her mouth pulled into a grimace.

"You okay?"

"Ugh."

"Having a flare?"

She blinked, frowning harder. "Yeah."

I'd been afraid of this. "Okay. What do you need?"

"Give me a minute or ten to see if my legs are going to work."

Everything in me wanted to panic at that. To bundle her up and take her to the nearest doctor. But she'd warned me that this happened sometimes. It would pass. Eventually.

I eased back to give her space, moving over to crank the radiator because I remembered that heat helped. Falkor took my place by the bedside as she slowly, painfully, pushed herself vertical. By the time she made it upright, her hair a mess about her shoulders, she was breathing almost as hard from the exertion as she had from hiking yesterday. I desperately wanted to help, but I was also a little afraid to touch her like this, so I curled my fingers to keep from reaching for her.

"Brace," she croaked.

Falkor locked his stance, and she used him to lever herself to her feet. She stayed where she was, swaying a little for seconds that felt like minutes.

"I need to get to the rug in the living room."

I had no idea why, but I wasn't about to argue, so I made sure the way was clear. At least it gave me something to do for a minute or two. She and the dog made their slow, careful way into the lounge.

"Can you scoot the coffee table over?"

I did as she asked, making space in front of the couch. With another whimper, she slowly lowered herself to the floor and stretched out flat.

"What are you doing?"

With a gentle tap, she dismissed Falkor and bent her knees, easing them to one side while her back remained on the floor. "Yoga. Torture. They're kind of one and the same when I'm in this state. But I'll be better if I move."

"Ah." What else could I say? "Do you want breakfast after? I've got coffee started."

"Coffee sounds great. We're going to be late for work."

"Well, you've got an in with one of the bosses. It'll be fine. Alex can cover."

I moved into the kitchen to pour a cup of coffee, so she didn't feel like I was staring. Then I sent a quick text.

CALLUM

> Parker isn't feeling well and is going to be late. Can you open today?

I wasn't even sure she'd be in at all, but I didn't add that yet. This was her call to make.

ALEX

Got it.

I sent up a grateful prayer that I hadn't needed to tag in Finn. He'd have been on deck to help as well, but he wouldn't have done it without more questions on the front end.

I drank down half a cup of coffee as Parker pushed herself through some gentle stretches. It was obvious she was in a lot of pain, but I bloody well wasn't going to keep commenting on it. I knew how much I felt like a freak when people got focused on my eye and couldn't seem to look away. I didn't want to do that to her.

By the end of the yoga, she was moving a little better.

"I got your clothes washed. I know you'll want to change before work, but at least you don't have to put on something that's still muddy."

"Oh, great. I'm going to need another shower. I need you to get me back to my place. I've got meds there that might help."

Might. Christ. But I kept my tone even. "Okay. We can do that."

While she got dressed, I put her coffee in a travel mug for the drive. I didn't think we had time for me to make something here. Maybe I could pick up breakfast from the bakery while she had that shower. She sipped her coffee slowly as I headed into the village. The haze of pain hovered over her, dimming everything about her. It worried me, and it took everything I had not to ask a lot of questions. I didn't want to upset her or make her feel pressured.

As I turned onto the high street, she finally lifted her head. "Is there an actual dog groomer in town? Because I think maybe we made a mistake not brushing him last night. He's got all kinds of snarls in his fur."

"We'll find one." I'd drive him wherever I had to so she didn't have to spend limited energy on it.

I parked by the kerb and got out of the Range Rover. I'd just opened her door and was about to help her out, when I caught motion in my periphery. Someone was lurking in her doorway. Instinct propelled me into motion, and before I even registered what was happening, I had the lurker pinned against the wall, my forearm across their throat. A moment's glimpse of furious dark eyes, before fingers jabbed hard into my armpit. Pain shot through my shoulder and down the back of my arm, but I didn't loosen my hold.

"What the actual hell?" The words came from Parker, and I froze.

So did my captive.

I finally looked at her. Because it was a woman I had pinned to the wall. One I recognized from photos in Parker's flat.

"Jade?" Parker's tone was a mix of shock and joy and resignation. "Holy shit. Callum, let her go."

I instantly backed off. I wasn't in the habit of accosting

women. Even women who evidently had the skills to defend themselves. "Apologies."

Jade offered one fulminating look at me before her focus zeroed in on Parker. An equally complex mix of emotions flitted across her face—frustration and worry and pleasure, before finally landing on understanding. She instantly moved to Parker's side. "How bad?"

"Like maybe a 6.5. Down from 8."

I could only assume this was some sort of pain scale they'd developed.

"All right. Let's get you inside."

Somehow I was made instantly superfluous to the efforts to get her upstairs and into her apartment. I could only bring up the rear, feeling utterly helpless as Jade took over, clearly knowing exactly what to do. And while I was glad someone knew how to help her... I wanted it to be me.

Upstairs, Jade took in the flat at a single glance before steering Parker toward the bathroom. "Into the bath with you."

Parker didn't fight it.

Feeling ten kinds of useless, I stayed where I was, just inside the door. "Do you want me to go?"

She glanced back at me, apology in her eyes. "No. I think we've all got things to talk about, if you can wait a bit."

"As long as you need."

They disappeared into the bedroom. I heard the bathroom tap turn on and the tub begin to fill.

"Where are your gummies?"

"Nightstand drawer."

Falkor padded out of the bedroom and came to lick my hand. He looked up at me as if to say, "I don't know what's going on, either." Absently, I scratched behind his ears. Parker had been avoiding this woman for weeks. And now here she was. What did it mean? Only that she'd finally tracked Parker down? Or was something else going on?

A few minutes later, the tall, lean black woman came out of the bedroom, leaving the door open, presumably so she could hear if Parker called. She crossed her arms. "So."

I fought the urge to mimic the motion. "So, you're the bodyguard."

"So, you're the boyfriend."

Given that Parker had just spent the night in my bed, even if it had just been sleeping, it seemed apt enough. "Aye."

Jade didn't respond to that, only stared at me as if she could see into my soul.

Parker called out from the bathroom. "I can hear you having a glower-off. Both of you behave!"

"I didn't realize you were dating your boss," Jade called back.

"Only one of them."

That made the other woman's lips twitch, just a fraction.

"How did you find me?" Parker asked.

"For all the steps you took to hide your tracks, you neglected to think that I'd actually watched all those Instagram and YouTube links you sent me with hikes all over creation. I remembered that several of them were hosted by a company owned by former military men. It just took me a little while to dig through the viewing history to track down which one." She chuckled. "You did extremely well disappearing for somebody with no training in espionage and evasion tactics."

"That something you have a lot of experience with?" I asked.

Her narrowed eyes flashed. "Oh, don't you worry your pretty head. I'm well qualified for my job."

I had a distinct impression that she was judging me and coming up undecided.

I felt much the same.

"J, be nice," Parker warned.

"I'm always nice. Until I'm not." There was a definitive edge to her, and no question she could handle herself.

She'd slipped off her jacket, and I caught a glimpse of a tattoo on her biceps. A globe with the edge of what appeared to be an anchor.

"Marines?"

One dark brow winged up. "Eight years. You?"

"Royal Marines. Fifteen."

That implacable face cracked just a little until she looked reluctantly impressed by that.

"Jade! Little help."

The bodyguard disappeared back into the bedroom.

Because I couldn't stand still any longer, I prowled over to the kitchenette to inspect the contents of the fridge. Parker needed to eat something. Finding eggs, cheese, and bread, I set about making some breakfast sandwiches. I was just plating them when the pair of them came back out.

Parker caught sight of them, and her face softened. "You didn't have to make breakfast."

"Least I could do. You should eat."

Jade looked mildly impressed that I'd made her a sandwich, too. "Thanks."

We relocated to the lounge. I was relieved to see that Parker looked less glazed and was moving a bit more under her own steam.

"So, what precipitated this visit? Is it that you finally found me, or is something going on?"

"Girl, you have to tell your parents. I can't keep putting them off."

Parker closed her eyes and blew out a long breath, her shoulders slumping. I wanted to put my arms around her, take whatever weight I could off those shoulders. But I wasn't sure this was something I could take on for her.

"Fine. I'll do what I probably should have done in the first place." She reached for the laptop on the end table.

"What are you going to do?"

She flipped open the laptop and began to click. "I'm writing them an email informing them I've moved to Scotland, and that I have a job and a home, and I hope they'll be happy and supportive."

Parker hadn't talked much about her family other than to say that they'd effectively smothered her, which had precipitated this whole adventure. But somehow I didn't expect them to take the news that well. Still, Jade and I stayed quiet, eating our sandwiches, while Parker typed up the email.

"Okay. It's sent." She looked at Jade. "You wanna take bets on how long it takes them to show up here?"

"I reckon that depends. How much sunshine did you try to blow up their asses about the wisdom of this decision?"

Parker stuck her tongue out in a gesture that said so much about her relationship with this woman. "A necessary amount. But when they show up, we'll be ready. Meanwhile, let me formally introduce you to Callum Quinn. Callum, this is Jade Washington, my bodyguard and best friend."

I grunted a hello.

Then we all stared at each other.

Jade was the one who finally broke the silence. "So now what?"

Parker finished her last bite of sandwich. "Now, we need to get to work, and I guess it's time for you to see what my new life looks like."

# CHAPTER 24

## PARKER

PARKER

Anybody up for an impromptu get together at the pub after work?

SKYE

Always.

PIPPA

I could go for a pint.

CIARA

I'm in.

SAOIRSE

Second the call for a pint. It's been A Day.

PARKER

Great. Make sure you grab a table with an extra seat. There's someone I want y'all to meet.

SKYE

Ooooo. :GIF of Chris Pratt from Parks and Rec with wow face:

SAOIRSE

:GIF of Flynn Ryder from Tangled raising an
eyebrow:

PIPPA

😊

They all obviously thought something else was happening. But
I'd sort that out when we got there.

CIARA

Falkor coming?

PARKER

Yep. 5:30?

CIARA

Patio it is.

PARKER

See y'all there.

"We're going where?" Jade asked.

I shut down my work computer. "Out to the pub. I want
you to meet my friends."

That wasn't precisely what I wanted. I *wanted* a chance to
talk to Callum alone to get a clearer handle on where we stood.
I'd slept in his bed. Nothing had happened beyond my using
him as my own personal teddy bear, but it had been intimate,
nonetheless. Then he'd been treated to me in the middle of a
flare, which we also hadn't gotten a chance to talk about
because Jade had shown up. He'd effectively declared himself
my boyfriend, which I wasn't opposed to, but I really wished I
had unequivocal confirmation of that fact.

Now my parents had been notified of my whereabouts
and that I'd started a new life here, which I expected to go
over like a lead balloon. I was anxiously waiting for the other

shoe to drop and for my carefully crafted world to fall apart, because I didn't see how my two disparate lives could possibly mesh. I was still avoiding my email and the phone calls that had started coming in. Honestly, the fact that I'd managed to avoid talking to my parents for an entire month was a minor miracle, and I knew I had the woman next to me to thank for it.

Jade had helped out around the office for the past two days. Alex and Finn had accepted my explanation that she was a friend in town without comment, but I knew they had questions. I owed them all kinds of explanations for what was coming. But those, too, would have to wait, because now that Jade was here, I couldn't just bail on her again. So I'd take her to the pub and introduce her to the girls.

Finley emerged from the back. "Need a lift?"

Callum and Alex were out on client excursions that had been booked well before Jade had arrived in town. Finn was barely back from his own assignment for the day.

"No. The weather's good. We'll walk."

Jade went brows up. "We will?"

Those brows said, *But you were flaring just yesterday. What the actual hell?*

"We will," I confirmed. "Are you ready for that rock climbing trip tomorrow morning?"

"Still checking ropes, but I'll finish up before I leave tonight. And I'll update the trip notes in the system."

"Good. I'll get those follow-up surveys sent out in the morning. Tomorrow's clients are supposed to be here by nine."

He nodded. "I'll be ready. You're sure you don't want a lift back to the pub?"

I hauled my purse out of the drawer. "Positive. See you tomorrow."

Falkor rose from his spot beside my desk, bending low in a

good stretch before padding over to give Finn's hand a lick. Finn obligingly scratched behind his ears. "Good lad."

Satisfied with his goodbye, Falkor swished his tail and assumed his position by my side. I snapped on his lead. "C'mon, pal. We're headed to the pub."

Jade said nothing as I locked up the front of the office. She simply fell into step beside me as I headed back toward the high street. The silence wasn't as comfortable as usual, full of all the questions neither of us had asked. After all these years together, it felt weird to have her on the outside. I wasn't deliberately trying to keep her there, but I'd been building this life on my own, and I didn't know how to incorporate her easily.

She waited until we'd hit the corner to break the silence. "You're actually over your flare."

"More or less. I'm hanging out around a 3 today." Uncomfortable but functional without the haze of fibro fog that had dogged me yesterday.

"That's a quicker recovery than usual for you."

I shrugged. "I walk everywhere here, so my body is used to moving more than I did at home. The five-mile hike Callum and I took the other day was overdoing it a bit, but in general, all the extra movement has been good for me."

"I'd say that's not the only thing good for you here."

Catching motion out of the corner of my eye, I smiled and waved at Mr. Patel, who ran the newsagent on the corner. "Is that a remark on the job, the village, or Callum?"

"To be determined. I'm just saying it seems like this new life agrees with you."

It was a concession I hadn't expected, even if I had been going out of my way to show her that this wasn't just some whim. That I'd really done something here.

"Yeah, it does. Not having to worry about my parents constantly has been a bigger load off than I expected. I can just... be, without worrying that they'll come barging in to intervene or overstep or smother me with their worries."

Jade frowned. "I guess we both just got used to that. I didn't realize it was as bad as it was. I'm sorry I didn't recognize you were drowning a bit."

I laid a hand on her arm. "You kept it from being worse. I appreciate that. But I needed to do this. Whether it was here or somewhere else. I needed some space from them and the expectations that go along with the Lawrence name. I absolutely love being just Parker here."

As we passed the bakery, Mrs. Byrne, the genius behind the pastries that I'd fallen in love with, was just locking up. "Oh, Parker, dear. I got in some gorgeous rhubarb today, so I'm making rhubarb and custard tarts tomorrow, in case you want to stop in."

I beamed at her. "You are a delightfully evil woman, encouraging my sweet tooth. Of course, I'll see you tomorrow, Mrs. B."

She winked. "It might be as I'll have some special treats for yon great beastie there, as well."

Falkor's tail picked up the pace as he trotted over to Mrs. Byrne for pets.

"Then we'll definitely be in tomorrow."

I was still smiling as I tugged my pup away from his love fest.

"Getting to know all the locals," Jade observed.

"Being on good terms with the supplier of my favorite addiction is just smart. And anyway, I like how small Glenlaig is. I like knowing my neighbors."

"Hell of a change from home."

She didn't say it, but I could sense the question she wasn't asking. If I stayed here, committed to what I was building, what would her role be in this new life? I didn't know the answer.

She'd been tied to me for so long, I didn't think she'd ever really thought about what she wanted to do herself. If she was no longer my bodyguard, would she have any desire at all to stay here? Would she want to pursue some other dream she'd never told me about?

I wasn't ready for the answers to those questions either, so I didn't ask.

We stepped through the door of The Stag's Head, pausing in the front entryway while our eyes adjusted to the dimness inside. I spotted Skye's boyfriend, Jason McKinnon, moving behind the bar. He seemed to be in deep conversation with Lochlan Reid, a local author who'd booked an overnight with us earlier in the month as research for his latest tartan noir thriller.

Zo Bassey hustled by, a tray of drinks on her shoulder. "Hey, Parker. The girls are already out on the patio, and an order for apps has been put in."

"Thanks, Zo."

I waved to a handful of other familiar faces as I wove through the tables, making my way out to the patio. Jade stuck close, scanning the pub in that way she had of assessing everyone and everything in it. She was more subtle than Callum. Then again, she'd been in civilian life a lot longer. I didn't think he'd ever be able to walk into a room and not look like exactly what he was—a man who could absolutely handle himself and anyone else.

We stepped out onto the patio. My friends looked up, expectation morphing to surprise, then brief disappointment, then on to curiosity.

Skye pouted. "I totally thought you were bringing Callum to introduce as your official beau."

I laughed. "If you think I'd be able to get Callum Quinn to show up as the only guy at girls' night, you are sorely overestimating my influence."

"Oh, I don't know," Ciara drawled. "He looked like he'd be pretty content to do anything you asked at dinner the other night."

"Finley hasn't stopped freaking out that he's actually smiling." Which was amusing, but I also could tell that beneath the ball busting he was happy for Callum. "Anyway, no, I want to introduce y'all all to Jade Washington, my bestie from home, who's here for a visit."

Jade shot me a meaningful glance before turning back to the others and offering a warm smile and wave. I made introductions to everyone, and we took our seats.

Saoirse pointed to the pitchers at the center of the table. "Pint?"

"Yes, please."

As she did the honors, Ciara leaned in, waggling her eyebrows. "Sooo, how was your hike? It was noted you didn't come home that night."

I knew what she was angling for and snorted a laugh. "Reality is a lot less salacious than you're imagining. The hike was great, but muddy, so we stopped at his house to give Falkor a bath before he got bog stench all over my flat. Then Callum went to heat up something for dinner, and I passed out on the sofa. So I stayed."

"Did he leave you on the sofa or move you to a bed?" Saoirse asked. "Inquiring minds want to know."

My cheeks heated as I thought about how it had felt to have him scoop me up like I weighed nothing.

"Oooo," Pippa crooned. "Did he tuck you in?"

"I mean... kinda yeah. He has a big bed."

"Wait, wait. Did he *cuddle*?" Skye demanded.

"Yeah."

Saoirse's gaze sharpened with interest. "Wanting to shag

you is one thing. Cuddling is something else entirely. I think our Mr. Tall, Dark, and Broody is smitten."

I couldn't stop the grin that stretched my lips. "Well, I guess I'm smitten right back."

Skye clutched her hand over her heart. "Awwwww."

"I love this for both of you," Ciara declared. "He's super protective of you, but in a totally good way."

Jade lifted her beer for a sip. "Seems like he's bucking to compete with some of Paisley's heroes."

"He's doing a damned good job," I admitted. Not that I'd come here looking for a hero, but I couldn't deny that I'd found one. I hadn't updated Paisley on the kiss or anything that had happened after. I knew that would lead to the Squee Heard Round The World, and she'd triumphantly declare she'd told me so. There were worse reactions, but I wanted to have some kind of confirmation before I let her in on things.

"We are all thrilled for Parker, but let's shift the topic away from men," Saoirse interjected. "Jade, tell us about you. How did you and Parker meet?"

"I hear definite southern in that accent," Skye declared. "Are you from Tennessee, too?"

"Georgia. Marietta. I did two stints in the Marines before I went to college on the GI Bill. That was where I met Parker."

"We were both in the same art history seminar," I explained.

"Yeah, except you actually liked that stuff. I was just clearing my humanities credit. You were the only reason I passed that class."

I sent her an affectionate smile. "And we've been besties ever since."

Jade tapped her glass to mine. "Damned straight."

Zo arrived then, with a tray full of appetizers for the table.

"Oh, these look amazing. Jade, you have to try the haggis balls."

"Do I?" She eyed the plate with suspicion.

"No lie. They're amazing," Skye added.

"I'll circle back in a bit to take your dinner orders."

"Thanks, Zo! Tell your dad I'll be back to give him hugs before I leave." As she headed back inside, Ciara explained, "Zo's dad, Dom, is the master of the kitchen here. He's basically the village dad who tries to feed everyone, and since it's my brother's pub and I worked here for a while, he's totally family."

"I love that about this place." With a happy sigh, I dipped a haggis ball into the whisky gravy.

"So, Jade, what sort of work do you do?" Saoirse asked.

"I'm in security."

Ciara nodded. "That seems so common post military. My brother also served with Callum, Finn, and Alex. All of them considered doing that after they got out. Ewan, Finn, and Alex all worked private security for my future sister-in-law on her last tour."

Jade speared one of the haggis balls with a fork and eyed it with suspicion. "Tour?"

"Her future sister-in-law is Elizabeth Duncan," I explained.

Her perfectly shaped brows winged up. "No shit? I love her music."

"She's absolutely lovely. I met her at the dinner party the other night. You'd like her. If you're here long enough, I'm sure you'll meet her." It was a roundabout way of asking how long she intended to stay. Chickenshit on my part? Absolutely. But I'd take the protection of the group to save myself from some tough conversations a little longer.

"Oh, please stick around so I'm not the last single person standing again," Saoirse begged. "I thought Parker was going to have my back there, but she's gone and gotten cozy with Mr.

Tall, Dark, and Broody, and I'm on my own again. It's getting old." She paused. "Unless you're not single, and I just stuck my foot in it."

Jade huffed a laugh. "I am also single. My plans are up in the air at the moment, but I'll be sticking around for the foreseeable future."

Translation: You gave me the slip once, but I'm not shirking my duty anymore.

*Understood.* I'd find a way to work with that.

"If you're going to be here for a while, you definitely need somewhere better to sleep than on my sofa. My flat isn't exactly set up for long-term guests."

"Oh, my cousins own a bunch of rental cottages," Ciara said. "We can certainly check with them to see if they've got one available."

"I'll definitely have to look into that." It wasn't a yes. Of course, it wasn't. She was my bodyguard. From her perspective, she couldn't do her job if she wasn't with me. If I'd brought her in from the beginning, we'd have found a place that would fit both of us. But that wasn't the choice I'd made, and we were both going to have to find a way to live with it.

# CHAPTER 25

## CALLUM

Because Parker had texted that she was hanging out with the girls tonight, I headed straight home after my guided hike. I could clean my gear just as well there as the office. For months, this had been my standard operating procedure, retreating to my cave where no one had any expectations of me. Alone was how I liked it.

But tonight my house felt emptier than usual. Suddenly I noticed how bare everything looked. How little of me there really was scattered around. I could blame that on my years of military service, on having been trained to travel light and not acquire much in the way of things. But it was more a reflection of the fact that I had so little in my life beyond my career and closest mates. And I'd deliberately held them at arm's length because it had felt safer than letting them in.

I hadn't wanted to let Parker in. But she'd worked her way past my defenses in that sweet, relentless way she had, saving me from so much more than just the bloody phone. She made me want things. Things I'd told myself weren't for a man like me. Things I still wasn't altogether sure I deserved.

She'd spent less than twenty-four hours under my roof, yet she'd managed to leave her stamp on the place, at least in my mind. I kept picturing her curled up on the sofa, her behemoth of a dog stretched out on the rug beside her. She took up so much space for such a wee thing, and damn it, I missed her.

I didn't know what Jade's continued presence meant for us. Or for Parker herself. I doubted she knew, either. Not that we'd had a chance to talk about it. But we would. We'd make it work. Parker Lawrence wasn't a weak-willed woman who'd let other well-meaning people dictate her life. Not after all the trouble she'd gone to in order to come here. I just had to be patient.

Not exactly my strong suit these days.

Wandering into my kitchen, I opened the fridge for a beer and pondered what the hell I'd eat for dinner.

The sound of tires on gravel pulled my attention to the front window. Parker had no car, so who the hell had come to interrupt my solitude?

I should've expected Finn and Alex. They'd been remarkably chill about the past few weeks, but clearly their patience was at an end.

I met the pair of them at the door, taking in the bag in Finn's hand. "Is that takeaway from Taste of Mumbai?"

"We all had clients today, so I didn't think any of us would want to cook."

"And we figured you'd be more inclined to answer questions if we fed you," Alex added.

"Fair enough. I've got beer."

They trailed me inside. Finn unloaded containers on the kitchen table, while I retrieved two more bottles, and Alex opened the cabinets, looking for plates. The scent of warm, exotic spices filled the space, making my mouth water and my stomach growl. "Please tell me you got samosas and garlic naan."

"I got enough food for a small army. I'm starving."

We settled in, filling our plates with fragrant biryani and at least three types of curry. I ripped a piece of buttery naan in half and dipped it into the lamb rogan josh.

"So, are you going to tell us what the hell is going on with Parker?" Finn asked cheerfully. "And I dinna mean between the two of you."

I'd held my tongue all these weeks, wanting to respect her privacy and give her the opportunity to tell them her story in her own time. But I no longer felt I had that option. My partners had a right to know about things that might well impact our business.

"Jade is Parker's bodyguard."

The piece of beef Finn had speared fell right off the tip of his fork as he stared at me. "I'm sorry. Bodyguard? What?"

"Why does Parker need a bodyguard?" Alex asked. "Who is she?"

I went brows up. "You haven't looked?"

"No, I respected her privacy. Even after setting up that whole untraceable communication system for her. Do I need to look?"

Did he? None of us were accustomed to functioning without full intel.

"I'm no' entirely sure. She hasn't said a whole lot about it, even to me. But the long and the short of it is that she has fibromyalgia, and her parents are very controlling. She insists not in an abusive sort of way, but out of a well-intentioned, overbearing concern. She wanted to throw off the yolk of their control, so she and Jade planned this six-month tour of Europe. Except unbeknownst to anyone else, Parker set up a whole second set of plans, with burner phones and new bank accounts, and she gave her bodyguard the slip and set out on her own."

"Jade is who she needed to contact without being traceable?" Alex asked.

"Aye. It took her this long to track Parker down."

Finn looked impressed. "I knew she had skills, but I didn't expect anything like this."

I broke open a samosa, allowing the steam to escape before I bit in. "Aye, well, Jade's been covering for Parker with her parents all this time, but that finally ran out, so Parker notified her family yesterday that she's gotten a job and started a whole new life here."

"So, now what?" Alex asked.

"Well, they both assume that her parents are going to show up, because they willnae be happy about any of this. I'd expect, based on the things Parker has alluded to, that they'll try to force her to go home."

Finn snorted. "Good luck with that. They have no idea they're about to encounter the Wall of Quinn."

"None of that tells me anything about who she or her family is," Alex insisted. "Whatever chronic illness she's got isn't a reason for any normal person to have a bodyguard. Do you want me to look into her family and see what we may be getting into?"

I scrubbed a hand down my face. We'd never run any kind of mission without proper intel, and I desperately wished we were better prepared. And yet... "Hold off for now. It probably will come to that, but I'd rather give her the chance to tell me—us—herself without violating her trust."

"Fair enough," he conceded. "That still leaves us with her bodyguard. It was one thing for her to show up the past couple of days and help around the office, but where does this go? Are we looking at hiring someone else? I don't know that we have that in the budget."

"I don't know. We havenae had a chance to really talk

about what any of this means since Jade got here. I'm no' sure Parker knows any more than we do." And I definitely felt weird and twitchy because so many things had simply been left hanging, without being fully defined.

"Seems like that's that, for now," Finn observed.

We lapsed into quiet for a bit, as we all dug into our food.

Alex was the one who broke the silence. "So Parker spent the night over here the other night."

I arched a brow and shoveled in some biryani. "It's no' what you think."

When he just stared at me, I shrugged. "It could have been, but it wasn't. We're... easing into things."

Finn narrowed his eyes. "You're different with her. Better. Less angry."

"It's pretty fucking hard to hang on to all that around her," I admitted.

"Not that I necessarily think this will happen, but just to play devil's advocate... what happens if she decides to go back?" Alex asked. "What if they pressure her into it?"

I had to fight down my body's instant demand for action. Because the idea that Parker would up and vanish as quickly as she'd come into my world left me shaken in a way I didn't expect.

"I dinna think she will. She's built a life across a bloody ocean because she doesn't want to deal with this. With them. She wants to stay for the job. For this life."

*For me.*

I didn't say it, but I had to believe that we were building something. I didn't entirely know what yet, but we'd just found each other. I couldn't just let her go.

Clearing my throat, I tore another piece of naan. "I willnae allow her to be forced into anything she doesn't want to do. Can I count on the two of you for the same?"

They offered sober nods.

"We've got your back, brother," Alex said.

"Always."

Knowing that was a comfort, even if I didn't always know what that looked like in civilian life.

But after we'd wiped out the mountain of food and the pair of them had left, the niggle that we were going into this prospective ambush blind wouldn't leave me alone. It drove me to my computer to do a little digging. I wasn't Alex. I didn't have his hacking skills, but I wasn't without some ability to research myself. I wanted to know who I was prospectively facing off with.

Even with the limited information Parker had shared with me about her family, it took me less than five minutes to track down her father's company. She hadn't been kidding. Meridian Global had interests in all sorts of businesses all over the world, with satellite offices on four continents. Anderson Lawrence ran a hell of an operation. A quick image search turned up photos of him with business leaders and government officials from all over. I pegged him in his late fifties, with graying dark hair, and a general aura of *I expect the world to behave in a certain way, so it does.* I knew the type. I'd come from exactly that kind of world before I'd walked away to pursue my own path and thoroughly ruined my grandfather's impeccable record for getting his way.

When Anderson Lawrence showed up to retrieve his daughter, he wouldn't be prepared to take no for an answer. We could run a tight literal defense, but somehow I didn't think that would do anything but antagonize the man. If Parker was going to be allowed to simply live her own life, we needed to get her parents' trust and support. And that meant playing by a different set of rules. Rules I'd done everything in my power to escape.

I had another prospective source of information on the likes of Anderson Lawrence. One that could probably tell me a lot more valuable information than whatever Alex might dig up. It just meant I had to sell a little piece of my soul to get it.

Was Parker worth opening that door?

I thought of the dozens of moments of joy I'd been witness to since she walked into my life—all her quiet triumphs—everything she stood to lose, and I reached for the phone.

He answered on the second ring. "Hello?"

"Grandda, it's Callum. I need your help."

# CHAPTER 26

## PARKER

Excited voices echoed through the lobby as the group of six university students who'd rented mountain bikes first thing this morning returned from their excursion. They were covered in mud, sporting various scrapes, and wearing expressions of exhausted satisfaction that told me they'd had a blast. Callum, Finn, and Alex were all out on guided trips, so the equipment check-in fell to me. That was fine. Jade was here, so she could wheel the bikes around to the back, while I looked over everything else.

"Did y'all have a good time?"

Ryan Boyle, the de facto group leader, beamed. "The best! I had no idea there were such good trails in this area."

"We'll definitely be back again." This came from... was it Melissa?

I grinned. "That's what we like to hear. I'm just gonna need to check over your equipment to make sure we've got everything before you can head on to whatever is next on your agenda."

"The pub. I'm starving," Nick insisted.

"Then I'll be sure to get you through as quick as I can. I hear they've got a really excellent trout special for lunch today." I grabbed my clipboard.

As I inspected the gear, Falkor went from person to person, passing out licks, gathering up head scritches. Most clients seemed hugely entertained by our unofficial office mascot, and he'd even ended up in some social media posts. I was thinking of designing a velcro patch with the Out of Bounds Scotland logo for his harness.

I was halfway through the group when I heard the bell over the door chime. "Be with you in a jiff," I called, not looking up from my clipboard. "Okay, Nick, your helmet's good. Just wheel around to the side and hose off those pedals. My associate will show you where to store the bike from there. But before you go, if I could just get you to initial here that everything's been returned..." I held out the clipboard, but the words died in my throat as another voice cut through the cheerful post-adventure chatter.

"Parker Anne Lawrence."

My lungs seized. I knew that voice. Had been dreading the next time I would hear it from the time I got on the plane in Nashville.

Clipboard clutched against my chest like a shield, I pivoted to find my parents standing just inside the door. Mama was impeccably dressed, per usual, in a designer pantsuit that probably cost more than my monthly rent. Daddy, too, wore a bespoke three-piece suit that fit his rangy frame to perfection. They both looked hideously out of place among all the gear and mud—as if they'd gotten lost on the way to a board meeting. The mix of concern and temper in their expressions did absolutely nothing to allay my anxiety.

Jade materialized, positioning herself between me and them, and I'd never been more grateful to have her by my side.

"Mama, Daddy. Welcome to Scotland." I kept my tone bright and easy, despite the way my heart had begun to gallop. "Feel free to take a seat or look around while I finish up with these folks."

It took far too little time to finish processing the last three clients. I was hyperaware of the fact that neither of my parents moved an inch, other than to recoil in disgust from Falkor's attempt to play ambassador. With a quiet command, I called him away, ducking down behind my computer for just a few extra moments, trying to gather my composure.

I'd known they'd do this; I just hadn't known when. Perhaps I could have made it easier on myself, if I'd bothered to respond to their flurry of attempted communication after I'd sent The Email. I might have at least been able to arrange the schedule so one of the guys was also here. But I'd wanted more time. I realized now that no amount of time would have prepared me for this.

I was so torn between wanting to rush over to hug them and to sink through the floor to escape their obvious disappointment.

*You did nothing wrong.* The reminder didn't do much to bolster my resolve as I squared my shoulders and prepared to face off with my parents.

"It's good to see y'all. How was your flight?"

Right. As if it made any sense at all to act like this had been a planned visit, and I'd known they were coming.

"Parker." Mama's voice wavered with repressed emotion. "I simply cannot believe you've done this. Baby, what were you thinking? Do you have any idea how worried we've been?"

"You haven't had but a few days to worry because you didn't even know what was going on. And as I said in my email, there *is* no need to worry, because I'm absolutely fine."

Daddy turned a fulminating glare on Jade. "I cannot

believe you helped her keep this from us. We trusted you to keep her safe."

Jade's shoulders tightened, that deeply ingrained military bearing coming to the fore, even as remorse flashed in her eyes. Before she could fall on her metaphorical sword, I stepped forward.

"Don't you dare blame Jade. I did this all on my own." I sounded a lot more confident than I felt, but I sure as hell wasn't going to let her take the brunt of their displeasure. "This is not her fault. I know you're worried. I know this is hard for you, and I'm sure I could have gone about the whole thing better. But if I had asked, you would have said no. You would have done everything in your power to stop me."

"Of course we would have." Concern bled through the temper as Daddy took a step toward me. "Parker, honey, you can't just pick up and move across an ocean. What happens when you have a flare? Who's going to take care of you? What if you fall?"

The familiar weight of their worry settled over me like chain mail, dragging me down, urging me to give in to old scripts. To acknowledge that I was helpless. That I needed their protection. And as much as I knew that wasn't true, I could feel the pull. Apologies trembled on my lips as my brain tried to come up with some kind of compromise that would make them both stop looking at me as if I was the world's biggest disappointment.

A warm heavy weight butted my leg. I glanced down at Falkor, who looked up at me with a steady, soulful gaze. Instinctively, I reached down to touch his head, stroking the soft fur around his ears and feeling a little more stable. Because, contrary to their belief, I wasn't alone.

"I'd like to introduce you to Falkor. My service dog."

"Your what?" Daddy asked.

"A service dog?" Mama's tone was full of shock and something that might have been bafflement. "For what?"

"For all those things y'all are concerned about. He's a mobility aid, and he helps me manage on my own."

The worried glances they exchanged proved they were struggling to process this latest revelation.

Mama stepped forward and reached for my hand. "Sweetheart, we understand you want independence, but this is so far away. I'm sure you can get him through whatever customs processes are necessary to take him home with you, but this is ridiculous. It has to stop. You need to come home."

Temper I could have met with temper, but this endless, well-intentioned concern had my chest constricting.

"Respectfully, Parker's not going anywhere unless she wants to."

Callum's quiet burr cut through the tension as he stepped up beside me. I hadn't even heard him come in, but his solid presence made breathing easier. His height and build dwarfed my parents, and I saw them both start at the sight of his scarred face and the milky left eye.

Mama's fingers tightened on my hand, and Daddy shifted forward, as if to put himself between us. Their instinctive protectiveness might have been sweet if it wasn't so frustratingly short sighted. I hated seeing anyone react to Callum as if he were a danger. Not when I knew the truth.

"And you are?" Daddy's tone held his particular blend of deceptively easy Southern drawl and CEO—the one he reserved for sizing up potential threats.

I could practically feel Callum bristling beside me, though his voice remained steady. "Callum Quinn. One of Parker's employers."

I resisted the urge to reach back and lay a hand on his arm to soothe. I didn't think that would help the current situation.

"One of?" Mother's gaze darted between us, no doubt noting our proximity. "Just how many jobs are you working, sweetheart? You know that's not good for you."

It took everything in my power not to turn straight into Callum's arms to hide.

"Just the one job. She's been an incredible asset to me and my partners here at Out of Bounds Scotland. She's revolutionized our business since she started, and is just generally an incredible person, as I'm sure you're well aware."

His effusive praise seemed to put both of them on their back feet.

"Yes, of course," Mama concurred, "but surely all of this is too much?"

"No, it's not," I insisted. "And even if it was, it's my choice to decide how much I can handle, because it's my life. It's my body. I'm not going to live in a bubble anymore, just because it makes y'all more comfortable."

Some of the bluster seemed to leave my father. His shoulders drooped a little. "Maybe we have been a little too overprotective in terms of how you live and manage your condition. But, Pumpkin, it is not safe for you to be this far across the world by yourself."

Safe? What the hell did they think was going to happen to me? I was so over the paranoia that went along with coming from money. I wasn't out there in the public eye. Nobody gave a crap about me or what I was doing.

The bell jangled again as someone else walked inside. A quick glance told me it was Alex.

Callum didn't miss a beat. "That's the thing, Mr. Lawrence. She's no' by herself. She has a support system here. Us and a wide array of friends who will step up as needed. Now, I understand you have concerns, and we're happy to allay them. Perhaps under more civilized circumstances? Dinner at my home? Where we can all speak more freely than we can in the middle of our workplace."

Dinner? At his house? Was he out of his mind?

My parents had the good grace to look a little chastened.

"This is not the way we should have gone about this," Mama conceded. "We shouldn't have ambushed you at work. Let's have a nice, calm discussion about this later. Dinner sounds lovely. Is there somewhere in the area we can stay?"

I didn't want them to stay. I wanted them gone. But I was far too polite and well-bred for that.

"Yes, there are places for you to stay." I circled around my desk. "Here's the number of the local B and B, and also to some cottage rentals. I'm sure someone has something available for a night or two."

"Dinner sounds fine. Tonight?" Daddy pressed.

"Seven o'clock," Callum concurred.

Insane. He was completely and totally insane, and he refused to meet my gaze as he reached for a pen and stack of post-its. "Here's the address."

Daddy nodded and turned to Jade, who'd been doing her best impression of a statue. "A word, Jade?"

She snapped to attention. "Of course, sir."

As they stepped outside, I sent up a prayer that she wasn't being fired on the spot.

Mama pulled me in for a gentle hug. Her embrace was light, as if I were made of spun glass. The care was familiar and appreciated, but I hated she didn't feel free to squeeze me tight as I knew she wanted to, so I was the one who squeezed.

"It really is good to see you, Mama."

"You, too, sweetheart. We'll see you for dinner tonight."

Once she, too, had stepped out of the office, Alex finally spoke. "I gather those were your parents?"

"Yep, here to tell me I'm grounded." I turned to Callum.

"Not that I don't appreciate what you just did, but... are you actually prepared to host a dinner for my parents at your place? Tonight? I mean, not that there's anything at all wrong with your house, but it's—"

He speared a hand through his hair, letting some of the frustration show. "Empty. Aye. I know. But that can be rectified." He pulled his phone from his pocket.

"Who are you calling?"

"Isobel. If we're going to pull this off, we're going to need a lot of help."

I wasn't sure there was enough help in the entire village to pull this off. Callum must have seen my skepticism. He curled his hands gently around my shoulders. "It'll all be all right. I promise. Trust me. I willnae let them bully you."

I slipped my arms around him, sinking into his embrace and feeling myself steady for the first time since my parents had walked through the door. "I do trust you. I just hope you haven't bitten off more than you can chew."

# CHAPTER 27

## CALLUM

My house was full of women who'd accepted my ill-advised call for help, and I had deep regrets. They'd come armed with curtains and artwork and even more furniture. Things I hadn't given a single solitary thought to since I'd moved in and covered the basics. But I knew better than to voice a single protest because when I'd called, they'd come, and judging by the flurry of activity, they absolutely understood the assignment. God help me. So when I got told to move or hang a thing, I did as ordered.

"No, no. A little higher. Riiiiighhhht... there."

Dutifully, I marked the height and position for the painting I'd been handed, while Charlotte Vasquez stood back, studying the overall grouping we'd started. Because my wall was suddenly full of art.

Charlotte ran the cottage rental business split between Ardinmuir and Lochmara. I'd only met her a handful of times, but the older Hispanic woman from Texas was an absolute powerhouse, and she sure as hell knew how to stage a place.

It hadn't surprised me that she'd come with Isobel and

Ciara. What had surprised me was the fact that the rest of the Ardinmuir Event Planning staff had shown up. Evidently, the prospect of getting their hands on a bachelor's house, in order to impress the pretentious parents of his girlfriend, was too great a lure to resist. Sophie MacKean was arranging fresh flowers. Her sister-in-law, Kyla—Ciara and Ewan's cousin—was rearranging my entire dining room to make room for a sideboard that they'd brought. Did they just have a truck full of furniture and accessories waiting on the estate for potential emergencies?

I didn't have any idea how many of the furnishings they'd brought in were on loan and how much they'd simply purchased and planned to bill me for. But as the afternoon wore on and my house started to look like a warm and inviting home, rather than a dusty afterthought with room to hang my metaphorical hat, I couldn't find it in me to complain. I could afford it, and anyway, Parker was worth it.

It was nearing six by the time Isobel dusted off her hands and looked around in satisfaction. "Yes. This will do nicely."

I was no longer standing in my house. The space had been absolutely transformed. Pillows and artfully draped throws softened the lounge. The furniture had been shifted, so the sofa faced the fireplace instead of the TV. A pair of Bergères chairs —and wouldn't my grandmother be proud that I'd remembered what those were?—had been added, flanking either end. The bookshelves on both sides of the fireplace now held decorative... things, along with my collection of books they'd unearthed from other rooms. All the windows were now framed with heavy curtains that softened the space and drew the eye. An eclectic assortment of art graced all the visible walls. The dining room had been turned into a proper place to eat, and a full tablescape had been laid out with dishes, utensils, and cloth napkins I absolutely didn't own. Elegant bouquets of fresh flowers filled vases and bowls at multiple points all over the house. The kitchen had been classed up with some kind of pitcher holding cooking utensils and bowls displaying a pleasing assortment of fresh fruit. A series of covered dishes were lined up along the island, as Afton Colquhoun, Hamish's wife, made last-minute notes about the proper warming and plating of the meal she'd catered. The women hadn't just stopped at the public spaces either. There was a fresh bedspread and pillows on my bed, and new fluffy towels hung in both the bathrooms. Not a single room remained untouched, and I recognized almost nothing.

"I had no idea it could look like this."

Ciara lightly punched me in the arm. "See? There's nothing wrong with having actual stuff."

"I owe the lot of you. But I need to kick you out now. They'll be here in less than an hour."

"Final instructions for the food are written on that notepad there," Afton said. "You can just drop the dishes back off another day, or send them back to the castle with Ciara."

"Thank you all. Truly." I had no idea whether Parker's parents would be impressed, but none of this would hurt.

"Good luck!" they chorused.

Then they stampeded out the door with as much haste as when they'd arrived a few hours before.

I didn't stand around gawking, instead heading back to make myself presentable to go with the house. It was far too late to get a haircut, but I could shower and lose the scruff I habitually didn't bother with. No reason to look any more like a pirate than I already did.

By the time I'd finished scraping off the partial beard, I stood in my closet, hips draped in a towel, wondering what the hell I should wear. Nothing casual. Parker's parents clearly weren't casual people, and given what my own intel had turned up about them, I knew I needed to present myself well. My kilts were at the back of the closet, shoved behind my dress uniform. I seldom had reason to wear any of them, but tonight seemed like as good an excuse as any to trot one of them out. Parker, at least, would probably enjoy it.

Bypassing the full highland dress, I chose a slightly less formal kilt and waistcoat. There was formal and then there was excessive. I'd be walking the line tonight, wanting to give the right impression of a man comfortable and in control of his world. The moment I slid it all on, I wanted to strip it off again. It wasn't really the clothes. It was the persona that went with them. The whole thing felt like a too-tight skin. One I'd shed years ago. But I'd endure it for the night because, no matter how far I'd run from this world, I knew impressions mattered.

A knock sounded on the door. It was early yet, so I suspected it was Parker and Jade. She'd wanted to help with today's mission, but we'd had too many clients who'd already been booked. Feeling unaccountably nervous, I wiped my hands on my kilt and went to answer the door.

Parker wore a dark green dress I hadn't seen before. Something in good fabric with a tailored cut that was a subtle indication of the wealth she seldom showed. She'd done something to her face with makeup, again subtle, that elevated her usual beauty to elegance, though the look was somewhat undermined by the way her mouth dropped open in an "O" at her first sight of me.

"Wow. You have a kilt." Her eyes dilated, and I knew that, for her at least, I'd made the right choice in attire.

My lips quirked. "I am a Scot. You look beautiful." I stepped back to let her into the house and shifted my focus to Jade, who'd gone for a sedate pantsuit that was cut in lines that would allow her to move. "Welcome to my home."

"Holy shit." Parker stood just past the entryway, staring. "I can't believe they did all this. Did you have all the elves from the North Pole helping today?"

"It certainly felt like it."

Jade took in the house. "Nice digs. I gather it's been duded up?"

"Almost completely overhauled," I confirmed. "They definitely understood the assignment."

"Seems like you did, too. You clean up pretty well, Quinn."

"Thank you." Abruptly, I realized Parker's shadow wasn't in attendance. "No Falkor?"

"Much to his disappointment, we decided it was wiser to leave him at home. We all know he's helpful, but I suspect my parents will see him as one big reminder that I *need* help. Since the goal is for them to acknowledge I'm an independent, functional adult..."

"Fair point." Checking my watch, I moved off toward the kitchen. "I need to baste the chops."

Parker gaped again. "You *cooked?*"

"God, no. Afton Colquhoun from Ardinmuir Event Planning catered. Cider-braised pork chops with herb-roasted new potatoes and baby carrots."

"Oh, that sounds delicious." Her gaze tracked me as I followed Afton's instructions. She was still staring as I straightened from the oven, and it wasn't with the faint and unmistakable shades of lust as when she'd first seen me.

"What?"

"You seem... different."

I twitched my shoulders at that. "I suppose I'm putting on a very old hat for the night."

Her big brown eyes searched my face. "I guess I'm not the only one who's been keeping secrets."

"No' a secret. No' deliberately, anyway." I gave in to the

urge to touch her, skimming a hand along her neck. "I promise I'll tell you later."

Her lips curved in a way that made me want to bend and taste them. "Holding you to that."

Fresh knocking sounded on the door. Bracing myself, I turned on the high society charm I despised and went to answer.

My smile felt rusty with disuse as I greeted them. "Mr. and Mrs. Lawrence. Welcome to my home."

"We're so pleased to be here. Thank you for having us, Callum." Parker's mother glided inside at my invitation. Her father followed, his gaze already darting around the space, assessing. And it was absolutely worth all of this afternoon's insanity to know that nothing would be found lacking.

"Can I offer you all a whisky? It would be a shame for you to come all this way and not sample some of the finest Scotland has to offer."

Mr. Lawrence unbuttoned his suit jacket and slipped both hands into his pockets. "I wouldn't say no."

"I've also got wine, if you ladies would prefer that. Parker? A glass of the Cab you like?"

After only a beat of hesitation, she smiled. "Yes, please."

Her mother also went for the wine, and Jade for the scotch. I moved to the sideboard, where the whisky I'd already had was now decanted into a cut glass bottle with matching lowball glasses.

"Perhaps we got off on the wrong foot this afternoon, Mr. Lawrence. I believe you know my grandfather. Alistair Brogan?" I arched a brow in question as I offered him the glass.

At the mention of my grandfather, I could see the instant he changed his assessment of me. I was no longer just Parker's boss. I had actual connections.

Parker caught my eye as I turned, and I knew her list of questions was growing longer by the second.

"I've not spoken to Alistair in quite some time. How's he doing?"

I moved back to pour the wine. "Well, I've not seen my family recently, but he was well when last we spoke."

"Mmm. Caledonian Trust was working on expansions the last time I saw Alistair. How's that going?" Mr. Lawrence asked.

I flashed a polite smile. "Oh, I couldn't say. I'm no' directly involved in the family business. I elected to pursue a career in military service instead." I gestured toward the dining room. "If you'd all like to take a seat. Dinner's ready."

"Oh, I'll help you serve." Parker followed me to the kitchen.

I sent up a half dozen prayers of thanks as I plated up the meal Afton had prepared, not only because it was beautiful and elegant in a way I'd never have pulled off on my own, but because it gave me a few moments to compose myself. Parked pressed a hand to my back before picking up a pair of plates and carrying them into the dining room. I focused on the lingering warmth of her touch as I picked up the remaining plates and did the same.

We got through the meal. I somehow managed to talk golf and investments and generally did everything I could to channel my younger brother, who'd given a shite about all these things. With every minute that passed, I could feel Parker's curiosity growing. But her parents seemed to relax as the evening wore on.

Not until I served the Cranachan for dessert did I broach the subject we'd all been carefully dancing around. "Now, I understand you have concerns about Parker having moved here. What can we do to put you more at ease with the situation?"

"Well, nice as this dinner has been, I don't see that there's anything you can do to change our minds. Our girl will be better off at home," Mr. Lawrence said.

"I'm a grown woman, Daddy. And I'm gonna need more evidence than your opinion to change *my* mind. Why are you so set against this?"

"Parker," her mother sighed. "Don't be difficult."

"I'm not a child. Stop treating me like one. If you have legitimate concerns, then lay them out, point by point, and let's talk about them. But if this is just because you don't like it, then I'm sorry, you're doomed to disappointment."

"Parker—" her father began.

"Tell her," Jade snapped. She'd stayed virtually silent through most of the meal, but her eyes flashed bright with frustration and no little temper now. "If you want even a remote prayer of getting her to agree to go home, you have to tell her why. Stop treating her like a child who can't handle the truth."

Parker's eyes went wide, and I gathered Jade seldom spoke out like this against her parents. "What are you talking about?"

Jade waited for a few moments to see if either of the elder Lawrences would speak. When they didn't, she set her spoon down. "Look, I need everyone to understand what we're dealing with here. For the past three years, Meridian Global has been dealing with increasing pressure from a consortium of Russian oligarchs and Chinese business interests who are trying to control shipping routes through the Arctic and the South China Sea. They started with 'legitimate' business pressure—heavy fees, restricted access. When that didn't work, they escalated."

She looked at Parker's parents. "Which is why you increased my scope from basic security to full protective detail." Her attention swung back to me. "They've successfully grabbed three executives' family members in the past year,"

Jade continued. "Two for ransom, one for leverage on trade agreements. And those are just the ones we know about."

My hands curled into fists. These bawbags would get their hands on Parker over my dead body.

"That's why she'll be better off in Nashville," Mr. Lawrence began.

"Nashville is the first place they'll look," Jade cut in. "They've had eyes on all your properties for months, which you know. Hell, that's why you doubled security at the gates. But here?" She gestured around us. "Nobody knows Parker's in Scotland. All the social media posting that's been done on the trip is down south. They'd never expect her to be here. And even if they did figure it out and somehow manage to get through me, they'd have to get through him." She jerked her chin toward me. "I'm good. He's better. Former Royal Marine with special forces training who would literally tear apart anyone who tried to hurt Parker."

Parker sucked in a breath, and Jade shifted her gaze back to me. "Tell me I'm wrong."

*Way to put me on the spot.*

I'd been very careful not to touch Parker or do anything to imply we were something other than coworkers, given that was yet another thing we hadn't discussed in terms of what she wanted her parents to know. But maybe they'd be more at ease if they knew protecting her wasn't just a hypothetical for me.

"You're no' wrong. Parker's safety is a very personal concern for me. There's nothing I won't do to protect her."

Deliberately, Parker curled her hand over mine where it rested on the table. "That would be the other reason I'm not willing to just pick up and go home."

Parker's mother lifted a hand to her chest, either to clutch the pearls she wore or cover her heart. I wasn't sure which. "You two are involved?"

"We are," Parker confirmed.

Jade turned her attention back to Parker's father. "Look, you've been sitting on all of this in some misguided form of protection, just patting her on the head as if she's an idiot. She's not. This may threaten my job, and honestly, at this point, I don't give a damn. I'm here to protect and support Parker, no matter what, and I believe she's safer here, under the protection of Callum and the rest of his team, who are all special forces, with experience in private security."

"And you," Parker added quietly.

"And me," Jade agreed. "Ten years watching your back, and I'm not about to stop now. But trying to force her back to Nashville? That's basically gift-wrapping her for them."

A muscle jumped in the older man's jaw, and I knew it was time to go back to being the Royal Marine. With no little relief, I let the thin crust of civility slip.

"Do you have the resources to research the prospective threat to Parker in a way that isn't going to alert your enemies to her presence? Because I do. My team had one of the highest success rates in the nation when we retired. Dinna mistake the fact that we run a recreational business now for any of us having lost our edge. We haven't, and we'll do anything necessary to see that Parker is safe. No one's getting to her through me."

Her mother laid a hand over Anderson's. "Honey, maybe this is the right thing. Her being here is certainly unexpected."

He scrubbed a hand down his face. "I don't like it, but you raise some valid points." His gaze fell on me. "And I expect you'd defend her even against the likes of us. That's what all this has been about, right?"

I inclined my head to acknowledge the point.

"All right. Then let's talk about how all this will work."

# CHAPTER 28

## PARKER

Mama wrapped me in a gentle hug. "Oh, I wish we could see you again before we go."

"If things are as dire as you fear, limiting contact for a bit is probably wise. You and Daddy are a lot more visible than I am." I thought all of this was overkill, but if I could use the situation to buy myself some peace, I would.

It had already been decided that they'd head straight back to the jet waiting in Glasgow, rather than staying the night. The crew would spread a rumor that they'd stopped only for repairs of some kind before heading on to the Meridian Global offices in Berlin for a day or two to throw off anyone who might be watching them. Was any of that necessary? I had no idea. The only thing that mattered was that I wouldn't be going with them.

Daddy was next. "We just want what's best for you, Pumpkin."

I pressed my cheek to his shoulder. "I know. And I swear I'll be careful. I'm in good hands here."

He pulled back to look at Callum, who was still giving off

weird Twilight Zone country club vibes. "I'm trusting you with her, son."

Callum gave his hand a firm shake. "I willnae let you down, sir."

With one last round of goodbyes, they were finally gone, and it was down to Jade, Callum, and me.

I loosed a long, slow exhale. "Well, that was... a lot."

Jade rubbed my shoulder. "I know we need to have a formal discussion about what all of this means, but for now, I expect you two have an overdue conversation that needs to happen."

She wasn't wrong. "Go ahead and take the car." Unlike me, Jade had seen the sense in picking up a rental. I still walked where I could, but Callum lived too far out. "I'll be home... eventually."

That could be later tonight or tomorrow morning. I supposed it depended on how this conversation went. I knew how I wanted it to end. How I'd wanted it to end even before I'd arrived to find him in that mouthwatering kilt.

Jade nodded and turned for the door.

"Jade?"

She paused, looking back at me.

"Thank you."

My friend flashed her gorgeous, fierce smile. "Anytime." With a quick salute, she slipped out the door, leaving me alone with a man who'd incited far too many questions tonight. One who'd gone above and beyond to have my back.

Without a word, I closed the distance between us, taking his hand and dragging him over to the sofa. He sank down, tugging me onto his lap, exactly where I wanted to be. I slid my arms around him as I'd been wanting to do all night. He wrapped around me, and we both sighed.

"I get to stay."

"Aye, you get to stay." He pressed a kiss to my temple. "I

wouldn't have let them take you away, but I'm glad it didn't come to that."

I tipped my head back to look at him. "Do you really think that I'm in any sort of danger?"

"I dinna know, but we'll find out." He stroked the hair back from my face, rough fingers grazing my cheek. "Either way, I'll keep you safe, no matter what."

"I know you will." I turned my face into the touch, soaking up the contact. "I don't know how to express what it means to me that you have my back." I found a smile for him as I nuzzled my cheek against his palm. "You did all of this—the house, the dinner, whatever this weird Stepford makeover was—to impress my parents. You hated all of it."

He opened his mouth to protest, but I laid a finger over his lips.

"You hated all of it," I repeated. "But you did it all anyway because you felt it mattered."

He kissed my finger. "You matter. More than anyone ever has."

My heart began to thud, slow and thick in my chest. "Callum."

"I wouldn't have done this for anyone else." He twitched his shoulders, visibly dropping the mask he'd been wearing all night.

"You come from a world like mine."

"Technically. It's been a long time. I'm what you'd call the black sheep. As the eldest, I was expected to follow in the family footsteps, so when I joined the Royal Marines instead, it didn't go over well. But I never had any interest in any of it."

I straightened. "You have siblings?" He'd said almost nothing of his family in the time we'd spent together.

"One brother. William. He took on everything I rejected, which is, perhaps, the only reason I wasn't fully disowned."

I tightened my arms around him, not knowing exactly how his family had hurt him, only understanding that they had. "Have you seen your family since you retired?"

"Just once." The way his body tensed told me that visit hadn't gone especially well. "But I called my grandfather to do my own form of recon on your dad."

If his world was like mine, then that kind of info gathering hadn't come without strings. "What did you agree to?"

He dragged a thumb across my cheek in a gentle caress. "Nothing I'm not willing to pay. We got what we needed out of this. You get to stay here and live your life."

I wanted to get started on some of that living here and now. Because this man had slain my dragons, and this princess wanted to celebrate. "Can I stay here tonight? With you?"

His hand stilled on my cheek, his eye going dark. "You can stay as long as you like."

I smiled at that. "Good." Then I leaned in and pressed my mouth to his, because I'd long since learned that in this I'd have to take the lead. He'd never push me. If I wanted him—and God, did I—I had to make it clear.

With a low hum in the back of his throat, he angled his mouth more firmly to mine, and his powerful arms circled me, somehow closing me in without pressing too tight. I loved how aware he was of everywhere we touched, not wanting to accidentally hit one of my trigger points. But I wanted to see what it was like having that absolute focus dialed fully to pleasure instead of pain.

"Callum?" I gently nipped his lip.

"Mm?"

"I want you to touch me. Everywhere."

With a growl, he tightened his hold on me, pressing heated kisses along my throat. On a contented sigh, I dropped my head back, inviting further exploration with his mouth.

His fingers worked their way under the edge of the neckline of my dress, testing the give of the fabric. When he found it had an elastic quality, he tugged, working it down from my shoulders to bare the top curve of my breasts. Wanting that greedy mouth on my nipples, I wriggled a little until the dress slid further down, baring my breasts fully. The almost feral sound he made had heat pulsing between my legs. I wanted his hands there, those massive fingers sliding into the heat he created. But before I could grab one to make it clear what I needed, he'd closed his mouth over one tight nipple. I cried out, spearing my fingers into his hair as he suckled. Pleasure spooled through me, making my limbs go warm and pliant.

I hadn't realized just how badly I'd needed to be touched. Needed this man's hands on me. Every inch of my body woke up and tingled, yearning for more. I wilted back, leaving myself open for him to devour anything he pleased. Callum feasted with his mouth and hands, inciting a riot of sensation with every kiss, every touch. And when my hips began to rock, seeking relief from the tension he built, he dragged one hand up my thigh, beneath the pooling skirt of my dress to cover my center.

On a cry of approval, I arched into the touch, spreading my legs wider, inviting more. His finger traced patterns over the silk of my underwear, driving me crazy while he continued to worship my breasts. Groping blindly, I covered his big hand with mine, pressing it close and moaning at the pressure that wasn't nearly enough.

"Need your fingers," I managed.

His good eye held a faintly maniacal gleam as he caught my gaze. "Aye, lass." Then he nudged the fabric aside and drew one blunt finger through the gathered wetness.

My hips bucked, and I whimpered. "More."

He eased one finger slowly inside me, and I thought I'd lose my mind. "Och, you're so tight."

"Been... long... time. Oh, God."

He bent his head, capturing one of my nipples again, laving it with his tongue as he mimicked the rhythm between my thighs. My hips rose and fell, and I could only hang on for the ride as he drove me ruthlessly up, adding a second finger to the first. He felt so good filling me up. Yet it wasn't enough. Not quite.

But before I could say a thing, he circled my clit with his thumb, the rough edges of the pad just grazing that sensitive bud, until I exploded with a cry. He held me through the rippling aftershocks, still working me with his fingers until at last I lay limp in his lap.

Feeling weak as a kitten, I stared up at him, taking in the look of adoration and total smug satisfaction on his face. A dreamy smile spread over my lips. "That was an excellent start."

"Start?" He barked a laugh.

"This isn't over tonight until we're both naked and mindless."

His good eye had gone black as midnight. "You're fucking incredible, you know that?"

"I certainly hope you think so on the other side. I want you to take me to bed, Callum."

He slid his fingers from me and scooped me into his arms. "As you wish."

# CHAPTER 29

## CALLUM

Already lightheaded from lust, I clutched Parker to my chest and strode down the hall. She took advantage of her position to trail nuzzling kisses along my throat, which only made me even harder.

"Woman, if you dinna stop that, I'll be flipping up your skirt and taking you against the nearest wall."

Her lips stilled against my throat, then she lifted her head to stare at me with unmistakable interest. "Really?"

Christ, she was going to kill me.

"That's no' how we're doing this tonight."

I wanted this to be good for her. I didn't make an issue of her condition, but it was never far from my awareness that she was effectively always in some measure of pain. I didn't want to add to that by being too rough or too fast. She deserved a bed, where she could be comfortable while I took her apart, one kiss, one touch at a time. Where I had the time and space to learn what she liked and what she didn't.

My step faltered as I carried her into the bedroom. I'd forgotten my room had been overhauled, too. I had a moment of gratitude for the overstep as I noted how much more inviting the plush duvet and pillows looked in the golden glow cast by the lamps on either side of the bed. There were more flowers here, in a vase on the dresser and smaller clutches on the nightstands. Their scents perfumed the air, mingling with the vanilla lavender scent of Parker's hair.

I let her slide slowly down my body, shuddering a little at the contact. Her hands came up to frame my face, drawing me down for another kiss that had the tether of my control fraying. My hands flexed on her hips, instinctively pulling her closer against the erection tenting the front of my kilt. With a moan of approval, she wriggled against me, dropping one hand to dip beneath the edge of my kilt.

I caught her wrist. "No."

Her pretty mouth pursed in a pout that had my brain tossing out vivid images of her on her knees before me, wrapping those same lips around my cock. "But I want to touch you."

Ruthlessly, I locked down my roaring libido. "No' yet. You first. Be a good lass and be patient."

Her eyes darkened. Intrigued by the reaction, I began to slowly drag her skirt higher. "Do you like the idea of being a good lass? Am I going to find you dripping for me when I get under this skirt?"

She swayed a little and laid a hand on my chest to steady herself. "Yes, but that's basically just a side effect of you saying anything with that voice in that accent. I'm pretty sure you reading a grocery list would turn me on."

"Does that mean you're walking around the office turned on?"

Her cheeks pinked. "Sometimes."

God, but I loved the sound of that. And hated it. How the fuck was I meant to function at work with the idea floating around my head that she could be wet for me at any moment?

Gripping the dress in both hands, I carefully tugged it up and over her head, leaving her standing in nothing but a bit of silk. Her breasts, freed from the stretchy confines of the dress, were full and proud, begging for my mouth. She was all soft alabaster skin, her dark hair cascading over her shoulders to brush the rosy tips of her gorgeous nipples.

She stepped into me, her fingers flicking open each button of my waistcoat and sliding it off. "You're getting a little behind here, Callum."

I took her hand and brought it to my lips. "Just appreciating the view. On the bed, gorgeous."

Hand still in mine, she stepped back, easing down onto the mattress and reclining onto her elbows. Keeping my gaze on hers, I crouched, hooking my fingers into the last scrap of silk keeping her from me, drawing the knickers down and off, until she was bare.

"Are you comfortable?" I rasped.

Parker worked her way more fully onto the bed until she was nestled among the pillows. She looked like a goddess, with her hair fanned out in a dark halo, her arms spread out on the pillows such that her breasts were offered up like the gifts they were.

Feeling far too restricted by my clothes, I dragged my shirt up and off, popping a couple of buttons in the process. Then I knelt on the bed, crawling up the length of her body. There was nothing between us but my kilt, and her eyes drifted shut as she absorbed the sensation of the wool brushing against her bare skin. Her lips curved.

"Do you like the feel of that?"

"I'm liking the feel of everything. I was just imagining how incredibly convenient kilts must be for quickies."

"There's nothing at all quick about what I have in mind, love." Bracing myself above her, I dipped my head to take her mouth again.

She opened for me immediately, her tongue tangling with mine. Her hands skated over my chest, exploring each dip and ridge of muscle, tracing every scar. I shuddered, absorbing the sensations. It had been so damned long since I'd been touched. So damned long since I'd felt wanted. And if she kept that up, she was going to make a liar out of me, because the sweet heat between her thighs was *right there.*

Tearing my mouth away from hers, I trailed my lips down the column of her throat, along her delicate collarbones and lower to those glorious breasts. I spent some time there, licking and sucking until each nipple was a tight bud in my mouth, and her hips began to buck beneath me. Only then did I move lower, draping her legs over my shoulders so I could settle between her pretty thighs and explore the promised land.

At the first brush of my tongue between her folds, she bowed up with a cry.

"Okay?"

"Dear God, don't stop!"

Smiling, I settled in to worship her with all the focus and attention she deserved. She was deliciously responsive and had no compunction about being vocal with her pleasure. I loved every second of driving her mad, until she flew apart again, crying out my name.

"Please," she gasped. "Please, I need all of you."

She'd brought light back into my world. Who was I to deny her anything?

I eased back only far enough to shuck the kilt and snag a condom from the nightstand drawer. Parker was already reaching for me. I finished rolling it on, and then I was in her arms, skin to glorious skin. Our mouths met and clung as we shifted and rolled until I was settled in the cradle of her hips, the crown of my cock just notched at her entrance. Trembling with restraint, I stared down at her, my chest so full it ached.

"Are you sure about this?"

Her hands framed my face, her thumb stroking tenderly along my scar. "I want this. I want you. Please, Callum."

I pressed into her, inch by slow inch, watching pleasure and need and something I desperately wanted to be more on her face. This was everything. She was everything.

I lost myself in the feel of her around me, in the look of her beneath me as I slowly drove her up yet again. Every sigh, every moan was music as we moved together. She was so slick and tight, her body fisting mine as if it had been made just for me. My arms began to shake from the slow, torturous pace I'd set.

Parker's hands pressed to my chest, over my heart. "I won't break." She jacked up far enough to nip at my jaw. "More. Harder."

"I dinna want to hurt you."

"You won't." Another fleeting nip of my jaw. "You won't."

The leash on my control snapped. I picked up the pace, driving into her deeper, faster. She cried out, but it was so clearly not in pain that I kept going, plunging harder, until the bed began to thump with the effort. Parker's legs tightened around my hips as she met me thrust for thrust, until suddenly she shattered, her whole body convulsing around me, a velvet fist that ruthlessly choked my cock until lightning shot down my spine directly into my balls and I came.

In the aftermath, I lost all sense of time. For a little while I wondered if I'd gone blind in the other eye, then I realized I'd collapsed on her, and my face was buried in her hair. Worried I was crushing her, I roused myself enough to roll off her.

She sucked in a huge breath.

"Are you okay?"

Two more big breaths before they began to even out. "I... am... fucking incredible."

Relief bled through me, and I melted back against the pillows, pulling her with me. I kissed the nearest thing I could reach... her shoulder. "That you are. Will you stay?"

I'd slept with her in my arms once before and had missed her ever since. I couldn't imagine letting her walk out that door after everything we'd just done. Especially as I aimed to find the energy to do it all over again before the night was through.

Parker shifted, snuggling against me. "Thought you'd never ask."

# CHAPTER 30
## PARKER

I ducked through the street-level door to my flat the next morning, praying no one had seen me make the run from Callum's SUV. He'd tried to walk me to the door, but I knew if he did, he'd kiss me again, and then we'd be giving the town grapevine even more to gossip about. We were unquestionably together now, but I still didn't want people speculating about our love life or talking about how I'd arrived home in the same outfit I'd left in last night.

I crept up the stairs, finally free to give in to the wincing. I was sore in places I hadn't known I could be sore. But for once it wasn't from a flare. My body felt deliciously used, and I couldn't deny that I was absolutely thinking about when we'd get to do it again. Which was crazy, because we'd literally just had each other again in the shower before Callum brought me home. I didn't have any idea how I was going to get through the workday without remembering every second of our time together. And after my admission about what his voice did to me, I suspected he'd be doing much the same. At least I had a little while to change and search out the scraps of my composure before I had to face Finn and Alex.

Just before I reached the top of the stairs, the door swung open. Guess there'd been no hope that Jade would still be asleep. I was saved from having to meet her gaze when Falkor bounded down the last few steps to greet me, his big floof of a tail swishing back and forth. He licked my hands and arms and whined.

"I know! I missed you, too, sweet boy. C'mon. Let's go back inside."

With a low *woof*, he scrambled back upstairs.

Feeling more than a little awkward, I followed, clutching together the lapels of the fleece I'd borrowed from Callum against the early morning chill. I'd texted Jade last night, of course, to let her know I wouldn't be home. Now I didn't know what to say. There was no question what Callum and I had been doing. It wasn't as if I hadn't had boyfriends I'd been intimate with in the past. But there hadn't been many, and the last one had been quite a while ago.

And everything about this relationship with Callum was different.

For her part, Jade wore an amused, knowing smirk as she shut the door behind me. "So, good night?"

My cheeks heated instantly, but I couldn't stop the simultaneous grin.

Jade grinned back. "Want coffee?"

"Please, God, yes." Callum and I hadn't taken the time for that life-giving beverage, being far more interested in squeezing every last drop of pleasure we could out of our limited alone time.

"I can see you've already showered. I'll go make a fresh pot while you change."

Self-conscious, I touched the wet tendrils of hair that trailed over my shoulders. "Thanks. That sounds fantastic."

By the time I came out dressed for work, the enticing scent of roasted beans perfumed the air, along with the rich, warm aroma of the Scottish butteries I'd gotten addicted to. A pair of them popped up from the toaster as I poured myself a mug of coffee.

Jade set the butteries on a plate and grabbed the raspberry jam from the fridge. "I figured you'd probably worked up an appetite."

Feeling awkward again as the heat in my cheeks dialed back up to about an eight, I clutched the mug between my palms. "Thanks."

Her dark eyes searched my face. "All I'm going to ask is if he treated you right."

As yet another memory of exactly how right he'd treated me scrolled through my brain, I shivered and smiled into my coffee. "Yes, definitely."

Jade nodded, settling back against the counter and picking up her own cup of coffee. "You're in love with him."

I startled hard enough that coffee sloshed over the side. I thought about denying it as I reached for a dishtowel to wipe up the spill. But this was Jade, my best friend, who knew me better than anybody.

"Yeah. Yeah, I think I am."

She nodded again, evidently satisfied with the admission. "Well, that works out, because he's sure as hell gone over you."

My heart gave a decidedly hopeful, giddy leap in my chest. "Do you think so?" Much as we'd shared, we hadn't said those words. I wasn't worried about where we stood. Where we were was so very good. But a girl never minded some reassurance.

Jade just arched one of those perfectly shaped brows. "Girl.

After everything he did to impress your parents? Yeah, that man is gone over you. Hook, line, and sinker."

He had said I mattered more than anyone ever had. In Callum-speak, that was tantamount to a definite declaration.

I spread jam over one of the butteries. "I know he's probably not what you or anybody imagined for me."

"I mean, no, but he treats you well. He looks out for you. That's the important thing."

"I know he can be gruff and taciturn and a little grumpy, but he's so different with me. He's not like that when we're alone."

"You're happy. That's what matters most to me. That, and that you're safe."

Abruptly, the elephant in the room that I'd been determinedly ignoring since last night popped back out of hiding. "Why didn't you tell me? About the stepped up security? Everything?" I didn't know if I would have changed how I'd handled my "escape" if I'd known, but I wanted to think I would've at least factored it in.

Discomfort flashed over her features. "I nearly did a million times. But for better for worse, your father is technically my employer, and he expressly asked me not to."

"What changed?"

"Honestly, it just reached a point where what they were suggesting was ridiculous. I meant what I said last night. You're safer here."

"The idea that anyone would know or care about me seems very out there to me, but either way, I'm grateful for everything you've done to make sure I can stay."

"Of course. You fit here. This may not be what anybody would've expected for you, but you fit."

I did fit, but that hardly assuaged the guilt I'd been feeling since Jade had joined me here. I dropped my gaze, tearing pieces off the second buttery. "I've been a crappy friend to you."

"What are you talking about?" Her girl-you-crazy tone made it clear she didn't agree.

"Your life has been tied to mine for ten years now. And I not only up and decided to change mine in a huge way without consulting you, I made your actual job harder and put that position at risk in how I decided to go about it. I'm sorry for that."

She angled her head. "I appreciate that."

"I shouldn't have made this big decision without taking you into account. Your life, your family, are all back in the States. You didn't sign on to pick up stakes and move across an ocean. If you'd prefer to be back in Nashville, or if there's something else you'd rather do, I'd completely understand."

I'd been afraid to ask what she wanted, but especially now, it was clear I was staying, and she deserved the chance to live her own life, independent of mine. Even if it meant I had to say goodbye to having one of my very best friends in my world every day.

Jade sighed. "Did I ever consider moving abroad? No. But I'm not opposed to relocating. Scotland's growing on me." One corner of her mouth quirked. "And if there are any more hot guys in kilts out there, I wouldn't be opposed to taking one for a ride."

I laughed, feeling the tension loosen. "Do you want me to put Ciara on that? Because I feel certain that if there's somebody available, she'd know."

"Let's put a pin in that for now. I'd rather get through the next few weeks without incident before I start thinking about anything else. Although I probably should start looking for a place. Your sofa's not bad, but I miss having a proper bed."

"Oh my God, yes, you need a real bed. We will figure something out."

Her eyes sparkled. "You could do a girl a solid and just move into Callum's bed and leave me yours. I feel like that's a win-win for us all."

"Damn it. I'd only just stopped thinking about sex, and now you've put it in my head again right before we need to leave for work."

"Sorry. Not sorry." She laughed. "Do you want to walk the whole way and see if you can work those kinks out of your system, or do you want me to drive?"

# CHAPTER 31

## CALLUM

I was late for work, but damn if I could find it in me to give a shite. Not when I'd had Parker warm in my bed all night and started my day coaxing her awake with an orgasm for an alarm —a state of affairs she'd breathlessly approved of before we'd moved to the shower to start all over again. Not surprisingly, that had done a hell of a lot more for my outlook on the day than the punishing multi-mile run I usually went for, rain or shine.

Finn was going to freak out because I couldn't seem to stop smiling. He and Alex would no doubt have plenty to say to me when I arrived. They'd seemed on board with the idea of me and Parker, but we'd taken a step we couldn't walk back from. I didn't think she wanted to walk back from it—not given how she'd lingered in the front seat of my Land Rover before finally making the dash for her flat. But they'd no doubt have concerns about how our relationship could impact our business. Which was fair. Right now, it was hard to see our relationship doing anything but improving the business. Because she was staying in Scotland.

I hadn't realized exactly how much anxiety I'd been carrying around the idea that her parents might talk her into leaving. I had no compunction about throwing myself bodily between her and anyone who tried to force her into anything. But I wasn't sure how I'd have combatted her making that choice for herself. Even if that choice had been made under some form of emotional duress.

But she'd chosen me instead.

Well, she'd chosen the life she was building here, which included me. Thank Christ.

I was one lucky bastard. I didn't know what I'd done to deserve the affections of a woman like her, but I was determined she wouldn't regret it.

Finn and Alex were already at the office, standing around the drink station with steaming mugs in hand. Their looks were decidedly conspiratorial as I stepped into the lobby, and I knew they'd been talking about me.

"Morning."

They exchanged a glance, then both went brows up in clear expectation.

When I only blinked at them, Alex prodded, "Well? How did the dinner go?"

After yesterday, it was entirely expected that they'd have questions. I'd allowed an entire troop of women into my inner sanctum and pulled out all the stops in the name of impressing Parker's parents. They'd done what they could to help, which had mostly been covering the excursions I'd been booked for, so I could handle the rest. They'd earned some answers.

Moving past them, I put on the kettle for tea. "Well, the dinner itself went well. Parker's no' leaving. That's the good news."

"Oh, is that all the good news?" Finn snarked. "Because

you're smiling an awful lot for a morning. Or for you at all. Frankly, it's rather terrifying."

Alex snorted. "You were late this morning. And our intrepid office manager hasn't made it in yet."

They were fishing. No question about it. Feeling a little awkward, I dumped a tea bag into a mug and cleared my throat. "We're together. She'll be along shortly."

I could leave it at that. Right?

To make sure of it, I shifted gears to what I wanted to discuss with them before Parker arrived. "There's something more serious that came up."

Their expressions sobered.

I quickly explained what Jade had revealed about the potential threat to Parker. "Her father is the CEO and owner of Meridian Global."

Alex's eyes widened. "Oh."

"Aye."

"So Parker is effectively an heiress?"

"Aye, that's more or less the gist of it."

Finn kicked back against the edge of her desk. "Huh. You two are better matched than I even thought at the beginning."

I rolled my eyes. My mates were well aware of all the reasons I'd walked away from my own family legacy. "Anyway, her parents' concerns are no' just about her potential physical limitations. They're concerned for her literal safety. Worried that she could be taken and used as leverage. Jade and I convinced them she'd be safer here, under our protection."

"Done," Finn announced.

"Aye," Alex concurred. "Anything we need to do to keep her safe. What do you need from us?"

"I need an assessment of how legitimate a threat this is. Which means I need you to do what you do best."

He nodded. "Understood."

"Jade will have more information. You can speak to her when she arrives."

"Speaking of," Finn muttered.

The door behind us swung open, and the women arrived. Parker caught sight of all of us clustered around the drink station and froze just inside the door with a deer in the headlights look.

"Um. Good morning."

Falkor made a low woof and trotted over to get his head scritches. Jade nudged Parker into motion, and she headed for her desk to stow her handbag.

"Sorry I'm late." The lovely blush that worked its way up her throat and over her cheeks told me she was definitely remembering all the reasons she was only just getting in. That promptly sent my brain down a rabbit hole of all the ways I'd made her flush with pleasure in the past twelve hours.

"So," Finn began. He ignored my sharp look. "We hear you're actually an heiress in hiding."

Parker's gaze shot to me. "You told them?"

I couldn't tell if she was upset about that. Maybe she'd have preferred I wait for her? "It seemed prudent, under the circumstances."

"Well, that saves me a step." She shut her handbag in a desk drawer. "Yes, technically, I suppose I am. But I'm not some spoiled little princess."

Alex pressed a hand to his heart. "We would never cast such aspersions."

"Aye," Finn agreed. "We just want to make sure you know that you're a part of the team, and we're committed to making sure you feel secure and safe."

With one of those smiles that told me she was feeling warm and squishy, she ducked under my arm and cuddled in. "I certainly appreciate that. I know none of you signed on for extra guard duty."

Finn shrugged. "It won't be the first time. Between Isobel and Ciara, we've had plenty of practice in our retirement."

She frowned. "I know you and Finn did security on Isobel's last tour. But what happened to Ciara?"

Alex's face closed up. "My past caught up to her."

"And we got her back and shut it all down," I reminded him. "She's fine, aye?"

He rolled his shoulders, visibly trying to shake off the memories that I knew would likely haunt him for years to come. "Aye. Well, under the category of other business, it seems like we really ought to talk about getting Jade on the payroll, at least temporarily. Because, obviously, you're not going anywhere."

"You are correct, sir." She stepped past him to start the kettle again. "To be clear, I'm still being paid in an official capacity as Parker's bodyguard."

"Aye, but you're still doing work while you're here. It's only fair," Finn argued.

She flashed a smile. "I won't complain about an extra paycheck."

"Having you here is ideal, actually," I said. "It'll relieve some pressure, as we're going into our busier season. That way, we can all three be out on jobs, and Parker's no' left alone in the office."

"I can't complain about that." With one more squeeze, Parker stepped toward her desk. "I'll get the paperwork drawn up. In the meantime, let's go over the schedule for the rest of the week."

# CHAPTER 32
## PARKER

With the lengthening daylight of late spring, our days at Out of Bounds Scotland were running longer. I still had official office hours, but the guys regularly didn't wrap their excursions and get their equipment stowed until well after five. So it was close to the dinner hour by the time Callum and I made it to The Stag's Head a few days after my parents had departed. Alex had finished whatever research he was doing on the credibility of an actual threat as pertained to me, so we were convening for what I'd been informed was a sit rep meeting. As Ewan was their former squad leader, we were having the meeting in the private party room at the pub so he could be in attendance. I really hoped this was just an abundance of caution and not some effort to soften bad news with good food.

Callum and I stepped through the doors, waiting for several seconds as our eyes adjusted to the dim interior. He stayed close, his broad hand on the small of my back. The din of conversation faded as the gathered patrons noticed us standing there. Beside me, Callum tensed. Instinctively, I tucked in closer to him, wrapping an arm around his waist.

"Parker!" Laura waved from behind the bar. "You want your usual, lass?"

I'd developed a serious fondness for the local ciders they had on tap. "A pint, please. We're gonna be in the back."

She shot me a thumbs up, and Callum began gently shepherding me through the tables.

"Oy, Quinn." Old William Fraser, who was eighty if he was a day, nodded from his regular corner spot near the dartboard. "Is your lass keeping you in line?"

Six weeks ago, I'd watched this man pointedly avoid Callum's gaze. Now his lips were twitching with a smile beneath his beard.

Callum huffed a quiet laugh. "She tries."

"Best listen to her, lad. A good woman's hard to find and worth holding onto."

He inclined his head toward William, even as his grip tightened on me. "Understood, sir. And agreed."

"Oh, Parker, love!" Mrs. Byrne beamed from a tableful of other middle-aged women. "Don't forget about Thursday."

"Wouldn't miss it!"

"What's Thursday?" Callum murmured.

"Somehow I got roped into their weekly knitting circle."

"Do you knit?"

"Not a day in my life. I'm hoping it's possibly just an excuse to feed me copious amounts of shortbread and share village gossip."

"Sure they're no' planning to ply you with pastries to tell them how you tamed the savage beast?"

I opened my mouth, then closed it again. "I hadn't considered that." With a grin, I bumped his shoulder. "They aren't very observant if they think I tamed you."

But there was no question people had been responding to him more kindly since we got involved. He walked around with less of an aura of "Fuck right off" and more "I probably won't bite if you approach me." I called that a win, considering where he'd started. Even Ewan had commented on the change last week, noting that Callum had actually managed a civil conversation with old Mrs. MacPherson about her garden without looking like he wanted to crawl out of his skin. The transformation wasn't dramatic—he was still fundamentally himself, gruff and reserved - but those tiny shifts felt like miracles to those of us who knew him well.

Everyone else, including Jade, had already arrived. They were clustered around the heavy wood table that dominated the room, various drinks already in hand.

"Ah, the guest of honor has arrived." Finn swept a bow. "We can begin."

"Maybe let's order food first," Ewan suggested. "Dom's only going to get busier."

"Fair point."

Callum and I settled at the table. Zo came in carrying my pint and another of lager for Callum, which I supposed must be his regular order. She took all our orders, then withdrew, shutting the door behind her.

Without additional preamble, Callum stretched his arm along the back of my chair and looked at Alex. "Well? What did you find?"

He settled back in his chair, his expression dialing in to a level of serious I wasn't accustomed to seeing. I wondered if this was how he'd been on missions during his military days.

"Right. So I've been looking into the situation with these shipping routes and the pressure campaign. It's bigger than just Meridian Global. There's a pattern of escalating tactics against multiple companies who've opposed the consortium's initiatives."

"What kind of pattern?" Callum's voice remained carefully

neutral, but I felt the tension in his shoulder where it pressed against mine.

"Started with the usual corporate strong-arm tactics—heavy fees, restricted access, regulatory pressure." Alex tapped one of the papers. "But in the past eighteen months, there's been a shift. Three executives' family members from different companies have been grabbed. One from Maersk Line, one from Hamburg Süd, and one from Pacific International. All companies that were blocking the consortium's expansion plans."

Grabbed. He meant kidnapped. Jade had alluded to that during the dinner with my parents, but I hadn't fully grasped the significance. My stomach clenched. "What happened to them?"

"Two were released after their companies made concessions. The third..." He hesitated. "That situation's still ongoing."

Which meant... what? An ongoing hostage situation? Torture? Murder? The possibilities churned in my stomach like curdled milk, and my imagination—usually my greatest asset— became my worst enemy as it conjured up one horrifying scenario after another. Suddenly, the plot of every international espionage thriller I'd ever read seemed less like fantasy and more like a blueprint for the brutal reality of global business. My fingers curled into my palms, nails biting into flesh, as I tried to ground myself in the present moment. Swallowing hard, I tried to keep my voice steady. "And you think Meridian Global could be a target?"

"Your father's company is one of the largest still actively opposing their initiatives. There've been six separate attempts to breach Meridian's network in the past month alone, specifically targeting files related to shipping contracts and route planning. And there are definitely people watching several properties connected to key executives."

"As I mentioned," Jade said.

"Aye. Your instincts were good. But..." Alex hesitated again.

"But what?" Callum prompted.

"There's chatter suggesting they're expanding their targeting. Not just going after the executives themselves anymore, but board members, key shareholders... anyone who might be able to influence company policy."

My head went light as the blood drained from my face. Callum's arm tightened around me, pulling me into the shelter of his body.

"So, in your estimation, the threat is credible?"

"Aye. I believe it is," Alex confirmed. "The good news is that Scotland would be very low on their list of possibilities. The company has no offices here. Certainly, they wouldn't be thinking of Glenlaig. Small village, tight community, everybody knows everybody. Strangers stick out. That's all in our favor. However, there are a few potential vulnerabilities we need to address in terms of how you could be tracked."

"Anyone monitoring her parents' movements could theoretically track them here," Callum said. "Even with the false trail being laid about them having stopped in Glasgow for repairs."

"If there's any chatter to that effect, I'll get an alert."

"What about my work visa?"

Alex nodded. "Aye. That's the second concern. The application's in process, which means there's a paper trail. Mind, it's buried in thousands of similar applications, but someone who knows what they're looking for could potentially find it."

"What else?" Callum's arm tightened fractionally around me.

"The YouTube channel." Alex grimaced. "We've been careful not to show Parker in any of the recent videos, but there are comments from right after she started where people noted seeing her in the background at the office. And there's the Instagram trail from her European trip—even though Jade's been maintaining the fiction that she's still traveling, someone dedicated enough could reconstruct her path and notice it went dead around the time she reached Scotland."

"Social media's the easiest to deal with," Callum said. "We can scrub any mention of her."

"Already on it," Alex assured him. "The work visa's trickier, but I've got some contacts in the Home Office who can help obscure the records a bit. The parents' travel... that we just have to hope wasn't noticed."

My pulse whooshed in my ears as the reality of all this began to sink in. My parents hadn't been unnecessarily paranoid. It wasn't just some out-there possibility. "So... what the hell do we do about all of this?"

"You're moving in with me." Callum's tone brooked no argument. "We can get your things packed up tonight. Your flat's small enough we can probably manage it in one trip—"

My spine snapped straight, and I pulled away. "Excuse me?" The words came out sharp enough to cut glass. "Did you just *tell* me what I'm going to do?"

He frowned at me, as if baffled by my tone. "It's the most sensible solution."

I shoved back from the table. "That's not the point. You don't get to just... dictate what I'm going to do. I'm still an independent adult. I specifically asked for your input, not your orders."

"Parker—"

I began to pace in the narrow confines behind the table. "No. I left Nashville precisely because I was tired of other people making decisions about my life without consulting me. You do *not* get to do the same damned thing. I won't be put in a fucking bubble again."

Callum scrubbed a hand down his face, his expression

shifting from determination to something softer. "That's no' what I meant to do."

"Isn't it?" I spat.

"No." He shoved out of his own chair, interrupting my pacing with his bulk. "This has nothing to do with questioning your capability—or Jade's, for that matter. I want you close so I can protect you." He curled his hands around my shoulders. "And I want you close just because I want you close. I want you in *my* bubble, with me, where I can see you're safe with my own eyes."

The intensity in his good eye made my breath catch.

"You... matter to me, Parker. More than I thought anyone could. And I will personally feel better if I'm your first line of defense. But you're right. I should have asked." He skimmed his hands down my arms to take my hands in his. "Will you move in with me? Please?"

There it was. The request instead of the command. The vulnerability beneath the protectiveness. How could I say no to that?

Besides, if I was being honest with myself, I'd been thinking about taking this next step with him anyway, almost from the moment I'd left his bed. I wanted to be with him, too.

"Okay," I murmured. "Yes."

From the other end of the table, Finn gave a sniff. I glanced in his direction to find him miming tears. "Oh, that's beautiful."

I rolled my eyes. "Oh, shut up."

"Well, you might as well brace yourselves. Ciara is going to demand you have a housewarming party," Alex warned.

I laughed and let Callum pull me in for a hug. "Well, courtesy of all the work she and the girls already did, the house is ready."

# CHAPTER 33

## CALLUM

"What y'all call summer and what we call summer back in Tennessee are *not* the same thing," Parker declared. "It's nearly July and I'm wearing *sleeves*, Callum."

Lips twitching at her vehemence, I turned to unlock the door to the house. "Is that a problem?"

"I mean, no. Although I don't know if I'll ever go truly swimming here. We get these temperatures in, like, March. By now it's bumping the backside of a hundred degrees."

I did the mental math. That'd be around thirty-six in Celsius. "That sounds verra unpleasant."

"That's why we have air conditioning. Really good air conditioning."

"We don't need it much here. A few days out of the year."

"Fair point. I'm getting used to having the windows open for the breeze. I still say we should have ceiling fans, just to keep the air moving. It's too quiet at night."

"You mean aside from your snoring?"

Parker gasped in only semi-mock outrage. "I *do not* snore."

"Aye, you do. You have the cutest wee snore. Just a little

snuffle." Especially when she was extra tired, which she usually was after one of our excursions. I expected more of that tonight, after the paddle boarding trip we'd been on most of the day.

"Take it back."

"It's adorable."

She poked me in the ribs. "Take it back, Quinn."

I gently trapped her hands. "Fine. You're the picture of decorum while you sleep."

Falkor made a groaning noise and gave us both some monumental side-eye.

Parker stuck her tongue out at him. "Nobody asked you."

Laughing, I let us all into the house.

It was midafternoon, and this time of year we had hours of daylight left, but I could already note signs of an impending flare in the way Parker's movements had slowed and the slight tension around her eyes. She'd stiffened up on the ride home and was favoring her lower back a bit. Not that she'd uttered a word of complaint. She seldom did, but over the past six weeks, since she'd moved in, I'd paid attention and learned. A good hot bath and some time on the heating pad might head off the worst of it.

"We should get cleaned up."

"We should start the chili for supper first," she argued. "The longer it simmers, the better it will taste."

"Fine. You're on chopping duty." I nudged her toward the stool at the counter and grabbed a cutting board and a knife. When she gave me a long, suspicious look, I shrugged. "You know I hate dicing the onions. Better for my eyes if you do them way over here."

It was a flimsy excuse, but she went with it, sliding onto the stool with a sigh and a wince she didn't quite manage to hide. I presented her with the onion and peppers and turned away to pull the mince out of the fridge. I set some oil to heat in a heavy-bottomed stew pot and began to brown the beef.

"What else do we need?"

*Thunk* went the knife. "Beef stock. Canned tomatoes. Bottle of beer."

While I reached into the cupboard for the tinned diced tomatoes and stock, Falkor trotted past me and opened the refrigerator door, carefully pulling one of the lagers from the door and bringing it over to me.

"That will never stop being weird." I took the bottle from him and gave him a scratch. "Thanks for the help, lad."

"Onions and peppers are ready," Parker announced.

I broke up the browning mince with a wooden spoon and added the onions and peppers to the pot. Giving the lot of it a stir, I moved to the sink to wash off the bottle. Just in case.

Parker abandoned her stool and headed over to the spice rack. She hissed as she reached for something on the top.

"Bath after this," I declared, plucking the chili powder and cumin down for her. "You had a big day."

"I had an amazing day. But yeah, bath sounds good."

Moving in what had now become a familiar rhythm, we finished dumping everything into the pot for the chili and set it to simmer on a low flame. Then we moved back to our bedroom. Because it was *our* bedroom now. Her things filled half the closet and drawers. Little signs of her were everywhere, from the jewelry scattered across the top of the dresser, to the romance novel on the nightstand on her side of the bed, to all the little pots and jars of girlie things that now took up more than half the counter space in the bathroom.

I loved it. Loved knowing she'd settled in here. With me. Loved knowing how well she fit into my house. Into my life. I simply loved her. Beyond all reason. And I was working myself up to telling her.

Without fuss, I drew the bath, adding in the bath salts with arnica and lavender she preferred for these sorts of days. When I'd bought this house, I'd thought the giant soaker tub the previous owner had installed was a monumental waste of space. But it was exactly what Parker needed. The fact that she sat on the edge of the bed as the tub filled told me she was definitely starting to feel the over-exertion.

"Need a hand?"

She scowled a little. "I can undress myself. I'm not a child."

"Hobbit, I can promise that I have never once thought you were a child when I was undressing you." I let the gravel drop into my tone, which had a satisfying blush rising to her cheeks. "I can appreciate the view, even when it's a look-don't-touch situation." She was in no shape for anything I might like to do with her tonight. And that was fine. I found I enjoyed taking care of her in every capacity.

"Fine. I'd appreciate a little help."

Carefully, I stripped her down, letting my eyes linger on the body I'd learned every intimate inch of these past weeks. I could still fantasize about next time. I had a long, long list of ways I wanted to pleasure her.

Before she could protest, I slipped my arm beneath her legs and scooped her off the bed.

"What are you doing?"

"Giving you bed-to-tub service." I carried her bride-style into the bathroom and carefully lowered her into the steaming water.

Her instant sigh as the water closed over her was as gratifying as it was arousing. "Oh, that feels good."

I turned off the water and crouched at the edge of the tub. "What else do you need?"

"You."

Damn if that word didn't shoot straight to my cock. "Parker," I rasped.

Her lips curved. "I didn't mean that. Although always that. I know I'm in no shape for the acrobatics required to take advantage of tub sex at the moment. But you would make for a very convenient heat source along my back, and there's room enough in here for both of us. Please?"

As if I'd deny her anything.

"I do appreciate your pragmatism." I efficiently shed my clothes and carefully sank into the water behind her.

It took a little finagling to situate her between my legs, but at last she lay back against my chest with a contented sigh. The water was just high enough to cover her nipples, and I used my hands to keep a steady wash of warmth over her chest. Despite the hopeful erection I was determinedly ignoring, this was comfortable, and I felt my own tension unraveling. I never seemed to be able to hold on to it long when Parker was around. And that was nothing short of a miracle.

She let her head loll back against my shoulder. "The tub was totally worth moving in for."

I pressed a kiss to the top of her shoulder. "Just the tub?"

Her mouth curved, though she didn't open her long-lashed eyes. "You're pretty great, too. Even if you're totally making up lies about me snoring."

My own lips pulled into a smile. That expression had become far more natural since she'd come into my life. "I know this wasn't precisely what you wanted."

She did open her eyes then, glancing up at me over her shoulder. "I don't like the reason we took this step, but don't mistake that reluctance for me not wanting this with you. Because I did. I do. I'm happy here, Callum."

It meant a lot to me to hear that. I knew I hadn't gone about getting her here the right way. But maybe I could make up for that now.

"I know the threat we all worried about hasn't materialized. And I'm grateful for that. But I can't say that I regret that it brought you here. Because I'm happy, too. I didn't think that was something I had the capacity to feel anymore. That's all you. Because you're fucking amazing. I have no idea what you see in me, but I need you to know that I love you."

Those big brown eyes filled with tears. "Callum. I love you, too." She tried to turn in my arms, but there wasn't room. "Damn it, you had to say it when I can't properly look you in the face."

Chuckling, I eased her back around. "You can look me in the face all you want later. I just needed you to know."

"I'm sorry we can't celebrate that appropriately just now."

"While I'll never turn down the opportunity to make love to you, that's no' why I'm with you and no' why I love you. You are the strongest, bravest, most amazing woman I know."

"Racking up the compliments, Quinn. I see you're making up for the snoring thing."

A laugh vibrated my chest as I wrapped my arms around her. "Seems I've got a way to go yet."

We stayed in the bath for a good long while, draining a bit and adding more hot water several times, until our fingers and toes wrinkled, and the enticing scents of chili grew strong enough to draw us out of the water. Parker had reached the limp noodle stage, so she docilely let me dry her off and dress her in some of her favorite lounge clothes.

I got her settled on the sofa with a heating pad and fixed us both bowls of chili while Falkor looked on with hopeful eyes.

"This is no' for you, lad."

"Oh, but he loves the chips," Parker argued. When she held one out, he bounded over, plopping his butt down and waiting patiently until she fed it to him. Then he stretched out below her on the rug with a happy groan.

This was my life now. A business that had grown to something we could be proud of, and a woman who understood and loved me to share my home with. I was a lucky bastard.

And if there was a voice in the back of my mind warning me that despite the quiet, the threat remained, I chose to focus on the now.

# CHAPTER 34

## PARKER

"So, how is living with our resident Tall, Dark, and Broody?" Ciara leaned forward, chin in hands. "He's certainly been keeping you to himself these past several weeks." The waggle of her eyebrows made it very clear how she imagined he'd been keeping me occupied. And, well, she wasn't entirely wrong, even if that wasn't precisely why I hadn't seen as much of the girls lately.

"Alex hasn't been bringing home daily reports?"

"What he deems worthy of reporting and what I'd expect from you are not the same thing."

I pursed my lips and sipped at my Coke while surreptitiously slipping a chip beneath the table for Falkor, who nipped it neatly from my fingers. "A girl doesn't kiss and tell."

Beside me, Jade snorted. "Honey, those fair cheeks of yours tell plenty."

"They *imply* plenty," Skye corrected. "But they don't give all the juicy details."

"*I'm* not giving all the juicy details."

"But you admit there are juicy details," Pippa pointed out.

I fixed her with a look. "Do you want to share all the intimate specifics of your love life with Zeke?"

"We did hear about that save a horse, ride a cowboy T-shirt," Skye said.

Pippa immediately sank down in her chair as we all began to laugh.

I plucked another chip off my plate and bit in. "I'm not going into specifics. But I will say that it's going well, and we're very happy. I love having all the one-on-one time with him." It was true. Even if I did occasionally feel the slightest bit stifled by the current security restrictions.

I was never truly alone these days. Callum or Jade or one of the guys was always with me, even though nothing had happened in all these weeks. I didn't know how long they intended to keep it up before the threat was declared... well, not a threat. But I definitely couldn't complain. Not when I was living with a man I loved, one who loved me. Not when my best friend was here in Scotland with me, embarking on this new life and risking hers to make sure I got to keep it.

"One-on-one time with men who are trained to focus like the Royal Marines is definitely worth appreciating," Ciara sighed.

I lifted my glass to her in a toast of solidarity.

"I hate you both," Saoirse said mildly.

"Hey, there's still one more available," I pointed out.

"Not if he were the last man on earth."

"So you keep saying." Ciara fixed her with a significant look before turning back to me. "But seriously, you've been so good for Callum. He's lightened up so much these past few months. The other locals aren't afraid to speak to him anymore. And Alex said he's even started joking with clients."

"Finn is still freaking out about all the smiling he's doing, so

I think Callum's doing it more just to mess with him." Jade paused. "Or maybe he's just imagining Parker naked."

"Jade!" Heat rushed to my cheeks, but I grinned and lowered my voice. "Both those things could be true."

Another gale of laughter overtook the table.

Jade straightened. "Oh, hey, I need to go grab something from my flat."

I hadn't quite finished my lunch, but I automatically pushed back the plate.

Jade pushed the plate back to me. "No, no. You stay put. I'll be back in just a bit, and then we'll head back to work."

She gave me a look that said *Sit. I know you're just coming off a flare.* She wasn't wrong. I'd overdone it on the paddle boarding trip. Courtesy of Callum's ministrations, I hadn't been fully down for the count, but I wasn't back to a hundred percent either, so I gratefully relaxed into my chair. "I'll be here, and I've got lunch."

"Appreciate it."

We all watched her weave through the tables.

"She settling in okay?" Skye asked.

"Yeah. And it worked out well that she's basically taking over my lease now that I've moved in with Callum. Easy on all fronts."

"It must be so great having one of your besties make the move with you."

I still felt a twinge of guilt at that, but Jade had insisted she was good with it. "It really is. I'm lucky to have her here. And I'm so grateful y'all all brought her into the fold."

"Of course we did. We've all had the experience of being the new person in town," Ciara said.

Pippa arched a brow. "You know everyone here from growing up."

"I never said I was new *here*."

"Oh Christ, is that the time?" Saoirse pushed back from the table, tossing some bills down. "I've got to get going, too. There's a whole herd's worth of vaccinations on my docket this afternoon over in Braemore. Ta, my loves."

We all waved as she practically sprinted out of the pub.

Ciara folded her arms. "Speaking of new or not so new, can we talk about Saoirse? She's resisted getting involved with anyone since she got here, acting like being in Glenlaig is temporary, but it's so clear she's going to take over her grandda's practice. I think she needs a man."

"*Does* she need a man?" I asked. "Or is that you're happily in love and want everyone to be equally happy and in love talking?"

"To be clear, I'm not saying she needs a relationship or a man to complete her, but I think she could benefit from some company that wasn't of the battery-powered variety."

Skye angled her head in concession of the point. "You want to play matchmaker?"

"She always wants to play matchmaker," Pippa pointed out.

"It's a small village. We have to get our entertainment somewhere. Now, who do we think likely candidates could be?"

Over the next fifteen minutes, we discussed options. I privately wondered whether there could be some kind of sparks with Finn, as she bristled like a scalded cat any time he came up, and it was feeling more than a little like the lady doth protest too much. But I didn't bring him up as a viable candidate. Mostly because I wasn't sure I wanted Ciara taking that bit between her teeth, and I had no idea how Finley might feel about the idea. By the time we'd finished our plates and the lunch hour was drawing to a close, we hadn't settled on anyone we all thought Saoirse would really go for.

Ciara shoved back from the table. "I've got to get back to the castle. We've got a client meeting with a new bride this afternoon, and I dinna want to be late."

"I need to get going, too. Zoom meeting with the home office," Skye said.

"And I need to get back to my coding," Pippa announced.

I needed to get back to work, too, but Jade still wasn't back from running over to the flat. The girls and I exchanged hugs, and I waved them off. Then it was just me and the dwindling crowd at The Stag's Head. What was taking Jade so long? She hadn't said what she needed. Maybe she'd gotten stuck on a phone call or something. Should I walk over to check on her? It was only a block. Neither she nor Callum had let me go anywhere alone since all this started, but surely I'd be fine in the middle of the village in broad daylight.

Even as I was trying to decide what to do, my phone vibrated with a text.

**JADE**

Hey, this is taking longer than I expected.
Head on back to work without me.

**PARKER**

Are you sure? Is there something I can help
with?

The reply dots started bouncing.

**JADE**

No, everything's fine. It's been quiet. Go
ahead and walk.

I hadn't planned to walk this afternoon, but my flare had lightened up considerably and the movement would probably do me good. Plus, I didn't want to pass up this opportunity for a little bit of normal. I missed my routine of walking to work to and from my flat. I'd lost out on that since I'd moved in with Callum. Laying down cash for my and Jade's portion of the bill, I waved to Zo and stepped out onto the high street.

The day was cloudy and a little cool. I couldn't get over highs in early July being in the sixties. Not that I was complaining. I decided to take a slightly different route back to the office. My usual one down the high street would take me past all the businesses I frequented and would most likely result in a lot of stops to visit. I didn't have the energy to make it all the way back to the office if I stopped moving. Just across from Village Chippy, I cut over a block to the first residential street. The quiet, tree-lined drive was lovely. Cozy. The sort of place where I imagined neighbors knew and looked out for each other.

Callum's house was so remote. It was lovely, and we'd put some effort into starting to clean up the garden. But there were no neighbors nearby. I understood that had been entirely deliberate on his part when he'd bought the place. No matter how much happier he might be with me, I didn't see him ever moving to a place that could be considered a neighborhood. He liked his privacy too much. God forbid somebody pop over to borrow a cup of sugar.

I was so amused by the mental image of that I didn't immediately register the sound of a vehicle approaching. Falkor tensed as tires crunched on asphalt, far too close for comfort. A white van screeched to a halt. The side door slid open with a heavy *thunk* and multiple sets of rough hands grabbed for me before I even understood what was happening.

My gentle, people-loving dog erupted into a frenzy of snarls and snapping teeth as he fought to protect me. I thrashed and bucked, trying to twist free of my captors' grips. The sharp yelp of pain and sudden cessation of growling had my heart seizing in my chest.

"Falkor!" I twisted and jerked harder, despite the screaming protest of my body. I had to see what they'd done to him. "Let go of me!"

I kicked out, connecting with something solid. A reverberation of pain shot up my own leg even as one of the men grunted. Small victories. But it wasn't enough. There were too many. Three? Maybe four? They hauled me into the van. The stale air inside reeked of cigarettes and unwashed bodies. I sucked in a breath to scream, but a rough hand pressed hard against my face, muffling the sound, and I felt the prick of a needle in my neck.

*No, no, no...*

My last coherent thought was of Falkor's silence as darkness washed over me, dragging me under.

# CHAPTER 35

## CALLUM

I hefted the last of the climbing gear onto the storage hooks, rolling my shoulders. Good session with the tourists this morning. The family of four had listened to instructions—always a bonus. We'd managed a safe but challenging climb that had made their two teenaged boys drop the affectation of boredom in exchange for whoops and smiles. That was what we liked to see. They'd be back. The whole job had been clean, uncomplicated. The kind of work I could still do without my limitations getting in the way. And I realized that my brain was finally starting to compensate for the lack of depth perception. It wasn't the same—not by a long shot. But it was better than it had been.

Maybe the doctors had been right about the need for time and patience.

I checked my phone for more texts, though it hadn't buzzed. All I saw was Parker's earlier message.

PARKER

Having lunch with the girls! Back in an hour.
🖤

Though I itched to see her—I'd been out since early this morning—I knew she needed this. Time away from all the security protocols and watchful eyes. Though she never complained, I'd seen her chafe at the restrictions. I'd done everything I could to offset them, to give her all the socialization she craved—God save me. But I knew it hadn't quite been enough. For better or worse, my woman was a social creature.

Still, it had been a little over an hour. She should've been back by now. Maybe they'd taken a slightly longer lunch. Or maybe her flare had kicked back up. It had been fading over the past few days, but what if it had gotten suddenly worse?

I squashed the quick surge of worry. Jade was with her, and Jade knew better than I did what to do for her, if that was the case. And if she was flaring, one or both of them would let me know. More likely, she'd just gotten caught up at the pub having a good time. She deserved that.

A booming bark pierced the quiet of the storage bay. But it was wrong, desperate, nothing like Falkor's usual cheerful greeting. The big white dog barreled through the open rolling door, barking frantically, his hackles raised.

Alone.

My gut clenched. Falkor never left Parker's side. Not ever.

The moment he spotted me, he charged over, limping slightly. Blood stained the fur at his shoulder.

Finn appeared in the doorway. "What's going on?"

"He's hurt." I dropped to my knees beside the dog, hands searching through his thick fur. The cut wasn't deep. Had he been clipped by a car? Gotten into some kind of fight with another animal? I was no vet, but I didn't think the gash had come from teeth or claws. The edges seemed too smooth.

Why had he left Parker?

"Where is she, lad? Where's Parker?"

Falkor barked again, limping toward the door. My fingers were already pulling up her contact on my phone as I followed. Straight to voicemail. Fuck. Was she hurt? Had her legs given out? I hit Jade's contact next, cursing when it, too, went unanswered.

Impatient, the dog grumbled at me and took my trouser leg in his teeth, pulling me along faster.

"Something's wrong. Parker was having lunch with the girls at the pub. She should've been back by now."

"You see where he takes you on foot. I'll grab my keys." Finn disappeared down the hall, and I broke into a run with the dog, my mind conjuring up increasingly horrific scenarios for what I might find.

But despite my vivid imagination, there was no cluster of vehicles in the road or emergency services loading her onto a stretcher. In fact, there was nothing at all on the residential street where Falkor stopped and circled, his cries growing more frantic by the second.

"I don't understand. What are you trying to tell me?"

I looked around for... anything. Signs of a struggle or evidence that Parker had even been here. This wasn't part of her usual route back to the office. Why had Falkor brought me here?

Finn drove up in his 4x4, Alex in the front seat. "Get in. We'll go check the pub."

I loaded Falkor into the back, still whining. "We'll need to call Saoirse to get him seen about."

"And we will, but he'll be all right for long enough that we can check this."

The drive to the pub took forever and no time at all. I scanned the streets, searching for any glimpse of her dark hair, her bright smile. But there was nothing, only the villagers I was coming to know despite myself, along with a dozen tourists strolling the sidewalks.

Zo looked up as we came in, her usual welcome dying on her lips at our expressions. "What's wrong?"

"Where's Parker?"

She flinched at the snap in my voice, but I wasn't capable of pulling it back. Not now.

"She left about fifteen minutes ago."

I zeroed in on what she hadn't said. "She left? What about Jade?"

"Jade ran back to her flat for something before they finished lunch. She didn't make it back."

A muscle in my jaw ticked. "So Parker left alone?"

"I mean, as alone as she could be with Falkor. What's happened?"

I was already moving as I heard Finn explain that Parker was missing and Falkor had been hurt and to spread the word around the village. He and Alex fell in behind me as we bolted for the flat down the street.

Everything outside the law office looked normal. The exterior door leading up to the flat was closed and locked. But everything felt too quiet. The silence scraped along my already raw nerves as I circled around to the alley beside the building.

A form lay crumpled against the wall.

I bolted forward. Blood matted Jade's close-cropped natural curls where she'd been struck from behind. Her eyes fluttered even as I touched her throat to check for a pulse.

"Parker?" Her voice was slurred and thick. "Where's—" Her eyes focused on me and widened. She tried to sit up, panic flooding her features as memory returned. "Fuck. No. They got the jump on me. Tell me she's not..." But the look on my face had her trailing off to a whisper. "No."

Pain shot up my arm as my fist connected with the wall, but I barely felt it through the rage and fear running through me like wildfire.

Despite every precaution, every protocol, she'd been taken.

Finn already had his phone out. "I'll call in some favors. We've got resources."

Alex helped Jade to her feet, steadying her as she swayed. "We'll find her. We're trained for this."

But all I could see was Parker's face this morning, sleep-soft and smiling as she'd kissed me goodbye at the office before I'd left for my climb. I'd promised to keep her safe. Promised nothing would happen to her on my watch.

Now she was gone, and I didn't have the first clue how we were going to find her.

Finn squeezed my shoulder. "Lock it down. You're no good to her panicked."

I exhaled a hard breath out of my nose and drew another in, my hands balled into fists. He was right, of course. I was trained to regulate my emotions so I could do the job. I was literally a deadly weapon, and I'd bring every ounce of my training to bear against the people who'd taken Parker. God help anyone who'd touched a hair on her head.

# CHAPTER 36

## PARKER

Pain shot through my body, dragging me closer to consciousness. Every inch felt leaden, disconnected from my fuzzy brain. My mouth felt like it had been stuffed with cotton, and my eyelids didn't want to work. I just wanted to sink back into the oblivion of sleep until this flare was over, because it was clearly a bad one. But fresh daggers of pain stabbed through my skull because I was... moving? Beneath me, a cold metal floor vibrated, each jolt making my stomach pitch. Every bump and sway sent pain pulsing through my body.

"—transmission is completely shot. Listen to that grinding —" A harsh Russian accent cut through my confusion.

Russian?

"Shut it! We need solutions, not complaints." This voice was deeper, angrier.

Memory slammed back like a physical blow. The walk back from lunch. The van. Falkor's desperate attempts to fend off my attackers. The sharp stab of a needle. Then nothing.

My brave boy. If they'd hurt him, I'd kill them myself. Somehow.

I had to believe he'd escaped unharmed, and that he'd gone to find help. The alternative was too awful to contemplate.

Despite my discomfort, I resisted the urge to wiggle or move, keeping my breathing slow and steady so they wouldn't know I was awake yet. I had to fight through this fog of pain so I could find a way out of this.

"There's an old sheep barn about half a mile down that track we passed." A third voice, younger. "Nobody uses it anymore. We could hole up there until—"

"Until what? The whole fucking village is probably looking for her by now. We can't make the switch point, can't risk the main roads with a van that's probably already been reported."

I cracked one eye open, just enough to make out my surroundings through my lashes. Rust had eaten holes in the van's floor, showing glimpses of pavement rushing by underneath. The fetid smell of old oil and exhaust fumes made bile rise in my throat. My hands were bound behind my back with what felt like zip ties, the plastic biting into my wrists every time we hit a pothole. Technically, I knew how to get out of that, courtesy of book research I'd helped Paisley with, but I had neither the leverage nor the energy to snap them, even if I had been alone, which I definitely wasn't.

The van lurched violently, and a grinding screech filled the air. My captors swore, their voices rising in panic.

"That's it. She's done. We've got to get off this road."

"Take that track up ahead. We'll find cover and figure out the rest."

The van turned sharply, and my body slid across the corroded floor. Pain flared through my shoulder as I hit the wheel well, but I bit back my cry. My head was clearing enough to notice details now—the sound of gravel under the tires instead of pavement, a musty smell mixing with the exhaust. Why did I know that scent?

"Sheep. I fucking hate sheep."

Wool. It was the scent of wet wool. I gathered we must've come to a stop near someone's farm.

I well knew that a huge chunk of the Highlands was rural, and sheep were around every corner. But I was getting the sense that we hadn't made it more than half an hour from the village before things started going wrong.

These weren't the organized professionals we'd feared might come for me. These men were scared, improvising, making mistakes. And that meant they'd be easier to find. Callum would be looking for me by now. So would Jade and everyone else.

My brain circled back to lunch. To the text from Jade telling me to go ahead. My stomach swooped again. She wouldn't have said that. Wouldn't have done that. What if these assholes had gotten to her first somehow? Prevented her from coming back to the pub for me?

Oh God, was she okay? Had they hurt her, too?

Tears pricked my eyes, and I struggled to hold them back.

Callum and the guys would find me.

They had to.

The van shuddered to a stop. Around me, everyone began to move. Doors slammed, followed by harsh whispers I couldn't quite make out. Then rough hands seized my arms and legs.

"Get her out. We'll have to carry her."

They hauled me from the van like a sack of potatoes. One of them—the one with the deep voice—slung me over his shoulder. The position sent fire racing through my joints, and I couldn't quite hold back a gasp of pain.

"She's awake," the younger voice said.

"Doesn't matter now. Keep moving."

My captor's shoulder dug into my stomach with every step as he trudged uphill. The zip ties cut deeper into my wrists as my body bounced against his back. Each jolt sent fresh waves of agony through my nerves.

"What do you want from me?" My voice came out raspy, my throat raw from whatever they'd used to knock me out.

No answer.

"Where are you taking me?"

"Quiet." The deep voice rumbled through his back, vibrating against my ribs.

Was there anything I could do to indicate we'd come this way? I couldn't reach my pockets and didn't know if anything was inside them still. Without my hands being free, I didn't have the flexibility to do much of anything. But I felt the slim band of my ring still on my right hand. The twining Celtic knotwork had been a purchase with my second paycheck. Maybe I could work it free? Under the guise of flexing my fingers to get the feeling back, I slowly began to work the band down my finger and over my knuckle. When it fell to the ground, none of my captors noticed. Possibly no one would ever notice, and I'd just given up one of my favorite pieces. But losing a ring was hardly my biggest problem at the moment.

We climbed for what felt like forever, the path growing steeper and rougher with each jolting step. The warm summer air had grown thin and crisp, carrying the distant bleating of sheep and the occasional rustle of dry grass. Through my sideways view of the world, I caught glimpses of the rugged hillside, all weathered stone and scrubby vegetation. A few lonely sheep dotted the upper slopes, their white wool stark against the muted browns and greens, but most of the flocks had already been moved down to lower pastures. At least, that was what I'd overheard some of the locals discussing at the pub recently.

Finally, a small stone building came into view—a shepherd's bothy, like the ones I'd seen in photos at the office. No electricity, no running water. Just four walls, a roof, and a fireplace. Perfect for shepherds during lambing season. Perfect for hiding someone who didn't want to be found.

My stomach lurched as my captor ducked through the low doorway, his broad shoulders nearly scraping the weathered stone frame. He dumped me unceremoniously onto what felt like an ancient wooden chair, the rough-hewn seat creaking ominously beneath my weight. The musty air inside the bothy carried decades of wood smoke and damp wool, the kind of deeply ingrained scents that made my nose wrinkle. This definitely wasn't like some of the bothies used by hikers all across the Highlands. Everything inside was so old and decrepit, I wasn't even sure that whatever farmer owned the land still used it.

"Please," I tried again, fighting to keep my voice steady. "Just tell me what you want." If I could connect with them somehow, get them to see me as a person, maybe I could reason with them. If this was about money, my father would certainly pay it.

The younger one started to speak, but the leader cut him off with a sharp gesture. "Shut it. We wait for new orders. That's all you need to know."

My heart sank. They were just the muscle, the grab team. Maybe they didn't even know why they'd taken me. That meant whoever was behind this was still safely hidden, still pulling strings from a distance.

I closed my eyes against a fresh wave of pain and nausea. Callum would be looking for me by now. But would he think to search way up here? Could anyone even find this place if they didn't already know it existed?

# CHAPTER 37

## CALLUM

My boots scuffed against the worn floorboards with a rhythmic thud that echoed my mounting frustration as I paced the length of the office like a caged animal. Each step marked another second Parker was gone, another moment slipping through my fingers. Another second I'd failed to find her, to do the one bloody thing I was supposed to be good at. She was out there somewhere, undoubtedly in danger, and every minute that ticked by took her further away from me.

"You're going to wear a hole in the floor." Alex didn't look away from his bank of computers, his fingers still flying over the keys.

He wasn't wrong, but that didn't mean I had to like it. I shot a glare in his direction and resumed my pacing.

The only thing keeping me from crawling completely out of my skin was the fact that this group wanted her as leverage. Hostage negotiations went better if the hostages weren't hurt.

They hadn't contacted Parker's father.

I had. That conversation had been the hardest I'd ever

faced. Her parents were livid and terrified. Justifiably so. I'd sworn to keep her safe.

I'd sworn I'd get her back, too. But I knew they'd believe it when they saw it.

Across the room, Finn and Ewan sorted combat gear. None of us had anticipated needing it again once we'd retired. But after Ciara had been taken last year, we'd made a few provisions for the just in case. We wouldn't be going after these arseholes unprepared.

The crackle of the police scanner drew all our attention for a moment. Anticipation quickened my already thundering pulse, but it was only another routine call—some drunk and disorderly at a pub the next village over. My teeth ground in frustration. Every false alarm grated on my already fraying nerves.

"Alex, tell me you have something." I'd asked the same thing in various ways two dozen times in the past half hour.

"Same as five minutes ago. Still working through traffic cam footage, trying to track the van's path out of the village. It's not like this is London, with a million and one cameras to draw from."

At Parker's desk, Jade worked her own contacts, dark eyes focused on her phone. She hadn't said much since Dr. Donaldson patched her up, releasing her against medical advice after putting four stitches in her head. The tight set of her jaw told me she was blaming herself every bit as much as I was—especially since we'd found her phone and seen the texts someone had used to send Parker out on her own.

My phone vibrated with a text.

SAOIRSE

The big guy is resting comfortably. His wounds have been cleaned and stitched. He'll make a full recovery.

I'd seen the doorbell cam footage Alex had pulled from one of the houses in the neighborhood. The dog had fought hard to protect Parker. I owed him a lifetime supply of whatever treats he wanted.

CALLUM

Thanks for letting me know. Parker will want to know when we find her.

I had to believe that we would find her.

SAOIRSE

Any news?

I clenched my fists, frustrated that the answer was still no.

CALLUM

Not yet.

SAOIRSE

I know you're doing everything you can. Just know I've got Falkor until Parker gets home.

I appreciated her faith in us. At this point, I needed whatever additional confidence I could get.

The police scanner squawked again. This time, the voice on the other end caught my attention.

"Dispatch, this is Campbell. Got a report about a white panel van seen up near Braemore about two hours ago. Caller says it was driving erratically, nearly ran him off the road. He just heard about the missing person alert and called it in."

My heart thundered against my ribs. Two hours. Christ. So much ground could be covered in two hours.

Alex had already pulled up a map. "That's heading northeast."

"How far could they have gotten in two hours?" Jade asked, rising from her chair.

"Too far," I growled. But it was the first real lead we'd had. "Call it in to your contact at Traffic Scotland. See if they can check cameras along that route. If there are any."

Alex nodded, already reaching for his phone.

"I'm driving up there. Maybe they left some sign we can follow."

Jade rose to her feet. "Not alone."

I started to protest. To point out that with her head injury, she was more likely to be a liability, but she cut me off.

"She's my responsibility, too. I'm coming."

The need to move, to do something, anything, clawed at my chest. But I forced myself to wait as Alex made his calls. We couldn't afford to miss anything by rushing in half-cocked. Waiting for the confirmatory intel could make the difference between finding them and not.

*Hold on, Hobbit. We're coming.*

We kitted up in silence, each of us falling into familiar roles. Jade's own military training showed as she slipped right into our rhythm. Comms check. Weapons check. Extra magazines distributed, though I really hoped we didn't have to use them. The muscle memory of a hundred missions kicked in as we loaded gear into the vehicles. The familiar weight of my tactical vest grounded me, focused me.

At last, I had something to do.

I took point, with Jade riding in the passenger seat of my Range Rover. Finn and Ewan brought up the rear in Finn's truck. We moved in a convoy along the route Alex had determined. He stayed behind, functioning as command center. My eyes swept the edges of the road in a constant scan pattern, compensating for my blind side. There had to be something, somewhere.

"I shouldn't have left her alone."

I didn't look away from the road as Jade spoke. "You didn't

leave her alone. You left her at the pub with three other people."

"None of whom knew there was a threat. I should've waited to run back to the flat after lunch, when Parker could have come with me. I was just trying to save her some steps. And now—"

"Wheesht. This is no' your fault."

"How can you say that?"

"Because if they were determined to take her, and they hadn't been able to disable you today, they'd have found some other way. This was only a matter of time. You and I both know that. And maybe we all got a little lax with the weeks of nothing at all. But blame doesn't help anything. It won't help bring her home. Only action can do that."

"Skid marks." Jade's voice snapped as she pointed to dark streaks scoring the pavement.

I slowed and radioed to Finn. "You see those?"

"Aye. Fresh ones."

We were less than half an hour from the village. No way had they been expecting problems this soon.

A quarter mile on, we spotted fresh tire tracks cutting deep into mud and gravel on a narrow track leading into the trees. Someone had been in a hurry. It was obvious this hadn't been a planned turn.

"Drive up or park a ways down and double back on fuul?" Finn asked.

"If they're hiding just inside the trees, driving up seems like a good way to get shot. Or at the very least, lose the element of surprise. Let's double back."

"There's a decent spot to pull off about a half a click further down the main road," Alex reported over the radio.

I hoped we weren't making a mistake.

Parking our vehicles where Alex had indicated, we armed

ourselves and made our way back through the woods, approaching in a standard sweep formation, weapons up, each covering our own respective zones.

The white panel van sat abandoned fifty yards in, screened by evergreens. Finn and Ewan split right, while Jade and I went left.

Clear signals rippled through the team. No movement. No sound. No hostiles.

"Clear," Ewan's voice was barely above a whisper.

I wrenched open the back of the van myself, but there was no sign of Parker.

Jade moved to the engine, her inspection swift and practiced. "Vehicle's dead. Something mechanical. They didn't plan to stop here."

I keyed my radio, keeping my voice low. "Alex. Van located. Foot pursuit. Area survey."

"Copy." Keyboard clicks. "Satellite showing two structures. Looks like a bothy northeast, two miles up. Outbuilding northwest, similar distance."

Finn's hand signals confirmed what I was thinking. They wouldn't separate with a hostage, so they were all headed to one location. But which one?

Wrong choice meant wasted time. Time Parker didn't have because as soon as they managed to regroup, she'd be gone.

"We could split up," Ewan began.

"Negative," Jade insisted. "There were at least three men in that video. If we hope to get her back without lethal force, we need all of us."

I considered. I didn't have any personal problems with dispatching every last one of them and hiding the bodies where they'd never be found. But without my military credentials backing us up, the authorities would frown on that. We didn't know if the assailants were armed. Attempting to take them down without deadly force meant more opportunity for things to go sideways. Parker could get hurt as collateral damage. That was unacceptable.

"We stay together."

The four of us moved up the muddy track in a diamond formation, with me in front, Finn and Jade behind, and Ewan bringing up the six. There were signs of multiple boots. Deep impressions in the mud—someone being carried. Was that because they were trying to control her or because she was incapable of walking herself?

Sunlight caught the glint of metal.

My heart seized. Parker's ring—the one she never took off and always fidgeted with during meetings.

I scooped it up, muscle memory warring with emotion as I secured it in my vest pocket.

"Contact sign," Jade murmured, pitching her voice for our ears only. "She's fighting."

The team tightened formation as we pushed up the trail. Every step, every movement, every breath was measured, controlled.

Years of training crystallized into lethal focus.

*Hold on, Hobbit. Your team is coming.*

# CHAPTER 38

## PARKER

I'd spent most of the afternoon listening to increasingly agitated phone conversations in Russian. Evidently, my captors were coordinated enough to have a satellite phone, because there was no way we had cell service up here. They didn't know I'd taken Russian in college. Just one semester. One of those "useless" courses my parents had complained about. I'd done okay with the speaking portion, but the different alphabet had been headache inducing, so I hadn't kept it up. The irony wasn't lost on me. While I couldn't catch everything, I understood just enough to gather that their original plan had gone sideways when the van broke down. They needed alternate transport, which was apparently proving difficult to arrange on short notice. Small mercies. That gave more opportunity for my people to find me.

The man I'd mentally dubbed "Captain Snarly"—I blamed Paisley's influence for that—kept checking his watch, his movements growing more agitated as the hours dragged on. Whatever timeline they were working against, we were falling behind. From what I'd pieced together, they were trying to coordinate with someone coming from Aberdeen, but it wouldn't be until dawn.

I'd lost track of time. With my hands bound behind me, I couldn't twist to see my watch, and I hadn't yet learned to estimate the time by light. The astoundingly long days at this latitude were still throwing me. And anyway, pain had a way of distorting the passage of time. My shoulders and arms pulsed with pain. This angle was awful. I'd tried to get my captors to at least retie my hands in front, but they'd only relented so far as to lash me to the chair instead. At least the bindings were loose enough that my hands weren't completely numb anymore.

As evening settled in—surely it was evening by now?—the tension in our makeshift hidey hole finally started to ease. Captain Snarly took another call. This time, his expression shifted from frustration to relief. He barked something that included "4 AM" to the others. The change in the bothy's atmosphere was instant.

The other men broke out some food from somewhere. Sandwiches and crisps that had obviously come from Mrs. Byrne's bakery. Jesus, they'd been in her shop. Had they been casing the whole town? How long had they been watching, learning my schedule and routine? And how had none of us seen them? Probably because we were at peak tourist season. Strangers were far more normal in the village this time of year.

Cans were cracked open, and I scented cheap beer. Two of the men started a card game, their low-voiced conversation punctuated by occasional huffs of laughter. The third dozed in a folding chair by the door, while Captain Snarly maintained watch, though even his attention had begun to wane. He'd stopped checking his watch every few minutes. They paid no attention to me, offering neither food nor threats.

I kept my expression carefully neutral, as if I hadn't the faintest idea what they'd said all day. But my mind raced, processing the implications. They were getting sloppy. More importantly, I knew exactly when they planned to move me. But what the hell could I do with that information? Even if I could miraculously get free, there was no way I could run. I wasn't even sure my body would carry me across the room right now. Which meant I could only wait.

Callum was coming. I believed that, down to my very marrow. The question was whether he'd manage to find me before dawn.

Every inch of my body throbbed. All the hours of being bound, first in the van, then to this chair, had aggravated my fibro, sending deep aches through my muscles and joints. The flare that had been waning this morning had returned with a vengeance, and dehydration wasn't helping. No one had offered me water since they'd nabbed me back in the village.

Exhaustion dragged at me, wooing me with a promise of a break from the pain if I just let myself sleep, but I forced my eyes to stay open. If anything happened, I needed to be ready. For what, I didn't know. But something. I'd had too many lectures from Callum and Jade about situational awareness these past many weeks.

At the rickety table in the corner, the card players had gotten louder, their volume increasing as they'd downed more beer. Even Captain Snarly had let down his guard enough to take the last chair, though he kept the sat phone close. The guard at the door hadn't moved in the past twenty minutes. His chin rested against his chest, his breathing slow and even. There hadn't been a single noise other than the occasional bleat of a sheep or the breeze rustling the trees. This whole place felt like the back of beyond.

Something in the air changed. A shift in pressure, perhaps? A storm rolling in? But as the hair on my arms rose to attention, I knew it wasn't a storm. At least not the usual sort. My senses jangled, that weird sixth sense that alerted prey when a predator was near. Nothing in the bothy had changed. Whatever was happening was outside. My heart broke into a gallop, and I worked to keep my breathing steady, desperate not to show any reaction.

There. Through a gap in the weathered wood of the shutters that had been drawn closed, a shadow passed, interrupting the light. Another followed close behind. Was it real or simply my desperate brain conjuring what I wanted to see?

I fixed my gaze on my lap, as if I were dozing.

*Don't look. Don't alert them. Don't give anything away.*

Another hand of cards was dealt. Captain Snarly shifted in his chair, but his attention stayed on the phone. The guard's head jerked up once, then settled again.

From the corner of my eye, I thought I saw another shadow. Deliberate. Silent.

They were here.

The world exploded.

Window shutters burst inward with synchronized precision, wood splintering as they crashed against the walls. Something metallic clattered across the floor, spinning and bouncing with an ominous rattle, followed by a sharp pop and the billowing of acrid smoke that burned my nose and throat. I held my breath, grateful for the warning all those tactical discussions with Jade had given me about what to expect. My heart thundered in my chest, but I forced myself to stay still, to trust they had a plan.

"Down! Hands where I can see them!" Callum's voice cut through the chaos, all command and barely contained fury.

Cards scattered, spilling over the edge of the table. A wooden chair crashed sideways into another, the impact sending both skidding across the floor with a terrible screech. The guard stationed by the door jerked awake from his half-doze with a startled curse, his bleary eyes going wide as he clumsily fumbled for the weapon at his hip. Too slow—far too slow to be of any use now. They'd taken advantage of the kidnappers' false sense of security. Now Callum and his team were turning the tables.

Bodies moved through the smoke with lethal grace, dark silhouettes dancing through the haze like something out of an action movie. I couldn't see clearly through the thickening gray clouds, but I didn't need to. I knew exactly who was who from the way they moved. The disciplined advance of my rescuers contrasted sharply with the clumsy, desperate scrambling of those who'd held me prisoner. Captain Snarly's cursing turned to choking as he inhaled smoke, his threats dissolving into a series of harsh coughs that gave me a tiny spark of vindictive satisfaction. At least until I began coughing myself.

The only thing I could think to do was throw my weight sideways, tipping my chair to the floor and praying the smoke wasn't as thick down here. More pain shot through my shoulder at the impact, but better that than catching a stray bullet. Eyes burning, I finally shut them, reduced to only listening to the fight.

Glass shattered. Someone slammed into the table. Someone's fist met flesh with a meaty thud. Shouts and grunts of pain filled the small space. Something cracked that I was deathly afraid was bone, an assumption backed up by the high-pitched scream that followed. More swearing—some English, some Russian. The thump of bodies hitting the floor, one after another.

Then silence fell, broken only by harsh breathing.

One heartbeat. Two. Three.

"Parker?" Callum's voice, rough with emotion.

"I'm here." My rasp of a voice was barely more than a whisper, but it was enough.

Boots crossed the floor with swift, purposeful strides, and then his hands were on the chair, righting it with infinite care. The zip ties fell away beneath his blade with a soft snick that made me flinch. And then I was in his arms, being hustled out of the building and into fresh air. He dropped to his knees, crushing me against his chest as he buried his face in my hair, his breath coming in ragged gasps against my scalp. His heart thundered beneath my cheek, matching the frantic rhythm of my own pulse as the reality of rescue finally sank in.

Absolutely everything hurt. My muscles screamed in protest at the sudden movement, and I was certain every nerve in my body was on fire. But I didn't care. He'd found me. I was safe.

"Christ. Oh, Christ, Parker." I could feel him shaking as adrenaline crashed through his system.

"I knew you'd come for me."

"Into hell itself."

Over his shoulder, I saw Finn, Ewan, and Jade securing my assailants, all of whom appeared to be either unconscious or dead. I found I couldn't much care either way.

"Falkor. What happened to Falkor?" I croaked.

"He's fine. The hero of the day, coming to get us."

"Thank God. I love you."

"I love you, too."

"I have to go to pieces now." Given his own relief at finding me in one piece, it seemed only fair to warn him.

He rumbled a noise that definitely wasn't a laugh and held me tighter. "You go right ahead. I've got you."

Only then did I let the tears fall.

# CHAPTER 39

## CALLUM

Parker lay sprawled on her back in our bed. If not for the gentle rise and fall of her chest beneath the duvet, and the tiny whiffling snore I'd never take for granted ever again, I'd have almost thought we'd been too late. She'd barely moved in the past twenty-four hours, and her already fair skin was so pale. She'd been medically cleared, but both she and the doctor had warned me she'd be crashing hard to sleep off the rest of the drugs and the fibro flare. Still, it was hard not to feel like I was sitting vigil as I waited for her to wake up.

Falkor lay with his head on his paws at the foot of the bed. She'd already been out by the time Saoirse had brought him home, and he'd immediately taken position as sentry and hadn't left her side. His dedication made my chest ache. He'd done his best to protect her. We all had. And we'd failed.

Sure, we'd gotten her back. But if we'd been any later... If we'd gone to the other location... If her kidnappers had managed to make their rendezvous point... Fifteen years of seeing the worst of humanity fueled the nightmares scrolling through my mind, even while I was awake.

*She's here. She's safe. We made sure of it.*

But for how long?

I hadn't been able to keep my promise to protect her. I'd sworn to her parents that I'd keep her safe, and I'd failed at that, too. Now that she was back, now that she was recovering, would she decide it wasn't worth it? That I wasn't worth it?

The thought of her leaving—of losing her—hollowed out my chest until it ached. She'd brought me back to life, made me feel again, and I didn't know if I could go back to the shell I used to be before her. But I could hardly blame her if she left. Not after what she'd been through.

The rhythm of her breathing changed, and her fingers twitched against the pillow. Was she finally waking up? Would she still want me when she did?

Her eyes fluttered open. For one heart-wrenching moment, I saw confusion and fear etched on her face. Then she spotted me, and her expression relaxed, her lips curving into a sleepy smile.

"Hey." Her voice was rough with sleep.

"Hey yourself."

Falkor whined and inched toward her in a belly crawl.

The moment she spotted him, she shoved herself upright and opened her arms. "My boy! My brave floof!"

The dog pressed against her, melting with joy and adoration. Parker held him tight, gently running her hand over the shaved spot on his shoulder where a neat row of stitches was the only remaining sign of his ordeal. "You were such a good boy. Such a good boy. I missed you."

"Saoirse says he'll make a full recovery. The gash wasn't deep. But no bracing on that shoulder until he's cleared."

As Falkor's tail thumped steadily against the duvet, Parker pressed her cheek to his head. "How long was I out?"

"Almost twenty-four hours. Here." I handed her a glass of water from the nightstand.

She drained it down in only a few gulps. And no wonder. She had to be dehydrated.

I took the glass back. "How are you feeling?"

"Little bit fuzzy still, but better." She straightened enough to meet my gaze. "Thank you for finding me."

Her gratitude hit me like a sucker punch to the gut. "I'm sorry I let them get close enough to take you in the first place."

She caught my hand and squeezed hard. "Don't. You didn't *let* them do anything. The only thing that matters is that you found me."

I brushed my lips over her knuckles, savoring the warmth of her skin. She was here. She was safe. I'd just have to keep reminding myself for a while.

I folded her hand gently between both of mine. "There's... quite a crowd waiting out in the lounge. Your parents flew in while you were sleeping. The team is here, too. Everyone's worried about you."

Her big brown eyes widened. "Oh. That's... a lot."

"I can send them all away if you're not up for it." It might take the entire team to force her parents to vacate, but my allegiance was to this woman right here.

"No, I know I need to catch up on what's happening. I just... need a bit to feel human again. And, please God, a shower."

"That can absolutely be arranged."

She started with yoga, which took somewhat longer than usual because she kept stopping to snuggle Falkor, who needed his own reassurance that she was okay. I didn't push. She'd get out there in her own time.

She took her time in the shower, standing beneath the spray until I was worried she'd fallen asleep again. But when she emerged, she was far more clear-eyed than she had been before, and color had come back to her cheeks. I thought taking time to do her hair and put on a little makeup was wholly unnecessary, but she pointed out that the more normal she looked, the less her parents would freak out. In theory.

I didn't think a little mascara was going to do a damned thing to mitigate her parents' reactions, but if she felt more armored up with cosmetics, who was I to stop her?

Once she'd dressed, we headed for the lounge, looking like we were in our own military formation, with Falkor on one side and me on the other, in case she needed support. She was moving slower than usual, but she was under her own steam, and now that she'd been awake a bit, she didn't seem to be dragging under the fibro fog.

The moment we entered the room, her parents surged to their feet. Parker's mother made a choked noise and rushed forward to embrace her. "Oh, baby girl."

"I'm okay, Mama. I promise." Her voice was muffled against her mother's shoulder.

The rest of the team hung back, giving them space for their reunion. Alex sat at his laptop, still running operations, his fingers flying over the keys as he monitored multiple screens of the mobile command center he'd set up in the dining room. Finn lounged against the wall near the window, keeping watch, while Ewan had positioned himself in the corner that gave him the best view of both exits. Jade occupied the chair nearest the door. All of them had taken tactical positions without discussion—some habits died hard. Even now, hours after the immediate danger had passed, they maintained their guard, a unit protecting one of their own. And there was no question they considered Parker one of theirs, even without her connection to me.

The positioning wasn't lost on her father, whose gaze had

lingered on each of them, clearly recognizing the military precision of their arrangement. He might not approve of his daughter being here, but even he had to see she wasn't unprotected.

I moved toward the kitchen because, after all the hours of sitting, I needed to do something. "Tea? You need to eat something, too."

Parker lowered herself to the sofa. "Tea and toast would be great. Thanks." Falkor leapt up beside her, laying his head in her lap.

I put on the kettle and prepped her mug, keeping one ear on the murmur of voices in case Parker needed me.

"—absolutely no reason you shouldn't come home with us right now." Her father's deeper voice carried.

My hands clenched on the edge of the counter. But this wasn't my fight. Not unless she wanted me to intervene.

"Daddy, I am home." Her easy, unperturbed answer loosened something in my chest. She still considered this home. Or did she mean Scotland in general?

"Parker Lawrence, you were kidnapped. It's clearly not safe—"

"Mr. Lawrence," Alex interrupted, "if I may? We've made some progress while Parker was sleeping that you need to hear."

I returned with her tea, fixed exactly as she liked it, and a plate of toast. She caught my hand and squeezed it in silent thanks.

Her mother's sharp gaze caught the gesture, but she remained focused on Alex. "What kind of progress?"

I settled on the arm of the sofa, close enough to touch but giving her space as we all waited for Alex.

Abandoning his array of screens, he moved in front of the fireplace, automatically falling into a formal stance for report-

ing. "The information Parker gave us about the 4 AM contact
was crucial. We coordinated with local authorities to set up a
sting operation and caught the Aberdeen operative who'd been
tasked with helping move her."

Parker blinked. "You ran a sting operation while I was
sleeping?"

Alex's lips twitched. "We had a busy night. Anyway, it
turned out she'd been documenting everything as insurance
against her own organization. She's been embezzling funds and
was paranoid about eventual betrayal. That documentation was
a goldmine. Detailed financial records going back five years.
Internal communications. Evidence of other operations.
Names, dates, account numbers—everything we needed."

Mr. Lawrence narrowed his gaze. "Everything you needed
for what? What exactly have you done with this information?"

Alex's smile was justifiably self-satisfied. "The money's
gone. Their operational accounts, their slush funds, their
reserves—all of it."

From his position by the window, Finn grinned. "Amazing
what you can do when you have access to their internal
network."

"Gone? Gone where?" Parker asked.

"An array of charities around the world supporting literacy
and women's rights. Plus a significant donation made to the
local animal shelter here in Glenlaig, after being filtered
through several shell corporations."

"So you've gone and stirred up the hornet's nest. How does
that help anything?" Mr. Lawrence demanded.

"The operative in Aberdeen had already set up what we
call a dead man's switch—a failsafe that would expose everything if anything happened to her. I've improved it. Any
attempt at retaliation now triggers full exposure of their entire
operation to all relevant governmental authorities, as well as

some competing factions who will take a dim view of many of the tactics they employed."

Jade leaned forward. "My contacts confirm the organization is in chaos. Their leadership is scrambling, their operations are frozen, and their people are scattering. There's so much blame being thrown around right now, they don't know which way is up."

"So... what does all that mean?" Parker asked.

I gently settled a hand on her shoulder. "We can't eliminate all risk, but we've made you too expensive—and too dangerous—a target now." It didn't feel like nearly enough, but it was what we could manage.

She covered my hand with hers, and some of the tension bled from my shoulders. But I still had to give her the out if she wanted it. "If you want to go back to the States with your parents, after everything that's happened... I'd absolutely understand."

Those gorgeous brown eyes narrowed as she looked up at me. "Callum Quinn, you noble idiot. Of course, I'm not going anywhere. You need me."

It was the God's honest truth. The steel in her tone made something warm bloom in my chest. God, how I loved this woman.

"I do at that," I managed. "More to the point, I love you."

Her lips quirked. "I know."

Both her parents sat dumbfounded.

"Your team did... all of that?" her mother asked.

"Aye," I confirmed. "I told you. We're verra, verra good at what we do."

Mr. Lawrence was staring at his daughter. "You're not coming home, are you, Pumpkin?"

Parker smiled up at me. "Tennessee isn't home anymore."

# EPILOGUE
## PARKER

"Happy anniversary!"

The shouted chorus of greetings was so loud, I almost stumbled right back out of the front door of Out of Bounds Scotland. Instead, I backed up into Callum, who'd driven us to work this morning. His big, capable hands steadied me as I pressed a hand to my galloping heart. "What is all this?"

"Has it been so long you don't recognize a party, sugar?" Jade asked.

The lobby had been festooned with streamers and balloons, and the entire crew was here. Finn and Alex grinned like idiots. Jade's own smile was smug, which meant she'd known all about this and maybe even had something to do with organizing the whole thing. Even our two newest guides, Imogen and Kieran, had gotten in on the action. Kieran caught Jade's eye and winked. I tried to hide my smile at the slight flush that crept up her throat. Kieran was a solid eight years her junior and thought Jade hung the moon. She thought the age gap was a deal breaker, but my money was on Kieran wearing her down with his unrelenting golden retriever energy.

"Y'all seriously didn't have to do this." But the protest was just for form because I spotted the veritable buffet of pastries spread out on the front deck.

"Of course we did." Finn stepped forward and wrapped me in a bear hug that lifted my feet clear off the floor. "A whole year of keeping this circus running? That absolutely deserves celebration."

"Put her down before you break her." Callum growled the demand, but the amusement in his tone totally undermined his effort to come across as a habitual grump. We didn't see that side of him much anymore.

I accepted more hugs as Falkor wagged his way through the group, collecting the pets and ear scritches that were his due, before settling into his corner with the new toy somebody had bought for the occasion.

"Remember what this place looked like a year ago?" Alex gestured at the newly organized retail section. "I couldn't find my own boots half the time."

"That's because you left them wherever you dropped them," Finn said. "Now Parker's got us so organized, even Callum can find things with his eyes closed."

"Aye, and that new software's a godsend." Callum's hand settled warm on my lower back. "No more double bookings or lost reservations."

"Speaking of bookings," Imogen chimed in, "we've got another corporate team coming in next week. That's what, the third this month?"

Kieran nodded. "The Instagram posts from the last lot went viral. My sister down in Glasgow saw them and didn't even realize it was us until I told her."

"That's all Parker," Jade said proudly. "She's the social media wizard. We're so busy now, we're having to turn people away."

"Which is why we hired you two," I reminded them, nodding at Kieran and Imogen. "Though I still think we need at least one more guide before summer."

"And maybe someone else to help you man the front desk," Finn added.

I went brows up. "Are you saying I can't handle the job anymore?"

"You are the organizational queen supreme. It's just these monthly team meetings you started have shown we're growing faster than we thought."

"The whole village is benefiting," Alex said. "Ewan says the pub's seeing twice the business from our clients, and Charlotte says their cottage bookings are up thirty percent."

"Not to mention how you've saved us with a proper beverage station. With actual coffee," Finn added reverently. "Not that instant rubbish we used to drink."

"And look at you." I bumped Callum's shoulder with mine. "Actually talking to clients instead of scaring them away."

"Och, I still prefer being out on the trails." But his smile took any sting out of the words.

"Good thing you've got me to handle the people stuff then."

"Good thing we've got all of us," Alex corrected. "We're a proper team now."

"No," I said. "We're a family."

Finn mimed wiping a tear. "That's beautiful."

"That also makes you the brother I get to tease incessantly."

"Careful, Lawrence. Turnabout is fair play," he warned.

Callum wrapped an arm around my shoulders. "Just try it, Patterson."

"Spoilsport."

I leaned into his warmth, marveling at how far we'd come. A year ago, I'd made a desperate gamble to escape my life. Even in my wildest dreams, I hadn't imagined that the life I'd build could look like this. Work I found gratifying, friends who made me laugh and feel supported, the world's best pooch, and a place in this village where everyone knew my name. With the active lifestyle I led here, I was the strongest I'd ever been. I still had flares and probably always would, but they were managed, and they weren't dictating my life in the same way they had before.

Most of all, there was Callum. The man I loved, who never ceased showing me every day how much he adored me in return. He anticipated my needs without babying me, something I'd never take for granted. We'd learned to read each other, and it had only made me fall deeper for this wonderful, flawed man who'd chosen me for his own. I'd stayed at the house with him. While it had begun as a necessity out of security, neither of us had wanted to backpedal once the threat had passed. And it had passed. The primary drivers of the consortium had been arrested by Interpol, and the remainder of the organization was in tatters, courtesy of the dead man's switch Alex had left in place.

On a personal front, Callum had finally introduced me to his family after Christmas. He'd been beyond anxious, but I'd done my Southern debutante thing and charmed them all. His mom, in particular, had been incredibly emotional when she'd thanked me for bringing her son back. I wasn't sure I deserved the credit for that, but either way, bridges were being built, and I couldn't see that as anything but a step toward healing whatever wounds he still had on that front.

"Earth to Parker," Jade called. "You're getting that misty-eyed look again."

"Can you blame me?" I gestured around the office, at this family I'd built. "Sometimes I still can't believe this is my life."

"Believe it, Hobbit." Callum pressed a kiss to my temple.

"Not to break up the love fest, but we do have clients

coming in an hour, and some of us probably do need to do some work," Alex announced.

I laughed. "I thought I was the taskmaster." But moved toward my desk. After all, these adventures wouldn't book themselves.

The morning flew by in a blur of bookings and preparations for next week's corporate group. Before I knew it, Jade was shooing me away from my desk.

"Go on. Kieran can handle the phones."

I glanced at Callum, who was already shrugging into his jacket. "Lunch at the pub?"

"We've got other plans." The corner of his mouth quirked up in that secret smile that always made my heart flutter. "Fancy a wee walk?"

"Always." I grabbed my own jacket, surprised when he headed for the back door instead of toward the village. "Where are we going?"

"You'll see."

He took my hand as we started up the slope behind the office, picking our way through the gorse. Falkor bounded ahead, secure in the knowledge that Callum had me, and he could be off duty for a bit. There wasn't precisely a path through the stand of trees, but Callum seemed to know exactly where we were going. Because of course he did. Sunlight filtered through the canopy, dappling his short-cropped hair. The climb was just steep enough to warm me up, but not so much that I'd regret it later.

"How have I worked here for a year and never known this was back here?"

"Most people stick to the marked trails." He steadied me over a fallen log. "This one's a bit of a secret."

We emerged from the trees into a sheep pasture, and I stopped dead in my tracks. "Oh, my God."

There, stark against the brilliant blue sky, stood a circle of ancient stones. Well, I had no idea if they were truly ancient, but they certainly looked it. They weren't anything on par with Stonehenge for size, but they had their own quiet majesty. Minerals in the weathered gray stone glinted in the sunlight, making me think fanciful thoughts of fairies and magic.

"How does no one ever talk about these being up here?"

"The locals know. They just don't advertise them. Keeps the tour buses away." He pulled me closer. "I thought you might appreciate them."

"They're incredible." I moved toward the nearest stone, reaching out to touch the rough surface. "Thank you for sharing them with me."

"Brought a picnic, if you're hungry."

I turned to find him pulling a blanket and plastic containers from his pack. "Ten out of ten for setting."

"Actually..." He set everything down but didn't move to open the food. "I brought you up here for more than just lunch."

"Oh?" I grinned, running my fingers over the weathered stone again. "Are we going to touch them and travel back in time?"

"I'm a lot more interested in the future." His voice had gone soft and serious in a way that made my heart skip.

When I turned around, he was down on one knee, and my breath caught. Falkor sat at attention beside him, tail sweeping across the grass.

"Parker." He cleared his throat, his focus dialed in only to me. "You walked into my life a year ago and turned everything upside down. Made everything better in ways I didn't even know I needed." His hand shook slightly as he pulled a small box from his pocket. "Marry me?"

Simple. Direct. Perfectly Callum.

"Yes." The word came out half-laugh, half-sob as I launched myself at him. "Of course, yes."

He caught me against his chest, overbalancing so we tumbled back into the grass. I kissed him hard, spilling out all of my unending joy. His hands tangled in my hair, and we melted into each other under, losing ourselves under the brilliant blue sky.

When we finally came up for air, he fumbled with the box, sliding a beautiful ruby ring onto my finger. A circle of tiny diamonds surrounded the center stone.

"It looks like the sun."

"Aye, that was the idea. Because you're my sunrise. You brought the light back into my life." He pressed his forehead to mine. "I love you."

"I love you too." I kissed him again, softer this time. "Even when you're being a grump."

"Especially then."

Falkor chose that moment to wiggle between us, clearly feeling left out of the celebration. We laughed, and Callum pulled us both close, right there in the shadow of the ancient stones where our future was just beginning.

# STINGER

## FINN

"Almost there, lad." I glanced in the rearview at Ajax, who lay on the backseat, head on his paws. The Belgian Malinois had been subdued since I picked him up two days ago. Made sense. He was grieving as much as any of us. More, maybe. Charlie had been his whole world.

"You're gonna like Dr. MacGregor." The words felt hollow, even to me. Truth was, I had no idea if Ajax would like her. Wasn't even sure I liked her, though that had more to do with the way she looked at me like I was something she'd scraped off her boot. But she was the best vet in the area, and Charlie would've wanted the best for his boy. I was determined to give him that in Charlie's stead.

Ajax's ears pricked at a passing lorry, but he didn't lift his head. Two years we'd served together in Afghanistan. Charlie and Ajax had been part of our squad. Brothers. Family. Now Charlie was gone, and Ajax... Christ, I hadn't seen him this low since that clusterfuck in Helmand.

"We're gonna sort you out, mate. Get you back on your

feet." And maybe, if we were lucky, we'd manage the same for each other.

The bell over the door jangled as we walked into the clinic. Ajax stuck close to my leg, head down, barely acknowledging the elderly spaniel and its owner across the waiting room.

"Good morning!" The receptionist's cheerful greeting faltered slightly as she registered my size, but she rallied quickly. "How can I help you today?"

I tried to dig up some of the charm I usually used to put people at ease, but I was running at low ebb, so I had to settle for adjusting my posture so I didn't loom. "Patterson. I've got an appointment for Ajax."

"Oh yes, the new patient." She beamed down at Ajax, who didn't even flick an ear in response. "Poor love. We'll get you feeling right as rain in no time."

I doubted that.

She pushed a clipboard across the counter. "If you could just fill these out for me? Standard new patient forms."

I took the clipboard and settled into one of the plastic chairs, Ajax lying at my feet without prompting. The forms were straightforward enough—breed, age, medical history. I had all of Ajax's records from his military service. Part and parcel of taking on a retired military animal. My pen hesitated over "owner's name." After a moment, I wrote my own. It felt wrong, but Charlie was gone. Ajax was mine now.

My handwriting had always been shite, but it was legible enough. I'd just finished when a vet tech appeared in scrubs covered in cartoon dogs.

"Ajax?" She consulted her tablet. "Come on through."

Ajax followed me down the hallway, his nails clicking against the linoleum. The tech—her name tag read "Jenny"—got Ajax's weight and directed us to an exam room. "Dr. MacGregor will be right with you."

Rather than taking a seat in one of the plastic chairs, I stood at parade rest, watching Ajax settle into his now-familiar dejected posture. Two weeks since the funeral, and neither of us was handling it well. But I had to do better. For Charlie. For Ajax. I knew we both had to grieve the loss and find our way to life on the other side.

Christ, I hoped Saoirse kept her claws in today. Every interaction we'd had through our mutual friends had been like oil and water. But for all she clearly couldn't stand me, I knew she was brilliant with animals. Had to be for Ciara and Parker to speak so highly of her. So hopefully she'd put aside that mystifying disdain for Ajax's sake.

The door opened, and Dr. MacGregor herself swept in, all long limbs and sleek blonde ponytail, looking far too posh for someone who dealt with sick animals all day. Her head was bent over the paperwork as she entered. "And who do we have here today?" She immediately dropped into a crouch beside Ajax, her voice going soft and gentle. "Hello, handsome."

That prep school voice did something unreasonable to my insides that I determinedly ignored.

Ajax didn't even lift his head as she stroked his ears. He was breaking my heart.

Saoirse straightened, and her professional smile faltered as she registered my presence. "Finley." The clipped tone was familiar enough, but there was something brittle beneath it. "I didn't realize you were Ajax's owner."

But I barely noticed because I was too busy staring at the dark purple bruise blooming around her right eye. Twelve hours old, maybe less. The swelling hadn't peaked yet. That kind of bruising—it'd be throbbing like a fucking bastard right about now.

Something dark and violent surged through my blood, a familiar rage I hadn't felt since my days in the service. I had no tolerance for anyone who'd lay hands on a woman. It went against everything I believed in, everything I'd ever fought for. And someone had more than put hands on this woman. Someone had hurt her, deliberately and with force. The kind of force that made my jaw clench and my hands curl into fists.

Before I even registered I was moving, I was across the room, my hand hovering just shy of her cheek as I stared at the mottled purple staining her otherwise flawless skin. The bruising was precise, targeted. This was no accident.

"Who do I need to put in a body bag?"

---

## Choose Your Next Romance

HOO BOY. Finley and Saoirse have been like oil and water this whole series, but we all know there's something underneath all that. I really hope they tell me what it is before June...

IN THE MEANTIME, I know you want to see more of Callum and Parker's happily ever after (read: more of the grump going squishy). Get their bonus epilogue straight to your inbox!

https://books.kaitnolan.com/x2sokanowl

If you'd like another grumpy sunshine romance to keep you company while you're waiting on the last Special Ops Scots book, feel free to check out *Grump in a Kilt* from the adjacent Kilted Hearts series! Or grab the entire Kilted Heart series bundle for less: https://store.kaitnolan.com/products/complete-kilted-hearts-ebook-series

# OTHER BOOKS BY KAIT NOLAN

**A complete and up-to-date list of all my books can be found at https://kaitnolan.com.**

### KILTED HEARTS
### SMALL TOWN CONTEMPORARY SCOTTISH ROMANCE

- *Jilting The Kilt* (prequel)
- *Cowboy in a Kilt* (Raleigh and Kyla)
- *Grump in a Kilt* (Malcolm and Charlotte)
- *Playboy in a Kilt* (Connor and Sophie)
- *Protector in a Kilt* (Ewan and Isobel)
- *Single Dad in a Kilt* (Hamish and Afton)
- *Kilty Pleasures* (Jason and Skye)

### SPECIAL OPS SCOTS
### SMALL TOWN MILITARY SCOTTISH ROMANCE

- *One Fine Night* (prequel)
- *Before Highland Sunset* (Alex and Ciara)

- *Beyond Highland Sunrise* (Callum and Parker)
- *Beneath Highland Stars* (Finley and Saoirse)
  Coming June 25, 2025

### BAD BOY BAKERS
### SMALL TOWN MILITARY ROMANCE

- *Rescued By a Bad Boy* (Brax and Mia prequel)
- *Mixed Up With a Marine* (Brax and Mia)
- *Wrapped Up with a Ranger* (Holt and Cayla)
- *Stirred Up by a SEAL* (Jonah and Rachel)
- *Hung Up on the Hacker* (Cash and Hadley)
- *Caught Up with the Captain* (Grey and Rebecca)

### RESCUE MY HEART SERIES
### SMALL TOWN MILITARY ROMANCE

- *Someone Like You* (Ivy and Harrison)
- *What I Like About You* (Laurel and Sebastian)
- *Bad Case of Loving You* (Paisley and Ty prequel)
  Included in *Made For Loving You* (Paisley and Ty)

### THE MISFIT INN SERIES
### SMALL TOWN FAMILY ROMANCE

- *When You Got A Good Thing* (Kennedy and Xander)
- *Til There Was You* (Misty and Denver)
- *Those Sweet Words* (Pru and Flynn)
- *Stay A Little Longer* (Athena and Logan)
- *Bring It On Home* (Maggie and Porter)
- *Come Away with Me* (Moses and Zuri)

## MEN OF THE MISFIT INN
### SMALL TOWN SOUTHERN ROMANCE

- *Let It Be Me* (Emerson and Caleb)
- *Our Kind of Love* (Abbey and Kyle)
- *Don't You Wanna Stay* (Deanna and Wyatt)
- *Until We Meet Again* (Samantha and Griffin prequel)
- *Come A Little Closer* (Samantha and Griffin)
- *Just Wanted You To Know* (Livia and Declan)
- *A Love Like You* (Juliette and Mick)

## WISHFUL ROMANCE SERIES
### SMALL TOWN SOUTHERN ROMANCE

- *To Get Me To You* (Cam and Norah)
- *Know Me Well* (Liam and Riley)
- *Be Careful, It's My Heart* (Brody and Tyler)
- *The Matchmaker Maneuver* (Myles and Piper prequel)
- *Just For This Moment* (Myles and Piper)
- *Wish I Might* (Reed and Cecily)
- *Turn My World Around* (Tucker and Corinne)
- *Dance Me A Dream* (Jace and Tara)
- *See You Again* (Trey and Sandy)
- *The Christmas Fountain* (Chad and Mary Alice)
- *You Were Meant For Me* (Mitch and Tess)
- *A Lot Like Christmas* (Ryan and Hannah)
- *Dancing Away With My Heart* (Zach and Lexi)

## WISHFUL MOMENTS SERIES
### BITE-SIZED WISHFUL ROMANCE

- *Once Upon A Coffee* (Avery and Dillon)
- *Once Upon A Rescue* (Brooke and Hayden)
- *Who I Am with You* (Dinah and Robert)

## WISHING FOR A HERO SERIES (A WISHFUL SPINOFF SERIES)
## SMALL TOWN ROMANTIC SUSPENSE

- *Make You Feel My Love* (Judd and Autumn)
- *Watch Over Me* (Nash and Rowan)
- *Can't Take My Eyes Off You* (Ethan and Miranda)
- *Burn For You* (Sean and Delaney)

## MEET CUTE ROMANCE
## SMALL TOWN SHORT ROMANCE

- *Once Upon A Snow Day*
- *Once Upon A New Year's Eve*
- *Once Upon An Heirloom*

## SUMMER FLING TRILOGY
## CONTEMPORARY ROMANCE

- *Second Chance Summer*
- *Summer Camp Secret*
- *The Summer Camp Swap*

# ABOUT KAIT

Kait is a Mississippi native, who often swears like a sailor, calls everyone sugar, honey, or darlin', and can wield a bless your heart like a saber or a Snuggie, depending on requirements.

You can find more information on this *USA Today* best selling and RITA ® Award-winning author and her books on her website http://kaitnolan.com.

Do you need more small town sass and spark? Sign up for <u>her newsletter</u> to hear about new releases, book deals, and exclusive content!